FIRST ST(
NEXT ST(,

CW01500554

There it stood in the middle of a massive
hangar—a big, beautiful silver rocket ship.
Its destination: the moon! On board would
be Hollywood playboy/rugged explorer Gil
Benson, along with his two trusted partners
in adventure, engineer Jerry Torrence and
Professor Crowley, the latter a noted atomic
scientist. Everything was set…the rocket
was ready to go. But two jealous women
seeking goodbye kisses is never a good
thing—especially on board a spaceship
that's about to blast off. So in the blink of an
eye Gil Benson's entire venture was turned
upside down. No one would have ever
guessed that a playboy bachelor, a pretty
red-head, and a Hollywood press agent
would end up in a rocket ship together
heading for the moon; but there was no
turning back—a lunar adventure was ahead
for them all. Who would then have imagined
that these three unlikely people would be the
ones to save Earth from possible
extinction…?

FOR A COMPLETE SECOND NOVEL, TURN TO PAGE 177

CAST OF CHARACTERS

GILBERT BENSON

He was known around town as a typical Hollywood playboy. But he liked to think of himself as a daring explorer. His bold plan: build a spaceship that would fly to the moon.

DIANA FENIMORE

A pretty red-head with the bluest of eyes who wanted desperately to break into show business. Her life dramatically changed when she met a hot shot publicity man and a handsome explorer

WILBUR WILLIAMS

This Hollywood press agent was a bit on the short and pudgy side; but he was known around town as the best publicity man in pictures—with a real eye for talent.

RUTH DELANO

Being MGM's vivacious, curvaceous pin-up sensation, she was a real attention whore, and always ready to have her picture taken and be at the center of attention

JERRY TORRENCE

Chief engineer and in charge of operations for the world's first moonshot, he was hard-boiled, dependable, and ever so ready to set foot on the moon.

PROFESSOR CROWLEY

As a well-known atomic scientist he was faced with a huge challenge—how to keep the world's first moon rocket from blowing sky high!

ALL ABOARD FOR THE MOON

By
HAROLD M. SHERMAN

ARMCHAIR FICTION
PO Box 4369, Medford, Oregon 97504

*The original text of this novel was first
published by Ziff-Davis Publishing*

Armchair Edition, Copyright 2016 by Gregory J. Luce
All Rights Reserved

*For more information about Armchair Books and products, visit our
website at...*

www.armchairfiction.com

Or email us at...

armchairfiction@yahoo.com

CHAPTER ONE

WILBUR WILLIAMS, Hollywood press agent, had a problem. She was a gorgeous redhead who wanted to break into pictures.

"Can you act, honey?" he asked her.

Diana rolled her blue, blue eyes and Wilbur almost rolled on the floor at her feet.

"Of course I can act," she said. "I've had two seasons in stock."

"You're beautiful," said Wilbur, with conviction. "I think you're a swell kid. I'd like to do something for you, honest I would. But tell me, baby—who referred you to me?"

Diana's eyes rolled some more. "Why everybody says you're the best publicity man in pictures," she said. "And so I naturally came to you..."

"It sounds like a line but I like it," said Wilbur. "Stand-off there so I can take a gander at you."

Diana obliged with a professional pose, lifting her dress above the knees, as required by every casting office. (Well, almost everyone.)

"Hmmm. Not bad. MacDonald body, Grable legs. Your eyes seem to be original."

Wilbur stood up to get a better view.

He was short, pudgy, and near-sighted.

"How long have you been in Hollywood?"

"A week."

"Where did you play in stock?"

"Milwaukee."

"Leads?"

"I walked on in 'Room Service' and I walked off in 'The Man Who Came To Dinner,' and I understudied the nurse in—I forget—oh yes, 'I remember Mama'..."

"I see—quite a variety. But you're beautiful, baby—there's no denying that. Have you got a date for dinner tonight?"

The blue eyes did another roll.

"Not yet."

"Well, you've got a date now. I want to give you more time. I'll See what I can cook up.   What you need is to go to dramatic

school—learn screen technique—let me give you a publicity build-up. But all this takes dough. Here's a sordid question—have you got any money?"

Diana's eyes stopped rolling.

Today the V-2...tomorrow the Moon Rocket! Even as you read, Man may be making the first try at space travel!

"No," she said.

Wilbur chewed for a moment on his cigar.

"Well, that makes things more complicated. Why do you girls always come to Hollywood on good looks and no money?"

Diana shook her head.

"How do you think I can afford to give you my services? I'm a busy man. I handle publicity for some of the biggest stars in the country. The streets are filled with good-looking dames who've got loads more experience. I'm sorry, Miss—what's your last name?"

"Fenimore."

"Fenimore? Hmm... Diana Fenimore. Yeah. It slips off the tongue. It'll look good in lights, too... Turn around, babe, let's see your profile..."

Diana revealed an impish nose and a cute, determined chin.

"All right—the dinner date stands. Meet me back here at my office at six. I can't promise anything, baby—but I'm sure as hell gonna try. You've got something. At least, it gets me...and I've been in this racket a long while."

Diana's blue eyes clouded up with appreciation. She reached in the bosom of her dress, unpinned a cloth purse, and took out a roll of bills.

"I was lying to you," she said. "I just wanted to see if you thought enough of my chances to do something for me on your own."

Wilbur choked on his cigar as she placed five hundred in bills on the desk before him.

"I've been around," she said, "and I know what it takes to crash Hollywood. One good publicity stunt will do it."

"Miss Fenimore," said Wilbur, his voice laced with respect, "you have just knocked me for a goal. You are not only beautiful but there is something inside that head of yours which is decidedly not sawdust. Do you mind telling me how you came by this bankroll?"

Diana's blue eyes made the complete circuit.

"I earned it," she said, "with a flying circus making parachute jumps."

Wilbur Williams, Hollywood's greatest press agent, nearly did a backward flip-flop in his swivel chair.

THERE was another man in Hollywood who had a problem. He was playboy Gilbert Benson, head of the Benson Aircraft Company, famous round-the-world flier, speed plane builder, financier, socialite, sports enthusiast, nightclub frequenter, ladies' man, and everything else he chose to be when the spirit moved.

Gil's problem was not money or girls or health or anything material. It was boredom. He was simply and completely bored stiff with everything on Earth.

"There must be other planets more interesting than this one," he had taken to remarking to all and sundry.

But no one seemed interested in Gil's speculations, least of all the feminine lovelies who sat with him under the moon and stars. They were interested in just one thing—romance. Each had her matrimonial hook baited to catch America's Number One Bachelor.

Some of Hollywood's most beauteous stars had given up in outraged despair after one night of astronomic indifference to their charms. But Gil didn't seem to mind. He'd date another hopeful the following evening and bob up at a different nightclub or private party, providing new gossip for columnists and candid camera shots for photographers who kept reporting him "that-a-way" about "this-and-that-a-one" until they realized that the fantastically popular Gil Benson was nonchalantly "playing the field."

"Something's happened to America's Leading Lady-Killer," a Hollywood columnist lamented. "He's not the same irresponsible, devil-may-care, life-of-the-party Benson and the glamour gals don't like it. We saw him at a cocktail binge the other night, surrounded by enough beauties to turn the head of any responsive male but Gil actually yawned in their faces and went home early. His few intimates say they think he must be working on a new invention—perhaps a new jet propulsion plane—which would partially account for his weird public conduct. If this is the case, girls, you'll have to face it. Gil is being true to his 'first love' and there just isn't anything you can do about it..."

The man who had elicited this comment read it in bed in his suite at the Beverly Hills hotel. The paper had been served to him with his breakfast, juicy morsels of gossip to be consumed with his prune juice.

Gil swore softly. Then he swore loudly. Finally, he threw the paper across the room.

"Damn it to hell. Do I have to have a playboy reputation all my life? All right—so I've got money. So I like to have a good time. So I can get any girl I want. So I'm news wherever I go—whatever I do. You'd think I never had a serious idea in my head. That I've never done a thing worthwhile. Nobody's fooling me. How many friends would I have if I was dead broke? How many girls? And, since I'm in the dough, how can I ever be sure that a girl really loves me? If anybody else wants to be Gil Benson, I'll sell out for ten cents on the dollar! I'd give everything I own to get off this Earth. If my space rocket works, I'll do it, too..."

He picked up the phone and jiggled the connection.

"Hello, operator. Get me my ranch in Arizona."

As he waited for the call, he examined himself in the mirror. Dark eyes, dark hair, white scar on his forehead from that plane crash, athletic build, handsome guy. At least everybody said he was. Nature had given him a good body and he'd certainly used it.

"Hello," Gil said into the phone. "This is Gil. Connect me with the plant and put Jerry on." He reached for a cigarette. "Hello, Jerry. How are things coming? Is the rocket set up on the launching site yet? Great... Have you tested the motors? You'd better be sure. If I'm going to the moon in that damn thing, I want a chance to get back. You don't think I'm crazy do you? You do?" Gil laughed. "Well, I don't exactly blame you... Tell the boys I'll be flying in this weekend, be seeing you..."

He hung up, talking to himself.

"Jerry's the best damn engineer in the country. If that rocket doesn't reach the moon, it won't be his fault."

The cigarette needed lighting. He fumbled for safety matches in his pajama pocket.

"When I'm ready to take off, I'll give these small-minded columnists something to write about. Playboy, eh...? I'll hand 'em a new title, 'Space Traveler.' See how they like that..."

The phone started ringing. Gil took down the receiver, laid it on the bed, and spoke into the mouthpiece.

"Hello. Wait till I light this cigarette." He struck a match, inhaled, and the tip glowed. "All right. Thanks for waiting. Who is it?"

"It's me, dear," said a woman's voice. "Be more specific."

"Why, Gil, darling. Do you have a hang-over?"

"Yes, I'm hanging over the bed to answer this phone. Is this Doris?"

"Dearest, you're wonderful..."

"I thought I recognized you."

"You didn't—it's Ruth!"

"I knew it all the time."

"Liar."

"What else could I say? What do you mean, calling me before noon?"

Gil liked Ruth Delano. She was MGM's new pin-up sensation. Vivacious, curvaceous brunette, high strung, demanding, but fun. Could have practically any swain in town—the country, for that matter—but seemed to prefer him. At least she was giving him the rush act.

"Haven't seen you for a week—but I notice you've been out with six other girls. When are you going to get off the 'I-Might-Marry-Go-Round' and let Hollywood settle down?"

Gil laughed. "Have you heard that old adage, 'there's safety in numbers'?"

"There's also confusion, darling. Did you ever try to pick one necktie in a hundred? No wonder you don't know your own mind. Now, if you'd just concentrate on me..."

"Let's leave personalities out of this."

"Gil—did you read Jimmy's column this morning?"

"Yes—damn it to hell!"

"Why, darling..."

"I'd like to go out with a girl once and not be interviewed or photographed."

"But maybe the girl wouldn't like it—especially if she's a star. You know it's great publicity to be seen with you."

"Do you feel the need of some more publicity?"

"Why, Gil—are you dating me?"

"No—I'm threatening you. At least you're frank about it. Where would you like to dine?"

"Ciro's?"

"No."

"Earl Carrol's?"

"No."

"Romanoff's?"

"I'll settle for Sardi's. A booth for two, a glass of wine—and you..."

"Poetic. How touching..."

Gil laughed. "Be beautiful. Anything in low neck. Hair done the way I like it."

"How is that?"

"Don't get technical. But leave off that perfume. I've got an allergy."

"Gil, darling—you sound like your old self."

"That does it. I'll pick you up at seven and break your neck."

"I'd love it!"

She hung up on him. Gil grinned and slammed down the receiver. The phone instantly rang again.

"Damn it to hell!" He took up the receiver. "Hello. I'm not in. Goodbye!"

CHAPTER TWO

SARDI'S, on Hollywood Boulevard near Vine, is quiet, respectable, secluded. Not so breast-beating a recommendation for the goggle-eyed Hollywood visitor, perhaps—who mistakes noise, indigestible dinner music, and people standing in line for tables as the only authentic atmosphere.

But to Sardi's, on this night, came two men with problems. They occupied booths with their respective dinner partners across the restaurant floor from one another. And neither, for the time being, knew that the other was present.

"You're beautiful, baby," Wilbur couldn't help saying again to Diana. "Don't hide your face with that menu. I want to see those eyes."

"I'm hungry," said Diana, "and I need my eyes to pick out my dinner."

"Well, hurry up and use them so I can plunge myself into their blue depths," said Wilbur.

Diana let out a gurgle of laughter.

"You are a very funny person, Mr. Williams—but I like you a lot."

Hollywood's greatest publicity agent was pleased with himself. He seldom went overboard for a dame. He'd seen too many of them come and go—with the emphasis on gone. But the redhead was fresh and new and different. And, with all else—a parachute jumper!

"I think I'll have shrimp cocktail, clam chowder and lobster a la Newburgh," said Diana, letting him have her blue eyes.

Wilbur gulped. "You certainly are strong for seafood..."

"I used to go with a sailor," she said. "Every once and a while I still carry the torch."

"That's very touching," said Wilbur. "I pay for your dinner and you sit there eating, with another man on your mind."

In the private booth across the way, America's Number One Bachelor was not having too private a time. Diners had sighted him coming in with MGM's ravishing raven-haired pin-up girl and they had gathered about with the usual autograph requests.

"What do you people do with these autographs after you collect 'em?" Gil asked.

"We trade 'em or sell 'em," said a freckle-faced Bobby-Soxer.

"Nice business," said Gil, "when you can get it. What's my

autograph worth on the open market?"

"That depends," said the Bobby-Soxer.

"Depends on what?"

"What you do next. If you should marry Miss Delano—the price of your autograph naturally goes up."

"Gil, dear—what an inducement," said Ruth.

"This is a frame-up," charged Gil. Then, turning to the Bobby-Soxer as all within hearing laughed, he said, "How valuable would my autograph become if I should make a rocket trip to the moon?"

"Now you're making fun of me," accused Miss Freckle-Face. "I don't think that's nice..."

"No, honest," Gil insisted. "I really am planning a trip to the moon."

Everybody howled.

"Gil, darling—stop ribbing the poor girl," scolded Ruth. "You'll lose an autograph fan."

Gil looked at her. "You think I'm kidding, too?"

"Of course, silly. And you'd better be careful. Some of these people are apt to talk this around and first thing you know, it'll get in the papers: 'Gil Benson Renounces Earth—Going to Live on Moon...' "

Gil gave a helpless shrug of the shoulders and handed out his last autograph to a little old maid schoolteacher who told him she hailed from South Dakota.

"Hang onto that signature," he advised. "It ought to bring you a thousand bucks when I land on the moon."

The veteran school "mom" shook her head.

"You can't land on the moon and you couldn't live if you did," she said. "Any schoolboy knows there's no air up there."

"All right, madam, have it your own way—but when you get back to South Dakota, you tell the Board of Education that Gil Benson says they'd better get ready to change their school books. I'm going to the moon—air or no air."

The little old maid schoolteacher backed warily away.

"I know where you're going," she said, "and it's not the

moon."

It was about this time that Press Agent Wilbur Williams, looking across at the departing autograph fans, saw who the celebrities were who were occupying the booth.

"Diana, cast your blue orbs over there—if you want to see Hollywood's leading pin-up—and America's most notorious playboy. That's Ruth Delano and Gil Benson—and Benson's a client of mine."

"A client," said Diana. "Oh, Mister Williams, that's thrilling! I know all about Gil Benson. He's my hero. What an aviator! What he's done for aviation... That flight around the world in three days...his plane factory...the new designs he's invented...and the way he's risked his life to test new models!"

Wilbur's lower jaw dropped, revealing one hundred ninety-five dollars worth of bridgework.

"Say, I ought to hire you to write his life story."

Diana's blue eyes were focused on Benson to the exclusion of all else.

"Oh, this is worth my coming to Hollywood just to see him in person. I've read everything I could about him...listen to him on the radio...seen him in the newsreels...and you say—he's your client? Oh, Mr. Williams—do you suppose you could introduce me?"

"Listen, baby—not so fast—and stop staring. That's never done in Hollywood—not much...! Be different! We've got to think this thing through. Gil Benson's a very eccentric guy. You rub him the wrong way and it's all off."

Diana took Wilbur by the arm.

"Don't you dare let him get out of here without my meeting him. It's fate. That's what it is. Did you know he was coming here tonight?"

Wilbur held his head.

"No, of course not. He usually picks a nightclub. He must be extra serious over Ruth Delano. See—they're holding hands—this is a bad night to break in on Gil, even if he is my client..."

"What have you been doing for him?" asked Diana.

"Me? You'll probably think he needs a publicity man like I need a haircut." Wilbur rubbed his expanding bald spot. "But Benson's peeved because the press keeps dubbing him a playboy and doesn't give him proper credit for his scientific achievements...so, he's hired me to do public relations articles for the slick magazines on his airplane factory, his research work in aerodynamics, his test piloting, his theories on stratosphere flying and that stuff. Pretty technical, if you'd ask me—but it pleases him and he pays big—so I should kick!"

Diana's blue eyes came back reluctantly to the little man at her table.

"Mr. Williams," she said. "If I were you, I'd feel greatly honored to be connected in any way with Mr. Benson. I think he's one of the greatest men in America...and it's just a shame that nobody really understands him."

"A FEW minutes ago, you were raving about a sailor," reminded Wilbur. "Ordering a meal in memory of him. Now your clam chowder's getting cold—and you're all heated up over another guy. I suppose, if Gil Benson was Clark Gable or Tyrone Power or Van Johnson, you'd really blow your top."

"I wouldn't give them a tumble," said Diana. "But aviation's my meat—and he's my idol. Mr. Williams—if you don't take me over and introduce me—I'm going over and introduce myself."

Wilbur pushed her back in the booth.

"If you lose your head, I'll lose mine, too. You let me handle this. If we work it right, you may get one of the greatest publicity breaks of your life. Just to be seen and photographed in Gil Benson's company has started many an unknown on her career..."

"Oh, I don't care about that where Gil Benson's concerned."

"Well, I do, young lady. I've taken you under my wing and Benson's one of my best bets to give you the right sendoff. You sit tight, make your eyes behave, and I'll go over and give him a build-up…"

He started out of the booth. "Remember," said Diana. "I'm your client, too. And I've already paid you…"

Wilbur groaned.

"You're forcing my hand on this. I hope I can put it over—but if Gil Benson kicks me the hell out of Sardi's—meet me outside on the sidewalk."

Gil Benson spotted his press agent edging between the tables toward him.

"Here comes 'Genius, Incorporated'," he announced to Ruth.

"Yes," said his dinner companion.

"I know 'Wee Willy Wilbur'. He's been hounding me to let him do my publicity."

"You could have a worse wolf on your trail," said Gil. "He's doing a job for me."

"For you?" said Ruth. "What could he do for you?"

"Write the kind of stories about me that I like to read," said Gil.

Ruth laughed. "You take your press comments too seriously, dear. Now me—I don't worry no matter what they say—just as long as I get mentioned."

Hollywood's greatest publicity agent was now within earshot. He had that "you've-got-to-be-glad-to-see-me" and "you-can't-turn-me-down" look which all successful press agents must wear.

"Hi, Gil," he hailed, from far enough away so that gawkers and potential clients at other tables might see on what close and familiar terms his friendship for America's Number One Playboy existed.

It was now time to throw a bouquet of recognition in the direction of Gil's dinner partner.

"Hi, Miss Delano. You look radiant tonight. Really chic. But I suppose Mr. Benson's already told you that…"

"He hasn't, as a matter of fact," said Ruth.

"Well, he probably hasn't gotten around to it yet," said

Wilbur. "The evening's still young."

With these preliminaries out of the way, Wilbur launched a direct frontal attack.

"Say, Gil, I'm going to ask you a terrific favor. You see that redhead I've been sitting with?" He pointed across the floor and saw Diana giving them her big blue eyes.

Gil looked and was startled as she smiled and nodded. "Who is she?" he asked. "Does she know me? Have I met her?"

"No, but she's dying to meet you," said Wilbur. "In fact, she'll be dead any moment, if you don't. She knows more about you than the Encyclopedia Britannica. She worships the air you fly in. Not bad to look at, is she? But she's got more than looks. Would you believe it, Gil, that little girl has made over two hundred parachute jumps."

GIL BENSON had been listening with an expression of annoyance but Wilbur had played his opening cards well. He produced the ace at the right time.

"That girl...a parachute jumper?" queried Gil. "What is this—one of your press gags?"

"No, Gil, on the level. She's traveled with Buzz Reynolds' Flying Circus."

"Then I've seen her make some of her jumps," said Gil. "She's all right. Bring her over. What are you waiting for?"

Wilbur hadn't played out his hand.

"Well, just this, Gil. Miss Fenimore's trying to break into movies. I realize this is asking a good deal but you know how much it means to have a picture taken with you. Would you mind?"

He gave a sidewise glance of apprehension at Ruth Delano who, as he surmised, was coming to a slow boil.

"You wouldn't mind, would you, Miss Delano? It'll only take a minute."

MGM's new pin-up girl was toying, agitatedly, with her fork. "Mind? Of course I don't mind," she steamed. "It's all up to

Mr. Benson."

Gil gazed at Ruth in amusement, then turned back to Wilbur. "I'm sure Miss Delano won't object to giving a poor girl a break," he said. "She was in the same boat once herself. Call your redhead over..."

Hollywood's greatest press agent could hardly conceal a look of triumph. "Thanks, Gil, old boy," he said. "I'll get you a special news release for this on anything you want. You, too, Miss Delano, even though I don't handle you."

"Be careful how you use words," snapped Ruth. "I wouldn't let you handle me if you were the last press agent on Earth."

"You'd love me if I were doing this for you," said Wilbur. "And some day, you'll love me yet..."

He hurried back across the floor in the direction of his booth, with the eyes of many curious diners upon him.

Diana's blue eyes now confronted him.

"Well?" they asked.

"It's all fixed," said Wilbur. "Gil's interested. He's seen you jump. Baby, if this works out, you'll be off to the races—and I don't mean Agua Caliente. Come on, Gil Benson's waiting..."

He helped a trembling Diana to her feet.

"Gosh," said Diana. "I feel more nervous right now than I do before a jump. I wonder what's the matter?"

"It's stage fright," said Wilbur. "That proves you're an actress. Take my arm, gorgeous. We're going places..."

He waltzed her between the tables.

GIL BENSON, watching, said to Ruth, "I get a kick out of that guy. He'll spend more time trying to put across an unknown than he will on his own business. You have to have a heart of gold to do that..."

"Or a girl who has sex appeal," said Ruth, eyeing Diana.

Wilbur was approaching their booth with his redhead.

"Miss Delano," he said, "I'd like you to meet a little lady who, I think, has got what it takes—Miss Diana Fenimore."

The two women eyed each other and neither one came off

second best.

"What does it take to parachute jump?" said Ruth. "I've often wondered."

"I saw your last picture," said Diana. "I wouldn't kid you, Miss Delano—it wasn't so hot."

Wilbur squeezed her arm. "She means the picture, not you," he hastily added. Then, turning quickly to Gil, he said, "Mr. Benson, Miss Fenimore...Miss Fenimore, Mr. Benson..."

America's Number One Playboy stood up and took Diana's hand. He looked into her big blue eyes and found it quite an experience.

If Ruth was boiling before, she was sizzling now.

"Mr. Benson," said Diana, as though his dinner companion no longer existed. "This is truly the greatest moment of my life. I've followed everything you've done in aviation—and when Mr. Williams told me he knew you...well, I just couldn't wait... I just had to get this chance to tell you how much I admire..."

Ruth was seized with a sudden coughing fit. She pressed a napkin against her lips.

"Did you choke on something, *I hope?*" asked Diana.

"Go right ahead," invited Ruth, with tiny icicles in her voice. "Don't mind me..."

Gil Benson was unperturbed. "Sit down," he said and they all slid into the half-moon, leather-cushioned seat. "You were saying...?" he prompted, smiling at Diana.

Her blue eyes sparkled.

"...how much I admired you," she said, "for the risks you've taken developing those new model planes. I heard you talk on the Hobby Lobby program when you said the day of space traveling was almost here. You really believe that, don't you, Mr. Benson?"

"I certainly do," said Gil.

"So do I," said Diana, with vibrant enthusiasm. "I just hope I live to see it."

Gil smiled. "You will," he said.

Ruth laughed. "You two should write for the comic strips."

"Gil, old man," cut in Hollywood's greatest press agent, "I know you're busy and we don't want to take up much of your time—but would you let me call the camera girl over and get a shot of you and Miss Fenimore together? It would mean a lot to this little lady."

Diana's face took on the color of her hair. "No, no, please, Mr. Williams," she protested.

"That's all right, baby," reassured Wilbur. "These things are done all the time in Hollywood." He snapped his fingers and motioned to the roving photographer.

"Mr. Benson," said Diana, "I hope you don't think...I want to make good in Hollywood all right...but that wasn't the reason I was anxious to meet you."

Ruth coughed lightly. "Of course not, dear—we understand."

THE woman photographer was at their booth.

"Okay, girlie," said Wilbur. "I want a couple of shots of Mr. Benson here, seated looking into Miss Fenimore's eyes. You know, the usual cozy twosome."

The photographer leveled her camera.

Diana stood up. Her face was flaming. "Stop it!" she cried. "I won't have it. Don't you dare take my picture...don't you dare!"

The woman photographer lowered her camera, uncertainly, while an audience of diners looked on.

"Well, well," said Ruth, "quite an actress."

"I mean it," Diana insisted. "I'm sorry, Mr. Benson. I'm terribly sorry." Hollywood's greatest press agent was flabbergasted.

"Take it easy, baby," he said. "You're kicking yourself in the face."

Diana pushed past Gil Benson and grabbed Wilbur's arm. "Get me out of here," she commanded.

America's Number One Bachelor held out his hand. "When am I going to see you again?" he asked.

"*Never...* " said Diana.

"How about this weekend?" said Gil. "I've got a ranch in Arizona." He took out a printed card with the state map on it and circled a spot with his pencil, handing it to her. "That's my location. Since you're a parachute jumper, why don't you drop in on me some time?"

"And break your neck," said Ruth.

Diana gave MGM's pin-up girl the eye. "You should drop dead, yourself," she said.

"Gil, I hope you don't blame me for this," apologized Wilbur. "I'm just an innocent bystander."

Gil Benson laughed. "This has been very enjoyable. I wanted to see you anyway. I'm about ready to break the biggest story of my life. You'll have to come to the ranch to get the dope."

"That's swell," said Wilbur. "I could stand a few days away from Hollywood."

"Good," said Gil. "I'll fly you to the ranch this weekend."

"Not me, you won't," said Wilbur. "I'm taking the train. I'm too close to the stars as it is." He turned to Diana. "Come on, Miss Fenimore. You've given me a delightful headache..."

CHAPTER THREE

GIL BENSON'S ranch was one of the show places of Arizona. It comprised ten thousand acres. Its great stone ranch house, with wide veranda and mammoth fireplace, could house thirty guests at one time. It had been built on the brow of a mountain overlooking a vast expanse of Arizona foothills and desert. Gil Benson raised prize cattle and horses but, in the last five years, something new had been added.

Beyond the sight of his ranch house and on a level, high plateau, some modern buildings had gone up. They housed newly designed, mysterious machinery and a research laboratory. Half a mile from this stretched row upon row of Quonset huts. In these simple dwellings lived skilled workmen and their families, brought to Benson-Bar Ranch to work on this secret project. There now existed a colony of over two hundred employees who seldom left the premises and who were pledged not to speak of their activities to the outside world.

Rapidly nearing completion was a new and odd-shaped building that resembled a skyscraper. It was twenty stories high, built against a steep rock incline.

Gil Benson's ranch was not on any regular air routes and few planes passed over this area. The private enterprise was fenced off from the rest of his ranch and carefully guarded. Visitors might express curiosity but they were not enlightened beyond the statement that Gil was experimenting with some new principles in aviation. Even his closest friends could not pry from him any specific details. Jerry Torrence, Gil's chief engineer in charge of operations, was hard-boiled and dependable.

The project, now in its final stages, had costs run into the millions of dollars, which Gil had taken from the oil wells, left him by his father. All supplies and equipment had been brought to the ranch by truck from the nearest spur railroad, forty miles away.

It was at this end-of-the-line junction that Hollywood's greatest press agent arrived, late this Friday afternoon, to find his client waiting for him in a station-wagon.

"Ye gods," said Wilbur. "If I'd known you were this far off from anywhere, I'd never have come. I began feeling lonely a hundred miles away and now I'm actually homesick for dear old Hollywood..."

"Most everyone feels that way when they first get here," laughed Gil. He was dressed in usual cowboy style, with brimmed hat, bright red shirt, open at the neck, and riding pants. "But you'll soon get over it."

"Not me," said Wilbur. "I can't stand being alone. I've got to be with people."

"*I'm* people," said Gil.

"You're not enough people," said Wilbur. "And this air out

here is too fresh. It hurts me to breathe it."

The station wagon was bouncing along at fifty miles an hour over the rough desert road.

"And another thing," complained Wilbur. "I told you I didn't like flying." His bag banged around in the back and he banged around on the seat. "I'm afraid you're trying to get even with me."

"For what?" asked Gil.

"For introducing you to that redhead," said Wilbur. "That was a great mistake and I admit it."

Gil dodged a boulder and the car almost left the road. "How is Miss Fenimore?" he asked.

"I hope she's left Hollywood," said Wilbur. "I gave her hell. Told her to go back to her stunt flying. Can you imagine a dame not wanting to have her picture taken with you?"

"It was quite a novelty. She interested me. I hope I see her again."

Wilbur almost fell off the seat. "Cut it out, Gil. I can't take any more..."

"I'm not kidding. I mean it. That girl really had something."

HOLLYWOOD'S greatest press agent groaned. "You tell me that now. After I've returned her money to her and told her to get out of my life. I guess I must be slipping."

They were nearing the Benson-Bar Ranch. It had taken a little less than an hour, which was considerably below par for this highway. As they approached the winding mountain road, leading up to ranch house, visible above, their attention was called to a low-flying plane that was circling around. Gil Benson slowed his car and peered out.

"Wonder who that is?" he said.

"I've got the only planes around here and nobody's supposed to be up." He stopped his car and got out to watch the plane's maneuvers. "No, it's no plane of mine. That's a four passenger Stinson. I don't like that. Someone's snooping around."

Wilbur slid out of the station wagon on his side and stared

skyward.

"What's the matter? You got something out here you don't want people to see?"

"You're exactly right," said Gil. "Not till I'm ready. That's why I brought you out here—to show you."

The plane, after twice circling the mountaintop, as though making sure of its bearings, was now climbing for altitude.

"The nerve of that guy," raged Gil. "I'll have to check that plane and see who it is…"

Wilbur looked worried. "My gosh, Gil—what are you making out here—atom bombs?"

"You'll see in a few minutes."

The Stinson, at about three thousand feet, suddenly banked sharply. Its cabin door on the earthward side opened and out shot a figure that plummeted downward, turning end over end.

"My God!" cried Gil. "Look at that…"

The plane, having discharged its human cargo, gunned away to the west. The figure, growing larger each fraction of a second, was falling about a quarter of a mile across the desert.

"It's suicide!" said Wilbur, covering his face with his hands. "I can't look."

"Pull that rip-cord, you damn fool!" Gil shouted.

Almost as he yelled there was the pistol-cracking report of a parachute blossoming out. The figure, clad in a blue jumping suit, was jerked to an upright position and swung crazily like a trapeze artist in the sky, at an altitude well under a thousand feet.

Wilbur took his hands from his eyes. "Gil," he said, "do you suppose…?"

"That's who it is!" exclaimed Gil Benson. "It's your redhead! Well, I'm a son-of-a-gun. She accepted my invitation…"

AMERICA'S Number One Bachelor started running across the desert toward the spot where the parachute jumper seemed destined to land. He was followed by the short-legged Wilbur whose street clothes and shoes were hardly a match for the rough terrain.

They got within half a city block of the chutist when she landed, kicking and wrestling with the parachute harness in an attempt to avoid hitting a mammoth cactus plant. There was not quite enough altitude left to miss it and she sprawled on top with the parachute settling over her like a collapsed umbrella.

"Hey, Diana…Miss Fenimore!" cried Wilbur. "Hang on! We're coming…"

Hollywood's greatest press agent stubbed his toe and made a landing of his own, tearing the knees out of both trouser legs.

Gil Benson arrived on the scene and circled the large cactus.

"Greetings to Benson-Bar Ranch," he called. "Are you all right?"

"Yes," said a somewhat irritated voice from beneath the parachute, "but I'm slightly uncomfortable. Get me down out of here!"

Gil reached up and grabbed the silken folds of the parachute, pulling them off the jumper. Diana was entangled in the harness, which, in turn, was caught in the cactus.

Gil Benson braced himself, gave a strong tug and she came down into his arms. He set her on her feet and helped her slip out of the chute. She looked up at him with her big blue eyes.

"You asked me to drop in some time," she said.

Gil laughed. "I sure did," he replied, "and I'm glad you're here."

Wilbur came limping up. "Look, Diana, you jump out of a plane and I'm the one who gets hurt. Look at my knees. You owe me a new pair of pants…"

Diana removed her helmet and shook out her red hair. "There was quite a wind at two thousand feet," she said. "I wanted to get down through it before I opened up. That wasn't a very good jump."

Gil Benson had rolled up the chute and put it under his arm. "It was a pip, for my money," he said. "And to show my admiration for your nerve, I'm going to let you in on the secret project of my life. There's not a soul knows about it but the gang on my ranch."

Diana smiled. "I'm all eyes."

Gil Benson looked at her. "You can say that again."

They started toward the car, with Wilbur bringing up the rear, as best he could.

"I should have stayed in Hollywood," he said, "where everything's phony. I'm not strong enough to face real life."

WILBUR WILLIAMS' redhead was assigned the Number One Guest Room in the ranch house of America's Number One bachelor. She needed only a few minutes to slip out of her flying togs and emerge in a stunning pair of green and gold slacks. When she reappeared all freshed up, with red hair and blue eyes aglow, she evoked whistles from all the wolves on the ranch.

"You're beautiful, baby," said Wilbur. "Or have I told you that before?"

Diana smiled. "You are very funny, Mr. Williams. But maybe I've told you *that* before."

"Well, let's skip the whole thing," said Wilbur. Then he eyed her again. "But you're beautiful, just the same."

This apparently was not far from Gil Benson's opinion. He immediately appropriated Diana and left Wilbur trailing along behind in a borrowed pair of pants which would have been four inches too long had he not turned up the cuffs.

Gil took them out past the other ranch buildings to a waiting jeep. He helped Diana in beside him and pushed Wilbur in the back seat.

"This isn't a disguised airplane, is it?" asked Wilbur. "I'm suspicious of you, Gil. Where are you taking us?"

"Just about half a mile. Get ready for a shock…"

Hollywood's greatest publicity agent moaned. "Listen, Gil, I'm not an explorer. I'm a writer. I don't know what you're up to but I want no part in it. You just tell me about it and I'll fix up a story. But, please, include me out…"

Gil laughed, as he spun around a rim of the mountain onto a smooth plateau, high above the desert.

"I can't describe the thing," he said. "There's never been anything like it on Earth. You've got to see it!"

Wilbur gave a helpless gesture and subsided.

Diana's red hair was blowing in the breeze. She looked very much the outdoor girl.

Gil Benson drove past long, low buildings where men were busy at work. They hailed him cordially as he went by and many watched the jeep out of sight.

"I've got a great gang here," said Gil. "There's not a man who wouldn't darn near give his life for me..."

"You've got a girl in the front seat," said Wilbur, "who darn near gave *hers.*"

Diana laughed. "A little jump like that was nothing. You should try it some time. It's good for your nerves."

"No, thanks," said Wilbur. "I'll take pheno-barbital."

They had now come into view of the towering wood structure erected against the mountainside. Two burly men stood guard at the locked door.

"Howdy, Mr. Benson," they greeted, almost in chorus, eyeing Diana and Wilbur.

"Open up, boys," said Gil. "I'm taking in my first visitors."

"Okay..."

The tallest of the two guards produced a key ring and inserted one key in the lock. The door swung open. Gil motioned for Diana and Wilbur to step inside. It was dark and cavernous. The door closed behind them as they both tried to accustom their eyes to the vast shadows.

"Don't be so mysterious," said Wilbur. "Give us some light."

Gil reached for the light switch.

"All right, you two, here it is..."

The large interior was suddenly flooded with illumination. Looming in front of them was a gigantic, unended, projectile-shaped metal body that pointed toward the heavens. Wilbur and Diana stared up and about, too petrified with awe and astonishment to speak.

"That's my Manhattan Project," Gil announced. "My closely guarded secret—the dream of a lifetime, about to come true."

"*A space rocket!*" cried Diana. "Oh, Gil—I mean, Mr. Benson—I think that's wonderful. Stupendous! There just aren't any words for it..."

Wilbur cleared his throat. "There's words for it all right. About a billion of 'em. This should be the world's biggest news story. Where are you going to shoot this thing?"

"*To the moon...*" said Gil. Hollywood's greatest press agent was getting more and more excited. "Boy, I can think of a million gags... 'All aboard for the moon.' Weekend excursions in space! Buy your round-trip tickets now. Get a load of green cheese. Visit the man in the moon! Brother, this is a *super-terrific-colossal-natural!*"

Gil Benson laughed. "I thought you'd go for this. What do you say we climb up this scaffolding and step inside?"

"Oh, can we, Mr. Benson?" said Diana. "I'd love to."

Gil led the way. They mounted a circular staircase, built around the mammoth rocket, which was painted black on one side with a glittering mirror-like surface on the other.

"Looks like a huge penguin," said Wilbur. "What's the idea of the two colors?"

"Black absorbs heat and this mirrored surface deflects it," Gil explained. "The sun would burn us up if we didn't turn our mirrored surface toward it part of the time. When we want heat, we roll over on the black side. In this way, we control the ship's temperature."

"Very fascinating," said Wilbur. "But where do you get this 'we' stuff? This isn't a man-carrying rocket, is it?"

Gil laughed. "Of course it is."

"You mean...now hold on, Gil...you don't really...are you actually going up in that thing?"

"Certainly...that's the whole idea. And two of my men have volunteered to go with me. That's why I designed and built it."

Wilbur gasped. "Well, this beats me...I can't believe it. You've probably made this rocket of papier-mâché or chewing gum wrappers. It's an advertising stunt. If you're really serious, Gil, this is *the most spectacular way to commit suicide ever invented...*"

"I don't think so at all," said Diana.

"Why, a hundred years from now we won't think anything of traveling to Mars or Venus or some other planet. The moon will just be a local stop."

They were still climbing.

"The Earth is my local stop," said Wilbur. "How far is the moon, anyway?"

"About two hundred thirty-nine thousand miles," said Gil.

Wilbur grabbed hold of the slender railing and looked down. "Brother, I'm close enough to the moon right now. How long do you expect it'll take to get there—if you make it?"

Gil smiled. "Not more than twelve hours."

DIANA'S blue eyes expanded. "Why Mr. Benson—do you mean it?"

Gil nodded. "I've had Professor Crowley working with me. He's an atomic scientist. We've solved the problem of fuel. Get this, Wilbur—it's the biggest feature of the space rocket story. *We've found how to extract the energy from a pound of gasoline.* We can create enormous power—enough to escape easily the Earth's gravitational pull. That's why this rocket only needs to be two hundred feet long. It could have been even shorter. Very little of its capacity has to be taken up with fuel tanks."

"I'm getting dizzy," said Wilbur, "and it's not the altitude." Then a thought struck him. "Holy smoke," he exclaimed softly. "Do you realize...of course you must...that you've developed atomic power? That same kind of energy can run ships and trains and machinery—everything. For cryin' out loud, Gil...you gotta be spoofing me. It can't be true. This is a story that's a little too big for even me. In fact it's probably too big for the world. This is what science has been aiming at for years and years."

"I know," said Gil, quietly, "and the day we take off for the moon, Professor Crowley and I will make known our process for transforming gasoline into energy to the United States government."

They had reached an elevation near the great nose of the rocket. Gil led them across a catwalk and flung open a tungsten steel door. They stepped into a rather spacious circular cabin, which contained bunks for sleeping built into the walls and soft, reclining seats, firmly fastened to the floor.

A passageway in the rear of the cabin led to other compartments: a small laboratory, a photographic room, and a machine shop on one side; and a galley and storeroom on the other. Behind these living and working quarters were the various units necessary for operating radar, television, radio, air-conditioning, production of oxygen and rocket power, all of which were controlled through a great instrument board set up in the forward part of the cabin.

"Say, this is all right," said Wilbur, looking around. "Just like being in a state room on board ship. But what's up and what's down in this thing?"

Gil laughed. "That's a problem," he said. "We'll have to adjust ourselves in relation to the position of the rocket at different stages of the trip."

Diana looked up at the glass dome of the cabin.

"What peculiar looking glass," she said. "It ought to give you wonderful visibility."

"It will," said Gil, "but it's not glass—it's a new kind of transparent plastic which resists heat. There's going to be considerable danger out in space from ultra-violet and shorter radiations from the sun. This plastic is practically opaque to the ultra-violet without impeding the necessary light. Of course, we're apt to run into meteorites which would come crashing through, but then they would pierce the metal walls of the rocket almost as easily—and this is a chance we'll have to take."

"It's tremendously exciting!" said Diana.

"*Exciting?*" said Wilbur. "Say nothing more, I'm scared as hell."

"I want to know all about it," said Diana. "Of course you have to be sealed up in this thing. How do you breathe?"

"We'll maintain an atmosphere of helium-oxygen," said Gil.

"That's fine," objected Wilbur, "but let's say you get to the moon and want to step out and look around. What then?"

For answer, Gil Benson led them into the storeroom small pantry alcove and pointed to three large strange looking, full length heavy metal suits, somewhat resembling a diver's outfit.

"These space suits will do the trick," he declared. "They contain a device for supplying oxygen and even a miniature walkie-talkie."

Hollywood's greatest press agent shook his head.

"You seem to have thought of everything, all right—but how about food and water?"

"We'll have to take that with us," said Gil. "Most of the foodstuffs can be dehydrated. I estimate that each person will need about a gallon of water per day. If all goes well, I don't expect to stay on the moon more than two weeks, the first trip."

"Listen to that guy," said Wilbur. "He sounds like a commuter already."

"There won't be anything to it in a few years," predicted Gil. "I just want to get the thrill of being the first one there."

"Well, brother, you're welcome to it. The only thrill I want is writing this up and saying I knew him when—and *if!*"

Diana's attention was drawn to the large instrument board on the forward wall of the cabin, containing a bewildering array of buttons, levers, and gauges. She walked over to it.

"Gosh," she said, "this looks more complicated than the gadgets on a Constellation…"

Gil Benson came over to her as she placed her hand on a lever.

"What's this?" she asked.

"That, young lady," said Gil, "happens to be the starting lever. When this ship is set to go, all I have to do is pull this lever down, the atomic power process begins—and we take off. It's so regulated that a shifting of this lever controls the speed. Fortunately, this power enables us to go as slowly as we desire, or as fast. You know, the friction of the air is so great that we could easily burn up like a meteor if we tore through our atmosphere at too high a speed. We only have to go seven miles a second to get beyond the gravitational pull of the Earth."

Wilbur did some figuring with a pencil on the back of an envelope. "Only seven miles a second," he said. "That's four hundred and twenty miles a minute—twenty-five thousand, two hundred miles an hour. Let me out of here. I can't stand it!"

"Oh, yes you could," said Gil. "The human body can stand any speed. Perhaps you don't know it—but this Earth is traveling around the sun at a rate of twenty miles a second—this very minute—and we don't even feel it. But what does affect us is a sudden change of speed. If an airplane pilot pulls out of a dive or makes a sharp turn, he's apt to 'black out.' And because we'll have to leave the Earth at a constantly increasing speed, the first ten minutes after our take-off are going to be tough. But once our top speed is established, we should be all right."

Wilbur shook his head.

"I still want out of here," he said. "*My* body's affected right now…"

Gil motioned toward the door. "Well, you've got the main points of the story, anyway."

"I've got so much my brain is congested," said Wilbur. "How soon do you want to break this story?"

Gil smiled as they started their descent of the scaffolding.

"Not till I send out my invitations," he said.

"Invitations," repeated Wilbur. "What are they for?"

Gil stopped and looked up the staircase at Diana and Wilbur who were following him.

"For my take-off," he said. "I'm throwing a big party and I want you to help with arrangements."

CHAPTER FOUR

RUTH DELANO came off the set at MGM after finishing a scene in her new picture: "To Have but Not to Hold." She was in a bad mood. Her leading man had flubbed some lines and she had been compelled to repeat the scene five times before a take.

"I don't know why I always have to get such rotten support," she said. "It's about time they were giving me some good leading man like Van Johnson. I'm tired holding up these newcomers."

The arrival of the studio mailman with a stack of fan mail did much to sooth Ruth's temper. She thumbed through the odd-sized envelopes. A large and distinguished appearing one, bearing the name "Benson-Bar Ranch," caught her attention. She slit it open and took out a handsomely engraved card. She shrieked at what she read.

GIL BENSON Cordially Invites You To Attend A
FAREWELL BUFFET SUPPER To Be Held At Benson-Bar
Ranch Next Monday
On the Occasion of His Departure by Rocket TO THE
MOON!
Arrangements have been made for your conveyance to the
Ranch by plane—from New York, Chicago, or Los Angeles
Supper at 6 P.M. with Take-off Scheduled at Midnight DRESS
OPTIONAL RSVP.

"Oh, no!" screamed Ruth. "He must be kidding! As well as I know Gil Benson, he never mentioned…yes, he did, too…but I didn't believe him… That night in Sardi's!"

"What are you raving about?" demanded Director Don Stevens.

"Gil Benson!" shouted Ruth, so that all could hear. She waved the engraved card. "The damn fool's going by rocket to the moon!"

The announcement created a sensation, which was increased when the studio doorman came in with a newspaper extra. He spread out the paper for all to see. MGM's pin-up girl took a look and let out another scream. A copyrighted, exclusive feature article by—of all persons—that little squirt of a publicity agent, "Wee Willie Wilbur."

"Oh!" cried Ruth. "This is too much. The idea of Gil letting that brassy Wilbur get a break like this... Why didn't he let me in on this secret? I was just out with him last night." She broke away from the excited actors and crew and ran to her dressing room. "Just wait till I get hold of that guy," she cried. "Just wait..."

She grabbed up the telephone. Gil's line at the Beverly Hills was busy. It continued to be busy. Finally Ruth, exasperated, got the hotel manager on the wire.

"I'm Ruth Delano," she identified. "I'm a very special friend of Mr. Benson's. I know he probably has lots of people trying to reach him this morning—but I've got to get a call through to him."

"I'll see what I can do, Miss Delano," said the hotel manager. "Hold on..."

Ruth held on...and on...and on. She jiggled the connection violently. The operator at the Beverly Hills came on the wire.

"Get me Gil Benson," Ruth demanded.

"I'm sorry, Miss Fenimore," said the operator. "Were you disconnected?"

"Miss Fenimore," raged Ruth. "This is Miss Delano... If Miss Fenimore is on Mr. Benson's line, get her off. What's she mean—holding up the wire this way?"

"I'm sorry, Miss Delano," said the operator, "the line is still busy."

Ruth Delano slammed up the receiver, then threw the phone across her dressing room.

AS GIL BENSON had carefully planned and surmised, the world reaction to his announced rocket flight to the moon was nothing short of terrific. His list of engraved invitations numbered a thousand. He was immediately besieged, yes— swamped, inundated, submerged by requests from thousands of others to be permitted to witness this greatest astronomic adventure in all Earth history.

Gil's small office staff at the Benson-Bar Ranch had to be reinforced. Foreign governments made strong representations to be allowed to have observers present. The F.B.I. immediately moved in to protect the Benson-Bar Ranch against invasion by secret agents and saboteurs who might wish to steal or destroy much of world value contained in laboratory, plant and rocket.

Gil Benson may have intended this project as a private enterprise but its scientific importance was too great for it to be kept in this category. Despite the remoteness of Gil's location in the Arizona desert, hundreds of humans sought to reach his Benson-Bar Ranch by every means possible and see and learn what they could. It became necessary for the Governor of Arizona to dispatch a detachment of state militia to draw a cordon around Gil's ten thousand acres and to challenge every unwelcome and uninvited visitor.

Newspapermen and photographers tried every trick in their experience and a few new ones, to get on the premises, but Gil Benson had decreed that no one would be permitted to take pictures or get information beyond the details given out in his official, authorized news release, until the night of departure.

Wilbur Williams, Gil Benson's press representative, thus became the most sought after and most important man, next to his client, in America. He had to close his office and go into hiding. He couldn't even stay in his own apartment.

"This is hell," he said, "but I love it!"

Ruth Delano, MGM's pin-up sensation, was going slightly mad herself. Gil Benson had left his Beverly Hills suite and gone into seclusion. The papers had reported that he was under heavy guard for fear he would be kidnapped or attempts made by crackpots and foreign agents on his life. The fact that his announced trip to the moon was now only two days away and that this event was causing such a tremendous stir in governmental and scientific circles, let alone the spellbinding effect on the public mind, had made it impossible for most of Gil's friends to reach him in person.

Reporters, however, had trailed Ruth Delano, as they had

every glamour girl Gil had been known to be interested in, with the hope that he would be seeking one or more of them out and could thus be caught and interviewed.

"I know that Gil Benson, if he were free to do so, would be getting in touch with me," Ruth told the newspapermen.

"Have you accepted his invitation to see him off to the moon?" asked a reporter.

"I certainly have," said Ruth, "but I don't mind telling the world that I love Gil and I'm going to try to dissuade him from taking such a risk." ·

"Would you go with him if he gave you a chance?" asked another interviewer.

"I should say not," rejoined Ruth. "Do you think I'm crazy?"

The newspapermen laughed.

"Who's this redhead Benson's been seen with lately?" fired one of them. "Do you know her?"

Ruth Delano stiffened. "Has he been out with her?" she asked.

"Oh, so you do know her?" shot another reporter. "Well, maybe you can give us a line on her. We saw them at Ciro's a couple of nights before this moon story broke and the lady wouldn't give out her name or permit any pictures. She's a mystery dame."

Ruth Delano was furious.

"And as far as I'm concerned," she blazed, "she's going to remain a mystery. I know nothing about the lady in question. And, if I did, I wouldn't tell you."

"Thanks, Miss Delano. You're very kind," said a reporter. "We know we can always count on you to give us the lowdown."

ON SUNDAY morning, one day before Gil Benson's projected trip to the moon, the Hearst papers came out with an entire section devoted to his life story. His daredevil experiments and achievements were depicted, topped off by the current rocket venture—but the most colorful emphasis was placed upon Gil's widely varied romantic interests.

Under the caption: "The Big Ten in Gil Benson's Life," the paper published ten photographs of ten different glamour girls with whom America's Number One Bachelor and Playboy had night-clubbed.

The question was asked:

"If Gil Benson reaches his destination and becomes the first real man in the moon, which of these Beauties will he choose to live with him in Lunar-Land?"

When Ruth Delano saw this story, she was pleased to note that her picture was given Number One Position—and the redhead was nowhere in evidence.

Early in the afternoon of the eventful day, the first influx of distinguished engraved card holders and especially permitted gatecrashers began arriving by plane and train and bus and car at the Benson-Bar Ranch. They were passed through tightly drawn lines of state militiamen who examined all credentials and turned back numerous imposters.

The desert, for miles around, was teeming with activity and filled with more humans than had ever been within miles of this area before. Coming in by air, many of the curious visitors could glimpse the rocket assembly plant and a mammoth canvas covering which concealed the spaceship. They could also see signs of something being done in the open level stretches around this apparent launching site. But, once arriving, all comers were carefully shepherded to the big ranch house and kept without the great fenced enclosure. Those who had come early with the hope of gaining special favor were forced to spend their time playing miniature golf, taking a swim in the pool, walking about the grounds or sitting on the wide veranda overlooking the Arizona desert.

Arrangements had been made with one of Hollywood's most celebrated caterers and a large tent had been erected near the ranch house from which the buffet supper was to be served. No accommodations were provided for this great crowd overnight, it being taken for granted that there would be no sleep on such an unusual nocturnal occasion.

Hollywood's greatest press agent was everywhere in evidence. In other words, he was all over the place. He had to be. Gil Benson had depended upon him to do the major planning for the event, to act as official greeter in welcoming this excited mob of celebrities, scientists, government officials and others of unclassified importance, in addition to being master of ceremonies at the unveiling of the rocket itself.

"This is a publicity man's dream," said Wilbur. "After this is over, my reputation won't be restricted to Hollywood. I'll be the world's greatest press agent..."

This afternoon Wilbur Williams was enjoying his authority. His client had told him to "shoot the works" in lining up entertainment and stunts which would amuse and beguile this thrill-expectant crowd. He was required to be a diplomat in the handling of various personalities and temperaments, but his Hollywood training enabled him to carry off this function with ease. He could say "yes" and "no" at the same time and mean both. And, if he didn't mean either, no one could tell the difference until it was too late.

GIL BENSON'S glamour girl friends, as they began arriving, gave evidence that each, in her way, had sought, through some ingenious design or quirk of evening dress attire or use of jewelry or hair-dress to carry out and express the moon motif. Then they stood off and jealously compared their own appearance with that of each new feminine arrival. This show and competition was worth coming miles to see, if only a minor prelude to the main event.

MGM's pin-up sensation was the last of the ten glamour girls to arrive. She had come by late afternoon plane from Los Angeles, in company with other Hollywood stars. When she saw "Wee Willy Wilbur" greeting guests at the entrance to the big ranch house, she hurried up to him, her white satin evening gown sweeping the flagstones. She was wearing diamond half-moon earrings and a diamond crescent in her hair.

Wilbur saw her coming and spoke first. "Well, Miss Delano," he called. "You certainly are a delectable looking dish..."

Ruth extended her hand as a peace offering and whispered in his ear, "Wilbur, darling—I'm depending on you to get me to Gil Benson right away."

"How's that?" said Wilbur, turning his head. "Try the other ear."

"You heard what I said, you little snob!" hissed Ruth. "If you know what's good for you, you'll do what I say..."

"Excuse me," said Wilbur, stepping to one side. "I think I see Eddie Rickenbacker coming."

Ruth caught his arm. "You can't brush me off this way. I've got to see Gil. I've simply got to!"

"He's very busy," said Wilbur. "He's not seeing anybody—not yet. Last minute preparations and all that sort of thing."

Ruth was beside herself and then some. "All right, you blackmailer. I'll let you handle my publicity. Now get to Mr. Benson..."

Wilbur grinned. "I'm not taking on any more accounts just at present. If Mr. Benson gets to the moon, this is going to be a full time job. I'm sorry, sweetheart; you're a little bit too late."

Ruth stamped her foot and broke a heel off her sandal.

HAL SPECK and his orchestra, one of Hollywood's name bands, had been hired to furnish the supper music. They were placed on the lawn by the side of the big ranch house where long tables had been set so that guests could find their own places after being served at the caterer's tent.

The sun was swiftly sliding beneath the rim of the western mountains as the orchestra struck up its first selection and the diners commenced assembling. Most of them, entering into the spirit of the occasion, were gaily wearing evening dress. They were looking hopefully for some sign or sight of their host, the highly colorful, unpredictable, perhaps slightly insane, at least foolhardy Gil Benson. But he did not appear, much to the particular wonderment and distress of his lady friends.

Dusk came rushing over the landscape and, with it, a small airplane which swooped low over the desert multitude and suddenly flashed, on its under side, a bright, white half moon. The effect was startling and brought exclamations of pleased surprise.

"Maybe that's Gil Benson," a guest suggested.

"It could be," said another. "You can't tell what he'll be doing next..."

But Wilbur knew it wasn't Benson or any part of his planned program. The plane circled twice more at a low altitude, flashing its luminous moon on and off. Then it turned back to the airfield and came in for a landing.

Wilbur dispatched a ranch hand in a jeep to see who had arrived. He returned, bringing a young woman in evening dress on the seat beside him. As she stepped down to the roadway and advanced toward the diners, Wilbur and all who saw her gasped their instant admiration. The front of the black velvet dress had a phosphorescent glow, which caused the design of a half moon and stars to stand out with stunning effect. Flaming red hair fell loosely and softly to the shoulders, banded by a single brilliant star at the forehead. Word of this gorgeous creature was passed back to those beyond sight of her and not a few left their tables to get a close-up view.

"Ye gods, Diana," said Wilbur, when he could get to her. "What are you trying to do—break up this party?"

"I'm awfully sorry to be late," Diana apologized. "But there was a dressmakers' strike in Hollywood. I almost didn't get this dress finished in time."

"Well, you've just about finished me," said Wilbur. "You're beautiful, baby. If I've told you that before, I say it again..."

Diana glanced quickly about her. She was conscious that she had captured the attention of all, that she was being "oh'd" and "ah'd" and "who-is-she'd?"

"Where's Gil?" she asked in a low voice.

"You can't get to him," said Wilbur, guardedly. "He's really installing some last minute equipment—the newest thing in radar loaned to him by the Army. He'll be lucky if he gets off on time."

Diana's blue eyes looked troubled. "That's too bad," she said. "I was in hopes he had seen my grand and glorious entrance…"

"You're not alone in that, baby. There are a lot of disappointed females here tonight." He nodded toward several, including Ruth Delano, seated two tables away. "I'd keep away from those dames if I were you. They're apt to hate you."

"I must get to Gil, somehow," said Diana. "I haven't gone to all this trouble for nothing."

Wilbur shrugged his shoulders. "Wish I could help you but no can do. Let me get you a plate of supper. Better get something on your stomach and Gil Benson off your mind."

He piloted her toward the caterer's tent, escorted by everyone's eyes.

WITH completion of the buffet supper, the tension of interest in Gil Benson's moon rocket was rapidly rising. Guests impatiently awaited transportation to the launching site, about a mile away on the high plateau on the other side of the mountain. A fleet of buses had been chartered for conveying purposes, back and forth. They stood lined up on the side of the private road, near the ranch house. Wilbur Williams had added a fantastic touch by having banners hung on each bus, with the printed words:

"TO THE MOON ROCKET"

This carried the suggestion that each visitor was going to make the trip, himself.

At nine p.m. a fanfare of bugles announced that the moment

had arrived for the first busload of spectators to depart for the rocket-launching site. Lines quickly formed and there was good-natured jostling to be in the first contingent.

The sight that met the eyes of all as they came around the mountain and looked down upon the plateau was unique on this Earth.

Towering skyward, like a shadowy specter, its bright black and white nose just protruding from its great canvas encasement, was the moon rocket. Its two hundred foot length was resting, in a semi-perpendicular position on a sleek runway built against the natural rock incline. Workmen, beneath, looking like pygmies, were arranging the guy ropes fastened to the canvas, preparatory to the unveiling.

In the great open space in front of the rocket, an outdoor amphitheatre had been formed with rows of several thousand folding chairs set up in a large semi-circle. There was a speaker's platform with railing and flag bunting at the base of the rocket and on one side of this stage, Hal Speck's orchestra had been placed. Standing beside the rocket was a great metallic portable stairway, its circular incline permitting workers and others access to any section of the spaceship. The area was illumined by strings of overhead lights and great Klieg lights, not yet turned on, were banked on each side of the aerial monster, ready to reveal its every detail when the canvas shield should be dropped.

The prevailing atmosphere of excitement took on the nerve-tingling quality of a championship heavyweight prizefight. Spectators to such events were lured by the promise of thrills in man's elemental combat against man. But in this case, interest was immensely heightened at thought of puny man's cosmic battle against the elements of time and space. This was a feast, a carnival, a state fair, a Hollywood opening, a sporting event, a launching and a new era exposition—all rolled into one. And Wilbur Williams' imagination and press agent wizardry had been equal to the occasion. How could a good publicity man, given carte blanche and an unlimited bankroll, miss?

Wilbur had arranged a program designed to acquaint his select audience with the nature and purposes of this first man-made attempt to escape the ball of Earth and explore the universe. With the crowd now fully assembled and sitting in expectant wonder, Hollywood's greatest press agent, as master of ceremonies, mounted the dais and, following an arresting fanfare, with the spotlights turned on him, began to speak.

"LADIES and gentlemen of Tomorrow," he said, his voice ringing out over the loudspeaker system. "You are gathered here tonight under the stars, but, presently, the rising moon will appear over the mountain top and very shortly after that moment arrives, you will witness the first take-off from this planet of a man-carrying rocket, bound for Earth's one and only satellite—two hundred thirty-eight thousand, eight hundred fifty-seven miles away...

"We are only sorry that the several billion humans on Earth cannot be spectators with you tonight, but many millions will observe the take-off through television, hear its description by radio, and see the event pictured in the newsreels. If Gil Benson and his two courageous associates reach their destination and are able to return to Earth, they will bring back with them information of staggering importance, not only to us now living but to those yet unborn.

"The era of interplanetary travel is just around the corner. Man has dreamed for centuries of flying to the moon. He first imagined that he might grow great birds to transport him there. Then he thought of attaching engines to these birds to aid in such a journey.

"And when man saw that the morning dew disappeared in the rays of the sun and seemed to be drawn toward the sky, he even dreamed up the idea of enormous bottles filled with dew— operating, I suppose, on the theory that all a space traveler had to do was sit on top of the bottle and he'd eventually be eating green cheese on the moon."

A thunder of laughter rolled up in front of Wilbur.

"You laugh at this?" he continued. "Well, how would you like to try to go to the moon in an iron chariot made of lodestone, the magnetic properties of which were calculated to be powerful enough to draw you upward...? Still rather primitive, you say? But give Man a chance. He hadn't been on Earth very long.

"The first hot air balloons came late in the Sixteenth Century. When a Frenchman introduced hydrogen gas to give them new lifting power, visionaries cried: 'Now for the moon!' But the closest approach was two miles above the Earth. Even so, this was progress.

"Next came the lighter than air ship, then the flying machine. The moon didn't seem so far away now. Maybe not, but Astronomy threw a monkey wrench into man's dream machinery. There was no atmosphere on the moon—no air or water. You couldn't breathe after you got there. And to get there, you'd have to escape the Earth's gravitational pull. There, little man, what are you going to do about that?

"Well, you people all know that Man came right back with the answer: "Rockets... Jet propulsion... A new fuel—perhaps liquid oxygen and alcohol... Maybe even atomic power—and, with the promise of atomic power—spaceships... What Man had dared dream, Man could one day accomplish!

"Which brings us up to tonight and the perfection of Man's dream.

"I give you now, the Number One Space Pioneer—the man whom Destiny has selected to fulfill the dreams of all men in all past time—your host and fellow human—Gil Benson."

THERE was a roll of drums and a mighty fanfare. At its climax, workers tugged the guy ropes and the great canvas covering billowed away from the gigantic spaceship, as floodlights suddenly beamed on. The smooth, glistening, streamlined surface, half-black and half-luminous, of this Goliath of the skies, was revealed to awe-inspiring view.

Emblazoned along each side, in mammoth letters, was its

name, *Goodbye, World*, first sight of which provoked shrieks of excited laughter.

A second mighty fanfare brought a focusing of lights on the cabin door high up on the rocket. It swung open and the figure of a man in evening dress appeared. He stepped out upon the platform of the portable stairway, at his elevation, and stood in front of a microphone. Beneath him a great roar of sound came involuntarily from the throats of all assembled. This figure stood quietly, for perhaps two minutes, looking down upon the ecstatic sea of upturned faces. Then he spoke.

"Greetings. I appreciate, in the name of Science and humanity, your acceptance of my invitation to be here tonight and the effort you have made to come long distances to witness our departure from Earth.

"Jerry Torrence, my chief engineer, and Professor Crowley, the atomic scientist, have elected to accompany me. We feel that, despite the known hazards and hazards yet unknown, we stand an excellent chance to reach the moon and, also, to return. We could not be so assured of such a possibility were it not for the fact that Professor Crowley, in working with us in our laboratory, has discovered a method for extracting the energy from a pound of gasoline..."

A great gasp of surprise went up from the audience, followed by almost unbelieving cheers.

"Yes," Gil continued, "you heard me rightly. The age of atomic power is here—and we are using it for the first time in our space rocket tonight. In five, maybe ten years at the most, thanks to the genius of Professor Crowley, this power will operate the machines of Earth and bring Mankind complete release from drudgery.

"Even apart from this, the United States Army is preparing to send unmanned space rockets to the moon, containing recording instruments and powered with liquid oxygen and alcohol as fuel. The advantage we enjoy, through use of atomic power, is that we do not require enormous weight taken up by fuel tanks and can carry, instead, more scientific equipment, supplies and such food and water as we will need on our journey.

"I'm indebted to the United States Army for the loan to me of their latest radar devices with which they are even now contacting the moon through high frequency waves which are bouncing back in something like two and four-tenths seconds.

"I'm also indebted to the General Electric Company of Schenectady for permitting me to install a hitherto untried sending and receiving radio set which beams radio waves of such high frequency that we are confident they can penetrate both the Heavyside and Appleton layers which surround the Earth, at respective levels of sixty and two hundred miles, so that we can keep in constant touch with this planet during our travels and while on the moon.

"These new instruments, in conjunction with the television apparatus we are carrying, will permit us to scan some of the moon's surface and project back to Earth the actual scenes as we are witnessing them. You know, of course, that television waves travel in a straight line and from the vantage point of the moon they can be beamed directly to Earth. In fact, could a television station be established on the moon, we could then beam all television shows to the moon and relay them back to Earth on a straight line so that they would be receivable everywhere."

THERE was a constant murmur of excited comment running throughout the crowd.

"I will have to leave it to reporters, photographers, and scientists to point out, in detail, the enormous possibilities and values to be derived from this moon trip—if we should be successful.

"Control of the moon is more important than you may think. Could an unfriendly nation eventually colonize on the moon, it could destroy any country on Earth by atomic bombardment. It will be our plan, upon reaching the moon, to lay claim to it as a possession of the United States of America. We are aware that certain foreign powers will soon be attempting moon trips of their own. We naturally hope to be first.

"And now, I know that all of you are wishing you might be permitted to examine this moon rocket at close range. We still have a little more than two hours before take-off time. If you are willing to climb these portable stairs, I will be glad to greet, you personally and let you pass in and out of the cabin. I must ask you to keep moving and to touch nothing. You will stay on the right, single file, going and coming. The guards will assist you.

"Welcome to *Goodbye, World...*"

Wilbur, in anticipation of the rush to be among the first on board the spaceship, had left the platform while Gil was speaking and, motioning to Diana to follow him, led her to the portable stairway.

"This is the best I can do for you, baby," he said. "You can be the first one up to see Gil."

Diana's blue eyes caressed him. "I could almost kiss you," she said.

"You're beautiful, baby," said Wilbur. "Remind me to tell you that some time when there's not a crowd around."

"Do you think Gil will like this getup?" she asked.

"If he doesn't, he's crazy," said Wilbur. "I mean crazier than he is now, if that's possible."

"He's not crazy," said Diana. "He's wonderful..."

She started up the steps.

Gil had just finished talking and the rush was on. Ruth Delano was among the first ten in line.

"I saw you tip her off," she called to Hollywood's greatest press agent. "That's no fair, Wilbur, and you know it."

Diana turned about on the steps and came down. She walked up to Miss Delano in the line.

"I heard what you said. You can see Mr. Benson first, if you want to. I've changed my mind. I want to see him last."

MGM's pin-up sensation stepped out of line.

"Oh, no you don't!" she cried. "You don't take advantage of

me that way. Go right ahead, dearie. I'll see him last."

The end of the line, still forming, was some distance away but Ruth Delano headed for it, with Wilbur's redhead following. Gil's other glamour girl friends looked on curiously from their positions in the line, as the two women passed.

"What goes on?" one of them called to Wilbur.

"Yes—what's up?" cried another.

"They're going to wait and see Mr. Benson just before he takes off," Wilbur explained."

"That's a good idea," said another glamour girl. "I think I'll wait, too..."

"Me, too," said another.

The contagion was on and glamour girls began stepping out all up and down the line, and trailing to the rear.

"Yikes," said Wilbur. "I told Gil it was dangerous to invite all those dames here. If they start fighting over him, he'll be lucky to leave Earth alive."

Ruth and Diana, reaching the end of the line and being good-humoredly kidded by various guests who sensed what was going on, turned to face one another.

"You first," said MGM's pin-up star, with mock courtesy.

"No, you first," insisted Diana.

"I'll see him last," said Ruth. "I'm sure Mr. Benson would prefer it that way."

"I would regret very much to have to use force," said Diana. "But I am seeing him last."

There was a flurry of shouts and the two rival women looked around to see almost a dozen other rivals descending upon them.

"You see what you started?" accused Ruth.

"I started...?" said Diana. "How dare you say that?"

She advanced toward Ruth but, before any damage could be done, the two were surrounded by other glamour girls, perhaps as pulchritudinous a collection of femininity as one seldom sees in any compact spot.

Reporters and photographers, quick to appreciate this fact,

went to work. Flash light bulbs popped as the girls struggled for positions at the end of the line.

"Girls! Girls!" shouted Wilbur, running up. "Remember—you are all ladies—or are you? Calm down... Take it easy... You won't look like anything when Mr. Benson gets to see you. Cut it out or I'll have the guards keep you off the rocket..."

This last threat had an effect and the beauties abandoned their bargain counter tactics. Ruth and Diana still brought up the extreme end of the line but declared a temporary truce by standing side by side.

"We'll see who's last when the time comes," said Ruth.

"And I know who that's going to be," said Diana.

MEMBERS of the state militia kept the line of distinguished guests moving rapidly past Gil Benson who stood just inside the cabin door and shook each hand. The guest then made a quick circuit of the cabin, with much of the equipment roped off. There was opportunity for only a good glance about and then he was ushered out the same cabin door and directed down the steps.

The time required for the end of the line to be reached consumed almost two hours, as was estimated.

It had been a fatiguing day for Gil Benson with all manner of last minute details, usual unforeseen happenings, and pressure of last earthly demands that could not be denied. Even now, as he was playing host, Professor Crowley and Jerry Torrence, his two rocket associates, were outside making final check-ups, to be sure everything was in order.

Everyone had something special they wished to say to Gil or some good luck charm to leave with him, all of which ate up additional seconds and energy. But America's so-called Number One Playboy, about to embark on what many privately termed "the greatest screwball adventure of his career," was understanding and gracious. Knowing human society as he did, he realized that he was still expected to live up to the public conception of him.

"Leave it to Gil Benson... Good old Gil... Nonchalant as ever... Acts like he's preparing to take off on a routine coast-to-coast flight in his plane... Nothing to it, according to him..." This was representative of general impressions expressed behind Gil's back—but, outwardly, he was greeted by a variety of well-meaning witticisms.

"Remember me to the man in the moon."

"Do you think you'll find any girls up there? If not, why go?"

"What's the matter, old boy—tired of Earth?"

"What're you going to do if the moon doesn't have any night clubs?"

"If Alaska doesn't hurry up, you'll be making the moon the Forty-Ninth State in the Union."

"Pick out a good piece of real estate for me up there."

"I know some people I'd like to send to the moon. Will you take 'em along?"

"The government should have gotten out a 'moon stamp' so we could mail letters to the man in the moon. Can you imagine what those stamps would have been worth—if you make the return trip?"

"If you run out of fuel will you come back on a moon beam?"

"I guess you'll be able to keep up your spirits—I see you're taking off while the moon is full!"

Gil good-naturedly parried such obvious wisecracks as these with a smile or quip of his own.

AS THOSE visiting the rocket reached the ground again, they resumed their seats to await the dramatic moment of its departure, all now excitedly discussing its mechanical marvels and thrilling at the thought that they had actually been inside a spaceship that might reach the moon.

"I was aboard the _Queen Mary_ just before she made her maiden voyage—also the _Graf Zeppelin_," said one. "But it never gave me a sensation like this..."

"And nothing else will," replied another. "When vessels start going to the moon and other planets, you've seen all modes of travel possible in the universe."

As they had been speaking, from over the mountaintop, could be seen the rim of the rising full moon. It cast an increasing white light upon the nose of the rocket pointed in its direction.

"Gives you an eerie feeling to think of shooting toward the moon in that thing, doesn't it?" remarked another guest, and shuddered.

Hollywood's greatest press agent, his collar wilted, his tuxedo wrinkled and his temper ruffled, pushed his way up the stairs, past the end of the line and Gil Benson's glamour girls so that he might reach his client first with a word of warning.

"How you holding out, Gil, old man?"

"Confidentially," said Gil, in a low aside as he was still meeting people, "I'll be glad when I can take off."

"Well, you may be sorry you haven't taken off already," said Wilbur. "Your girl friends are just outside. They're coming in a bunch—and they've got blood in their eyes..."

"What do you mean?" asked Gil.

"They each want to bid you the last farewell," said Wilbur. "It all started with Ruth and Diana—then the rest followed. Boy, get set for a stampede..."

Gil laughed. "Wilbur—you just haven't learned how to manage women."

"Not when they're like that redhead or Miss Delano," Wilbur admitted.

"Leave 'em to me," said Gil. "Are they here now?"

There was a hubbub of female voices.

"That's them," said Wilbur.

"Let 'em in," ordered Gil.

The steel door was half shut and the last guest had been ushered out, with only the feminine contingent remaining of the great number who had tramped up the stairs, around the cabin and down to Earth again.

"Okay," said Wilbur, swinging open the door. "You asked for it…"

In came the glamour girl avalanche… A blonde in the lead gave one cry, "Oh, Gil, darling!" and threw her arms about his neck, kissing him rapturously on the cheek. She was pulled away by a tall brown-eyed, auburn-haired girl who kissed him on the other cheek. This girl was almost instantly replaced by a short, vivacious brunette who had to jump off the floor to encircle his neck. She found Gil's lips, a bit one-sidedly, and clung to him, smearing lipstick. But now the girls were coming by twos instead of ones and Gil's face looked bruised and battered with all shades of purple and red imprints.

"Hey!" he called out. "Not so fast. One at a time. I want to enjoy this…"

There was a jabber of comment.

"Oh, Gil—you're wonderful!"

"My man in the moon!"

"I'm going to miss you, darling…"

"It's cold up there, dear. I'll give you a warm reception when you get back…"

"Be careful, sweetheart, don't take any chances…"

"Don't forget me, Gil. I'll be mooning for you!"

FINALLY, with the initial assault over, only Ruth and Diana remained who had not bestowed their affectionate regards—and each had held the other off. The glamour girls shrieked at sight of their lipstick handiwork as Gil, glancing at himself in a wall mirror, gave a helpless gesture and sank down in a chair.

"You've got me, girls," he said, not even trying to remove the abundant evidence of impetuous osculation. "I'm done in. For once in my life, I've got enough kisses to last…" He looked up and grinned. "…until the next ones come along."

This brought the threat of another direct frontal attack but he held up a restraining hand.

"It's great to see you all here," he said. "You all look gorgeous. I mean it—each one of you different and lovely."

Some of them laughed. "Well, maybe just a little shopworn after that wrestling match," Gil conceded, "but still lovely... I guess you know now that I've had a lot on my mind these last few years...and you've all helped me enjoy my spare moments. I like you all a lot and I've had some great times with each one of you. Let's hope we can have some more—when I get back..."

"You said it, Gil. I'll be waiting for you."

"Remember my phone number."

"Call me first, Gil. I haven't seen you lately."

"You're a great guy, Gil. You've given us all a break."

"May the best girl win..."

Hollywood's greatest press agent stepped forward.

"Sorry, girls. You've just about wrecked Gil now. It's only half an hour till take-off time...so would you mind...I know parting is such sweet sorrow—and all that stuff, but..." He began gently pushing them.

The glamour girls started moving toward the cabin door but each had to shake Gil's hand and kiss him properly this time...and each one naturally tried to outdo her predecessor in planting the kiss to be remembered.

Ruth and Diana stood by, looking on.

"This is disgusting," said Ruth. "I wouldn't make such a scene in public."

"And you're not going to make one in private, either," said Diana.

"We'll see about that," said MGM's pin-up star.

WILBUR, at last, having herded everyone out but Gil's two most ardent admirers, looked toward them, worriedly.

"Come on, you girls, make up your minds!" Then he turned to the guards standing near the door. "Okay, soldiers," he said. "These two are the last ones. You can go, now."

The militia men nodded and stepped out.

"Gil," said Ruth. "I'm afraid you're going to have to choose between us. This Miss Fenimore has been acting like a wild woman. She seems to think she has some special claim on you."

"Oh, no I don't," denied Diana. "But you wanted to see Gil first—so I offered you my place in line and said I'd see him last—and you didn't like it..."

"That's true, Gil," testified Wilbur. "Diana could have been first in..."

"You keep out of this," charged Ruth. "It was all a trick. Miss Fenimore's a little smoothie...I'm surprised, Gil, that you'd let her..."

"That does it," interrupted Diana.

Wilbur's redhead leaped forward, pinioned a startled Ruth's arm behind her back and, applying pressure, ran her across the cabin to the door.

"Out you go!" she said.

"Gil, are you going to let her get away with this?" shrieked Ruth.

Diana's action had come so fast that Gil Benson and Wilbur Williams had been unable to restrain her.

"Help!" cried Ruth.

"Let go of her!" Gil shouted.

But Diana, giving a final push, shoved MGM's pin-up girl out onto the portable stairway and, before Ruth could recover her equilibrium, Diana reached out and pulled the heavy door shut, clamping it in place.

"What do you think you're doing?" an amazed Gil demanded.

Diana wheeled, eyeing the man who was about to take off for the moon and Hollywood's greatest press agent.

"I'm sorry, Gil—but I just couldn't take any more from her. You may love her and all that but..."

"Open that door and let her in."

"I won't," she defied.

Gil Benson made a grab for Diana. She ducked and ran to the front of the cabin. He followed.

"I'm going to have to put you out of here."

"You'll have to catch me first..."

Gil lunged. She dodged again but he caught her mass of red hair. Diana reached out and grabbed hold of the instrument panel. He yanked to get her free. Her hand closed over a lever, pressed it down...

"Let go of that!" yelled Gil.

The spaceship gave a great lurch. Hollywood's greatest press agent, America's Number One Playboy and a redhead who wanted to crash Hollywood—went crashing to the floor.

"Now you've done it," Gil cried.

"Done what?"

"We're off!" he said, *"to the moon..."*

CHAPTER FIVE

THE sudden and unexpected departure of Gil Benson's moon rocket, *Goodbye, World* caught radio announcers, television operators, newsreel cameramen, photographers, newspaper reporters, and the audience of invited guests totally by surprise.

There was a frightening roar, a brilliant flash, a white vaporish cloud—and it was gone...

The closest eyewitness to this dramatic and unscheduled disappearance was MGM's pin-up sensation, Ruth Delano, who saw the huge rocket vanish in one great blinding swish, almost from her grasp. The force of its take-off was largely spent downward but the air repelled in its, wake sent the portable stairway rolling and careening. It swayed dangerously but did not tip over.

At the base were two men who had intended to be passengers on this trip to the moon. They were Gil Benson's chief engineer, Jerry Torrence, and the atomic scientist, Professor Crowley. They had just started their ascent to board the rocket when the blast of atomic power sent it hurtling into space.

In the split second that followed, everyone was too dumbfounded, horrified, and stunned to move or speak. Then, when the realization of the apparent catastrophe had come, humans once more began to function, many excitedly and incoherently.

The radio engineers were frantically trying to get their networks cleared so that the account of this terrific happening could go out over the air.

The eye of the television camera, cheated of its mechanical vision, could only scan the bare launching site where the mighty spaceship had been.

Photographers were shooting the uncanny cloud of white vapor, which still hung in the night air, obscuring the full moon.

Newspapermen, at portable typewriters and telegraph keys, were trying to compose a lead that would adequately describe the unbelievable thing that had just occurred.

As for the distinguished guests themselves, largely untrained in the meeting and reacting to tragedy, this stupendous and unheralded take-off had been all but nerve shattering.

Somewhere in space, only one minute after its departure, Gil Benson's *Goodbye, World* was tearing through the Earth's atmosphere, heading for the moon, without having waited to say goodbye.

"Ladies and gentlemen of the radio audience," an on-the-spot announcer was saying, "The space rocket has gone. We don't know yet what happened but it left unexpectedly and ahead of schedule. We don't even know who was on it although we are reasonably sure Gil Benson was aboard. But Professor Crowley and Jerry Torrence, his two associates, were left behind.

"Even now, we can't believe it. We hardly know how to begin to tell you. We didn't expect to go on the air with this event until fifteen minutes before midnight when the spaceship was supposed to depart. It is quite obvious that something suddenly went wrong.

"The last visitors, some girl friends of Gil Benson's, had just left the rocket and one of them—we're trying to find out who she is—was still up on the stairway adjoining the ship when it took off. It's a miracle she wasn't killed.

"We hope, in a few minutes, to bring Gil Benson's two

associates to the radio and get their possible explanation of this tremendous mishap... Stand by, ladies and gentlemen...we're just being given some special information..."

The radio announcer's voice broke off and there followed a spine-tingling silence as listeners throughout the world waited and wondered.

AT THE scene of the rocket-launching site, there was still pandemonium. All channels of communication were confused and clogged. Everyone was now trying to talk at once, to give his version or conjecture of what had happened. A frantic Jerry Torrence and Professor Crowley were being besieged from all sides to explain, as best they could, what had occurred. They were finally dragged in front of a microphone.

"Here you are, ladies and gentlemen," said the announcer, coming back in the air. "I have with me now Gil Benson's two right hand men, Professor Crowley and Jerry Torrence. These two gentlemen are best qualified to tell us what took place. As you all know, this spaceship left Earth ahead of schedule and without warning. Professor Crowley is the atomic scientist who developed the atomic power that was to be used on this flight. Professor, can you hazard a guess as to what happened?"

The voice of Professor Crowley had a noticeable quaver in it.

"Someone would have been compelled to shift the starting lever. I'm reasonably sure that Mr. Benson would not have done this."

"Is it possible, Professor Crowley," questioned the announcer, "that Gil Benson may have decided, at the last moment, he shouldn't permit you men to take this risk with him—and that he elected to go off alone?"

"No, I doubt that very much," said Professor Crowley.

"Mr. Torrence, what do you think happened?" asked the announcer.

Gil Benson's chief engineer was also shaken.

"It's pretty hard to figure," he said. "Everything was ready for the take-off. I noticed when we started up to board the rocket that the cabin door was suddenly slammed shut. I saw a woman standing above on the stair landing and then—*woosh*... Just like that—the rocket was gone."

"Could some form of sabotage be a possible explanation?"

"No, I don't think so. Of course, we can't be sure about anything yet. It's a terrible thing."

"Thank you very much, Mr. Torrence and Professor Crowley. Ladies and gentlemen, you have just heard from the two men closest to Gil Benson, who were supposed to make the moon trip with him. They are at a loss to know how this spaceship could have taken off prematurely... And now, ladies and gentlemen, we are bringing you the woman who so narrowly escaped with her life and who was the last to leave the ill-fated rocket... Ladies and gentlemen—this is MGM's movie actress, Ruth Delano... Well, Miss Delano—you've just gone through a frightful experience. I don't want to tax you too much, but the whole world is anxious to learn as many details about this catastrophe as possible. Do you have any idea what happened?"

MGM's pin-up sensation was trembling, half from shock and half from indignation.

"Yes, I have," she said. "I think a woman is behind this."

"A woman," said the announcer. "How could that be?"

"There's a woman in that rocket," revealed Ruth. It's a redhead!" She became hysterical. "I hate to say this, but we quarreled over Gil Benson...and she threw me out..."

"Threw you out? You mean—from the rocket?"

"Yes—she's a terrible person—a wild woman. The men couldn't do a thing with her."

"Men—what men?"

"Mr. Benson and Wilbur."

"Compose yourself, Miss Delano, if possible," soothed the announcer. "You say there was a woman on the rocket and now you mention a man named Wilbur. Are you sure...?"

"Yes, of course I'm sure. Wilbur Williams—Mr. Benson's press agent. He's gone, too. All three of them."

"You don't say," said the announcer. "Now we're beginning to get the picture. You think this woman...?"

"I'm positive," cried Ruth. "She's caused this, somehow. She pushed me out and shut the door and locked it before the men could stop her. They must have struggled with her... She's irresponsible...she was a parachute jumper!"

"A parachute jumper!" exclaimed the announcer. "What was her name?"

"Diana somebody," said Ruth. "I don't know... Oh—I can't talk any more. Gil Benson was my dearest friend. Excuse me, please...I'm feeling faint..."

Ruth Delano permitted willing hands to lead her away.

IN THE cabin of Gil Benson's moon rocket, five seconds after the takeoff, wild things were happening.

"I don't want to go to the moon," cried Wilbur. "I don't want to go anywhere. Let me out of here!"

"Lie down," ordered Gil Benson. "Both of you. Crawl over to those bunks. Strap yourselves in. Hurry up!" He dragged himself to the instrument panel, grabbed the starting lever that also regulated the rocket velocity, and turned it to a slower speed. "We're ascending too fast. Our bodies can't stand it..."

"I can't breath!" gasped Diana. "I feel faint..."

"My head," moaned Wilbur. "I'm dizzy..."

"Oxygen," said Gil. "We're going to need oxygen...I can't see..."

A gray mist was forming in front of his eyes. The pull of gravity under their terrific initial acceleration was almost blacking him out. His hand groped toward the instrument panel and pressed a button. There was a whir of machinery in a rear compartment of the rocket. A mixture of helium-oxygen began flowing into the cabin.

Wilbur was flat on the floor beside his bunk.

"My legs...my arms!" he gasped. "They're so heavy...I...I can't lift them..."

Diana had fallen into a chair, her back braced against it. Her face was contorted. She was trying to fasten a strap around her but arms fell useless at her sides.

Gil was on his knees and clutching the control lever, making a tremendous effort to stay conscious. His eyes were fixed on the instruments, dials, and gauges.

"Let's go back," panted Wilbur, fighting for breath. "Get us...down...out of here..."

"Can't," said Gil. "We're...in...for...it...now. We've got to go...the whole way..."

With the speed of take-off reduced to what it should have been, at three times the pull of gravity instead of the extreme high of six, the physical bodies of the three space passengers began to regain their normal functioning. This too rapid acceleration had greatly reduced blood pressure in the brain and had threatened possible rupture of blood vessels as well as affecting their breathing and momentarily deranging their circulation. As the three commenced to emerge from this first harrowing crisis, with the rocket now under control, knifing steadily upward through the Earth's ever-thinning atmosphere, they stared speechlessly at one another.

LOOKING up through the great forward dome of the cabin, they could see the glowing features of the moon. They had already reached such an altitude—free from lower level dust particles—that the moon now presented a sight never before beheld by human eyes. It was actually frightening to look upon—a jagged ball of sublime desolation—a fantastic pockmarked, ugly, leering, luminous face. Each second, it seemed, its rugged contour of shining peaks, yawning craters and barren rocky deserts became more and more distinct. They were traveling now in the bright, reflected light of the moon, which cast an awesome illumination over the cabin.

Wilbur finally spoke. He turned reprovingly to Diana. "Baby, this is all your fault," he said. "If this is your idea of a publicity stunt, you won't live to cash in on it." A dire thought hit him. "My gosh," he added. "And I won't either..."

"I'm terribly sorry," said Diana. "I didn't mean it. Honest." She looked toward Gil Benson. "I know, Gil, you'll never believe me."

"I'm afraid I won't," said Gil, grimly, his eyes on the instrument panel. "It's very peculiar that you grabbed the one lever that could have sent us off—the lever I identified for you that weekend at the ranch."

"I was mad and I was excited," said Diana. "I didn't know what I was doing."

"And, because a woman lost her head," said Gil. "I'm about to lose a life's ambition and the world may lose the possible benefits of this scientific project."

"I said I was sorry," Diana repeated. "I don't know what else I can do now."

"You can jump overboard," said Wilbur. "You can blame me, Gil. I ruined your rocket trip the day I introduced you to this baby."

Gil Benson, satisfied that the spaceship was operating on automatic pilot, as it should, turned away from the controls. "Well, I'm stuck with you two," he said, "and I've got to put up with it—but it's not going to be easy."

"We'll do anything we can," said Diana. "I know something about mechanics. And I'm not afraid—much."

"I'm afraid—*period!*" said Wilbur.

"I don't know what I'd be good for on a trip like this. I guess I'm just going along for the ride..."

Gil smiled. "Well, you're good for a laugh, anyway," he said. Then he glanced at his wristwatch. "We've been up exactly six and one half minutes."

"Is that all?" groaned Wilbur. "Ye gods! I'm ten years older."

"If my calculations are right," said Gil, "we'll be getting beyond the gravitational pull of the Earth—in about three more minutes."

"Let's go back to Earth," begged Wilbur. "Where is it, anyway?"

Gil pointed to a cabin window. "You can see it best on this side," he said.

The three space travelers looked out. So much had been happening of immediate concern to them that they had temporarily forgotten the Earth.

"Holy Smoke..." exclaimed Wilbur. "It's enormous! But, my gosh, it looks like it fills the sky below. Or is it below? Boy, would I hate to have that fall on us..."

"It looks flat," said Diana. "No, I can see now, it's curved around the edges. But is it dark?"

"It will be dark," said Gil, "until we get out of the Earth's shadow and can see the sun."

"How interesting," said Diana. "I'm beginning to like this. Please forgive me, Gil. I'll make up to you for what I've done. I don't know how, but I'll do it." Then she started laughing. "Your face, it's still covered with lipstick. Here, let me wipe it off." She looked about on the floor for her bag.

"I haven't time for that now," said Gil. He returned to the instrument board and studied the dials and gauges.

AS HE did so, Wilbur cried out, "Hey, Gil! Something's happening... My body's getting light. I feel like a feather. Gill what's wrong now?"

"Hang on," said Gil. "We're out of the Earth's atmosphere."

"I've turned the power off. There's no more gravity. We're falling through space toward the moon..."

As Gil was speaking, their bodies were becoming lighter and lighter, till they seemed to have almost no weight at all.

"Oh—there's my pocket book!" said Diana. It had lifted from the floor and was floating past her.

"I feel silly," said Wilbur. "Like a run-away balloon."

"You'll have to get used to it," said Gil. "That's the way you're going to feel for a long time. I anticipated this condition. That's why I placed this railing around the cabin to hang onto. In just a minute, I'll get you something that will help."

Gil, sliding his hand along the rail, half floated to the rear of the cabin where he entered the galley that contained food and other supplies. He presently emerged with three pairs of iron-soled shoes. He handed one pair to Wilbur but let go of them too soon and they floated toward the ceiling.

Wilbur released his hold on the bunk and tried to stand. His body followed the shoes. "This is a fine how-do-you-do," he said.

Gil reached up and grabbed him, pulling him down with ease. He placed one of Wilbur's hands on the rail.

Diana was seated, gripping a chair.

"Oh, Wilbur," she said, "you looked so funny up there." She shifted her position, relinquished her hold, and took off herself. "Oh, catch me, somebody!" she cried. Her figure rose lazily toward the ceiling, turning a complete somersault.

"Not half so funny as you look right now," said Wilbur. "While you're up there, baby, will you get my shoes?"

They were floating along beside her. Diana obligingly extended her hands and retrieved them. Gil worked his way along the railing to a point where he could reach up and grab Diana's dress, which was now over her head.

"You're beautiful, baby," said Wilbur. "I've never noticed it so much before."

Gil pulled Diana down and rightly upended her. She handed Wilbur his shoes.

"I'd slap your face," she said, "if I weren't afraid of letting go of this rail."

Hollywood's greatest press agent clutched his bunk, fastened the strap around his body, and began putting on the iron-soled shoes. "I don't see what good these are going to do," she said. "They float just like everything else."

"You'll find out in a minute," said Gil. He handed a pair to Diana. "Put these on," he commanded.

"These clumsy things?" said Diana. "They're not my style."

"Suit yourself," said Gil, "but the next time you go to the ceiling, you'll stay there."

Diana put the shoes on.

Gil, slipping on a pair of these specially made shoes, himself, returned along the railing to the instrument board and then pressed a button. He turned to Wilbur and Diana.

"Now put your feet flat on the floor."

They did so, wonderingly.

"Unstrap yourselves," he ordered.

This done, Wilbur and Diana exclaimed their surprise. They remained seated, apparently fastened to the floor.

"There's an awful pull on my feet," Wilbur reported.

Gil grinned. "There's a magnetic field on the floor of this rocket," he said. "We figured it would act as a substitute for the field of gravity and that anything made of iron, or attached to iron, would feel a downward pull."

Wilbur stood up. "This is swell," he said. He lifted one foot from the floor. It floated out in front of him. He put it down and it stayed down. Then he lifted the other foot. He looked slightly ridiculous but he could navigate. "This will take a little practice," he announced, quite proud of himself, "but it's a great idea, Gil. It'll work."

Diana preferred to remain seated for the time being.

"Would you be interested to know how many miles we now are from Earth?" Gil inquired.

"I'm afraid to ask," said Wilbur. "I can't stand being up high. It took all the nerve I had to climb those stairs into the rocket."

Gil was looking at his instruments calculatingly.

"We've been gone from Earth about twenty minutes now and we're about nine thousand miles away."

"Nine thousand?" said Wilbur. "That's terrible..."

Gil smiled. "If our take-off, the first few seconds had not been faster than planned, thanks to Diana, we would not have been quite so far away. We're really running slightly ahead of schedule."

"I'm glad of that," said Diana. "I hate to be late places."

Gil's face sobered. "We've been so busy thinking about ourselves—what do you suppose the people are thinking back on Earth—especially Professor Crowley and Jerry Torrence...? They must be about out of their minds."

Wilbur grinned, foolishly. "Why don't we write them a postcard," he suggested. "And say, 'Having wonderful time. Wish you were here...'"

Gil turned to his newly installed radio set. "Well, what have we got all this equipment for? Might as well find out right now whether these high-frequency waves can get through to us or to Earth. The experimental station at Schenectady was set up to keep in touch with this ship. They may be trying to make contact this minute."

Gil adjusted the dials for reception and listened. There was a low humming sound and a slight crackling. In the comparative quiet of the silently plunging spaceship, a voice suddenly boomed out.

"Calling Station Moon... Calling Station Moon... Spaceship, *Goodbye, World* Come on in..."

Gil gave a great shout of exultation. "Thank God... They've done it. They've beamed their waves through the ionic shield! This means there are no longer any space limits to communication."

Wilbur and Diana, equally excited, got up and walked exaggeratedly toward Gil. He had now turned on his high frequency transmitter.

"This is Station Moon," he spoke into a microphone. "Calling Experimental Station G.E. Schenectady. Spaceship, *Goodbye, World*. This is Gil Benson... Come in, please..."

He shifted over to receiving and waited, anxiously.

The booming voice again: "This is Experimental Station G.E. acknowledging... Greetings. Carl Mack speaking. This is great, Benson... Every top man in G.E. is standing by... We're all thrilled! Are you okay? Over..."

Gil Benson's attention was now centered on sending and receiving. He worked the dials back and forth as his two fellow space travelers listened, breathlessly.

"This is Station Moon... Spaceship, *Goodbye, World*... Rough start, but all okay… How are you getting me?"

The answer came hurtling back. "Coming in clear…Army radar station in New Mexico has picked up your spaceship…is following you… Whole planet excited… Any message?"

Wilbur touched Gil's arm. "Tell someone to pick up my shirts at the laundry," he said.

"Shut up," said Gil. Then, into the transmitter, "This is Station Moon…Gil Benson… Message: Get word to Professor Crowley and Jerry Torrence. Tell them start of flight accidental. One of guests touched starting lever… Two passengers aboard—Miss Diana Fenimore and Wilbur Williams."

"There's your publicity break, baby," said Wilbur. "Your name will go all over the world. If I was only on Earth I could fix it for you fine. 'Beautiful Redhead Takes Off to See Man in Moon. Objective: Matrimony.'"

"You must think I'm awfully hard up," said Diana.

The booming voice from Earth again: "Message being relayed… Question: When do you estimate arrival on moon?"

Gil Benson consulted the time and his instruments.

"At present rate of acceleration, we should arrive in vicinity of moon in about nine and one-half hours from starting time… Will keep you advised of progress. This is Gil Benson…Station Moon…Spaceship, *Goodbye, World* now signing off…"

Gil cut off the power in his radio set and wheeled joyously about. He seized Diana and lifted her lightly over his head. It required only the slightest exertion to do this since her body had no appreciable weight.

"You crazy redhead!" he cried. "Do you realize that you are seeing history made? That you've just heard a man in space, traveling over twenty-five thousand miles an hour, talking to someone on Earth?"

"I know something more wonderful than that," said Diana.

"What's that?" asked Gil.

"I'm out here in space, talking to that very man," she said.

"Ye gods…" said Wilbur. "What a time to get romantic…"

CHAPTER SIX

NOT since Charles Lindbergh's historic flight from New York to Paris in 1927, had there been such world interest in a space adventure as there now was in Gil Benson's spectacular rocket attempt to reach the moon. It had taken Lindbergh something over thirty-three hours to cover a distance of approximately 3,600 miles in flying from Roosevelt airport, Long Island, to LeBourget field, just outside of Paris. Whereas, Gil Benson, thanks to the stupendous advance of science, would reach the moon, a distance of 238,857 miles, if all went well, in a little over *nine hours*. This was incredible but startlingly true.

It was front-page news in smashing black headlines that radio operators on Earth had actually talked with Gil Benson from thousands of miles out in space. It was immensely thrilling to contemplate that radio communication could now be maintained throughout the entire journey and that, hour by hour progress of the rocket, *Goodbye, World* could be reported through radio and news bulletins, as issued from Schenectady. Plans were being rushed with the hope that radio and television could bring to the people of the Earth a first-hand account of actual vision of the pioneer landing of a human being on Earth's barren satellite.

Gil Benson's time of arrival was estimated as taking place about twelve noon, New York time, or nine in the morning, Los Angeles time. Peoples throughout the world were busy computing his moment of arrival as it pertained to their own time, so that they would have the unparalleled thrill of seeing and hearing this event, did such a spectacle prove to be possible.

An enterprising television producer hit upon the plan of later bringing all Gil's glamour girl friends to the studio and projecting their alluring images to the moon, with the query: "Don't you wish you were back?" As a stunt, this idea received feature space in papers with pictures of the beauties Gil Benson had left behind.

But Diana Fenimore, the mysterious redhead, the dark horse in the field of feminine heartbeats, who had actually accompanied Gil Benson on his moon adventure, usurped the limelight. She sent news hounds sniffing in all directions for information concerning her and their trail finally led to Buzz Reynolds, head of the Buzz Reynolds' Flying Circus. When interviewed concerning his former parachute jumper, Buzz said she was the greatest, natural daredevil show-woman he had ever met and that she would do anything for a thrill.

"I can well believe," declared Buzz, "as Miss Delano has suggested, that the redhead deliberately planned and executed this take-off in the rocket so she might make the trip. It sounds just like her. I don't envy Gil Benson. To have that redhead with him is as dangerous as the moon trip itself."

Rival press agents, however, were not sorry to learn that Wilbur Williams had left Earth with his wealthiest and most notorious client. Competition would be a little less steep now in Hollywood's make-believe and big build-up alleys.

"If dear Wilbur doesn't return," said one of his most caustic rivals, "we'll hold a memorial service and shoot a rocket to the moon with a wreath in it."

Ruth Delano had been compelled to absorb considerable ribbing for her dramatic relation to the moon rocket's departure. She had added a new version to the age-old role of "the girl who had been left behind."

Pictures of MGM's pin-up star clinging piteously to the towering portable stair rail and staring bewilderedly into space had been published in all the early morning papers. One caption writer had titled the photograph:

DARING REDHEAD SNATCHES MAN INTO SKY FROM
UNDER VERY NOSE OF RIVAL

Ruth Delano tore this paper into shreds when she saw it and it is well she was not playing a dramatic scene at the time for she most certainly would have bitten her leading man.

"TO THINK this would have to happen to me," she raged. "Something like this could actually ruin my career. If I could get hold of that red-head, I'd scratch her eyes out…"

But Ruth Delano's chances of gaining such satisfaction were diminishing at the rate of four hundred and twenty miles every minute…

In the moon rocket, 51,000 miles out in space, it was 1:30 a.m. Arizona time by Gil Benson's wristwatch. Each moment was increasing the tension on board. The newness of the experience, which had brought about temporary exultation, was now giving way to realization of the growing perils, known and unknown of such a voyage.

Gil, compelled to press his unskilled passengers into service, had assigned Diana to keep the log of the trip under his dictation, and Wilbur had been shown how to carry on radio communication.

"It's sure going to be tough without Jerry and Professor Crowley," he said. "You've both got to be ready for all emergencies. We can't tell what may happen any minute…"

The sky had long since changed its color from blue to black. In this strange, dark firmament, the stars shone out with a fierce brilliance. The pitted face of the moon became more and more clearly etched each passing minute, its crazy quilt of craters and jagged peaks standing out like the three-dimensional pictures in a stereoscope.

The Army radar set had been placed in operation to scan space in all directions, to detect any possible meteors that might be flashing across their path.

But now a new and startling effect began to manifest itself. The Earth, directly behind them, was an immense dark ball, around which an increasing bead-like corona of sun's rays had been observed for some time.

These rays suddenly flared into gigantic bright tongues of flame, leaping thousands of miles out into space. The Earth became a huge black spot against the much larger body of the sun, the light from which was now so dazzling that their eyes could not stand the sight.

Gil, almost blinded, fumblingly opened a panel in the cabin wall and took out some dark-lensed glasses, which he put into the hands of Diana and Wilbur.

"Put these on," he ordered. "We're passing out of the shadow of the Earth and the sun's going to be terrific. I'll have to turn the bright side of the rocket toward the sun to deflect the light and heat or we'll be cooked in here."

He switched on the atomic power and grabbed the directional lever. The ship responded and all gasped their relief.

WILBUR spoke into the microphone: "Hello, Earth... The sun just hit us and, for a few seconds, I thought we'd lose our eyesight. Boy, you can certainly see the sun's rays out here! There isn't any atmosphere to stop them and they come shooting at you like liquid fire. I can't see Earth now at all. I don't even dare look in that direction. You'd think half the sky was on fire. If there's a cold spot on the moon, I want to get to it... Gil Benson has just shifted the bright side of our ship toward the sun and this helps plenty. I thought you were going to hear our flesh frying for a moment but we're okay now... Stand by, please..."

Diana, at Gil's bidding, was recording: "Traveling in a vacuum...no resistance to our movement...ship in free fall, can be held on course whether head-on or side-wise...power needed only to change position...has been turned off now..."

Wilbur resumed his broadcast: "Here I am again... I'm looking off toward the moon. With my back turned to the sun's side of the ship, I can take off my dark glasses... Gil wants me to explain that since there is no air where we are, and no dust particles to reflect light, you can't see the sun's rays until they hit something... Of course they're hitting the moon and I'm getting an eyeful of it...but all around the moon and everywhere else— it's inky black, except for the stars and, boys and girls, there's billions of 'em... What am I saying...? Trillions... Decillions...

Septillions... I can't count 'em... And are they bright?"

Wilbur's running commentary was broken into by Gil who cried out, "Radar! It's picked up something..."

An object was appearing on the radar screen.

"It must be a meteor," said Gil. "It's some thousands of miles away and it's coming at us from the sun side. That means we won't be able to see it till it passes us—but it could cross our path." He explored the object with his radar beam. "Its size is enormous!" he announced, "and it's traveling thirty-five miles a minute! We may have to change our course to keep it from hitting us..."

"If it isn't one thing," said Wilbur, "it's another, out here." He spoke into the microphone, "Hello, Earth... A meteor is going to pass us...I hope. Gil Benson says it's a big one. He's checking it on the radar. We're watching for it but we can't look in the direction it's coming on account of the sun. If it shoots between the sun and us, we'll never see it, but if it passes on our other side, we might catch a glimpse...oh, MY GOSH!"

Gil Benson and Diana cried out in horror at the same time. Flashing into view on the side of the ship away from the sun, but caught in its rays and glowing brilliantly with reflected light, a monstrous object of fantastic irregularity filled the sky in front of them, blotting out the moon and stars. For an awful moment it seemed as though they were running head-on into it. They ducked instinctively, expecting oblivion, but in the same split second, this wild roamer of the black void went tearing on beyond and to their left.

IT WAS thousands of miles away from them, yet too close for comfort. Gil switched on his atomic power motors and veered hard to the right. "We're in danger," he said. "If we hit any of those fragments, we're goners..."

"What do you think, Gil, are we going to miss them?" asked Diana.

"I'm playing safe," said Gil. "I'm making a ten thousand mile detour around that baby. Better get on the radio, Wilbur, and tell them we're still here."

Hollywood's greatest press agent returned to the microphone. He was still mightily shaken and when he tried to speak he was too weak to make a sound.

"Hello, Earth," he finally managed to whisper. "This is *Goodbye, World* and, brother, it was almost goodbye for good. A big meteor just missed us. Stand by...I can't talk yet...I swallowed my voice..."

At seven o'clock in the morning, Arizona time, Gil Benson, after careful computing, announced that they were now on what he termed their "last lap" toward the moon. They had traversed about 200,000 miles from Earth and, within two more hours, barring necessity for another detour to evade possible meteors, they should be over the moon's surface, preparing for a landing.

Most of the journey had been made with the instruments set at automatic pilot. Even so, it had been a nerve-trying night, if one could refer to time in space as "night," but it helped the three travelers from Earth to keep their minds fixed on time, as it existed in the part of the universe from which they had come. The tension was still on but it had eased somewhat through their having become more accustomed to the conditions and hazards they were required to face.

Wilbur had even been able to assume a fatalistic point of view. "Oh, well," he philosophized, "if a person has to die, I suppose it doesn't make any difference whether you die on Earth, in space or on the moon. You're just as dead one place as the other."

"That's a cheerful thought," said Diana. "I wonder if something happened to us all inside this spaceship and it missed the moon, would it keep on going in space forever?"

"It certainly would," said Gil, "unless and until it should come within the gravitational pull of some planet in which case it would probably become a minor meteor and burn up through friction in the upper atmosphere of that body. Of course, if the planet was like the moon and had no atmosphere, the ship would crash on it—and that would be that!"

"Let's get off this subject," said Wilbur. "I'm sorry I ever started it." He put his hand to his stomach. "Say," he said. "I feel funny down here. I guess I must be hungry."

"Me, too," said Diana. "I'm glad you mentioned it. How about it, Gil? Isn't it time for breakfast?"

Gil Benson grinned. "How do you think we're going to eat out here?" he asked.

"I don't know," said Wilbur, "but we've got to do it. I'd like a cup of coffee and some ham and eggs."

"Which you're not going to get. You watch these instruments and I'll bring you something."

Gil left the control board and walked across the cabin with his steel shoes clinging to the magnetized floor. He entered the galley and came back carrying three large sized tubes as well as three strange appearing collapsible rubber liquid containers. Wilbur eyed them, unappetizingly.

"No tooth paste for me," he said, wryly. "I'm not that hungry. And I don't need a hot water bottle, either."

"Then you're not going to eat," said Gil. "This is the only way it can be done properly where there is no gravity." He handed Wilbur a tube and a container and did likewise to Diana.

"WHAT'S in these things?" Wilbur asked.

"You've got a preparation of chocolate fondant in the tube and some of Arizona's finest water in the rubber bag," said Gil. "And if you're smart, you'll put the end of that tube in your mouth and squirt its contents into you."

Wilbur and Diana looked at one another, then commenced unscrewing the caps on their tubes. They placed the ends, as instructed, in their mouths and squeezed the tubes. Their cheeks bulged. They chewed and swallowed.

"Tastes pretty good," Wilbur admitted.

"It's nourishing," Gil replied. "And that's what counts on a trip like this."

"What would happen if I poured some of this water out?" asked Wilbur, removing the cap from the liquid container.

"Try it and see," said Gil.

Wilbur squeezed the sides of the rubber bag and a round globule of water oozed from the funnel-like opening, floating toward the ceiling, under impetus of the squeeze.

"Good gosh," he said. "Is that funny?" He tried it again, like a small boy, pointing the mouth of the container toward Diana. Another round globule of water emerged and headed toward her.

She put up her hand to ward it off. At contact, the surface tension of the water was broken. It spread out in squashy fashion and crawled wetly over her hand and arm.

Diana shrieked. "Oh, how awful!" she said.

Gil laughed. "You see how difficult it would be to pour drinks? Food wouldn't stay on plates and water wouldn't stay in a glass. At the least touch they would go elsewhere."

"Well," said Wilbur, placing the liquid container to his mouth and taking several swallows, "if I have to return to my baby days, I guess I can do it."

Diana and Gil followed suit and all three soon finished their light breakfast in outer space.

Then Diana stood up. "All right, boys," she said. "Give me your 'dirty dishes.' I want to be the first stewardess on a spaceship. I'll take these to the galley."

"Put them in drawer number ten," said Gil, handing her his empty tube and deflated liquid container.

Wilbur did likewise. "Don't drop these," he warned.

"How can I?" smiled Diana.

Clutching containers and tubes so they wouldn't get away from her, she crossed the cabin floor with elaborate steps and disappeared into the pantry.

"What a woman," said Wilbur. "Can you imagine the big offers she'll get if we make it back to Earth?"

"Don't look so far ahead," said Gil. "We could easily crash on the moon."

Wilbur paled. "Well, it was just a passing thought," he said. "Ye gods, Gil, you tell me that just when I'm commencing to feel relaxed."

"Can't help it. We'll soon be entering the gravitational field of the moon. Then I'll have to start the atomic motors to keep from approaching the moon surface too fast. Fortunately, we can cruise with this spaceship at slow speed but this is still a mighty big piece of metal to get down out of the sky, especially since I've never had any experience in doing it before."

Wilbur moistened his lips, nervously. "Maybe we'd better not try to land," he suggested. "Maybe we can just fly close to the moon, take some pictures, and beat it back to Earth..."

Gil flashed a smile. Then seriously he said, "That wouldn't help us any. It's going to be even tougher landing on Earth. We'll have to dip in and out of the Earth's atmosphere a number of times, circling the Earth while doing it, and slowing up our velocity so we won't burn up like a meteor. I'd rather get my first practice in right here."

Hollywood's greatest press agent picked a raveling off his coat, released it, and watched it stand idly in space.

"Oh, well," he said, after a moment, "it was nice knowing you. I suppose all things must end sometime—including me."

Gil stood up and looked toward the galley. "I wonder what's keeping Diana?" he said.

As he spoke he heard her exclaim and two of the liquid containers came floating through the doorway.

"She's probably made a mistake and put herself in the drawer," said Wilbur.

Gil grabbed the containers out of the air and took them with him into the galley. He saw Diana frantically pushing the various contents of drawer number ten back in as all were trying to bob out.

"These darn things," she said. "I can't do anything with them..."

"Take it easy," laughed Gil. "The harder you push them in, the faster they'll come out. Do it gently, like this..."

He blocked the articles with his hands and fitted them quietly back into the drawer where they gradually subsided. Then he pushed the drawer shut.

"Give me gravitation," said Diana. "This is an all-fired nuisance."

She looked up at Gil. "Your face, young man! That lipstick! I can't stand it another minute...the thought of all those other women kissing you..." she added.

Gil grinned. "They gave me a terrific send-off," he said.

Diana slipped the strap of her pocketbook from her arm. She carefully opened the bag, rubbed her handkerchief over a stick of cold cream, and turned to Gil.

"Hold still, now," she directed. "I'm going to clean you up. If you should land this way, you might give the man in the moon a lot of wrong ideas."

America's Number One Playboy submitted good-naturedly to a vigorous facial massage.

"It's hard to get off," said Diana. "You'd think they'd branded you."

"Please leave my skin on," said Gil. "This is the only face I've got."

Diana critically surveyed the result of her labors. "There, I guess that will do," she said. "But isn't this all slightly ridiculous? We three people from Earth going to the moon in evening dress?"

"Do you put on your old clothes to go visiting?" asked Gil. "I think you have exactly the right attire. That's a stunning design, by the way—the moon and those stars. Are you sure you didn't have it designed purposely for this trip?"

Diana's blue eyes had not lost their ability to speak for themselves. "Why, Gil," she said, with just the right reproof in her voice. "How could you? You know that was all an accident—although I'll admit I stowed away on a trans-oceanic plane once..."

Gil tried to translate the meaning in her eyes and gave up. "I can't figure you out," he said. "What kind of a woman are you?"

Diana smiled. "I'm just a woman who's been cheated," she

said.

Gil frowned, wonderingly. "Cheated?" he repeated.

"Yes," said the girl with the red hair and blue eyes. "I didn't get a chance to kiss you goodbye. Do you suppose I could welcome you to the moon?"

Her face was upturned to his and her lips were suddenly alluring. Gil Benson was a man of action. While there was no gravitation, there was certainly attraction. They clung to each other as though they were conscious of their fall through space—and when the clinch was broken, Diana whispered, "Shall I record this in the log, Mr. Benson?"

"No," said Gil, "this is our own private scientific experiment."

"Then let's continue our research," said Diana.

They kissed again and, as they did so, Hollywood's greatest press agent appeared in the doorway, calling, "Hey, Gil, come quick!" He was excited to begin with but he was even more excited when he saw this. "Holy smoke…! Excuse me… What goes on here?"

"We just wanted to see how it would feel," said Diana, "to kiss in space."

Wilbur advanced toward her. "That's a great idea," he said. "Let's try it…"

For once, the girl with the blue eyes was taken aback—but she was game. Wilbur gave her a resounding smack.

"How did it feel to you?" she asked.

"Terrific," said Wilbur. "Let's try it again…"

Gil tapped Wilbur's shoulder. "We've fooled around enough," he said.

"Oh, say, Gil," exclaimed Wilbur. "I was coming in to tell you. I think I've discovered a new moon. I was looking off on the sun side through my dark glasses…there's something out there…it's tremendous…"

"LET'S have a look," said Gil, leading the way into the cabin, followed by Diana and Wilbur. All adjusted their dark glasses and stared out.

"My, yes," said Diana. "There it is. A big crescent! Funny we never saw that before."

"That's not another moon," said Gil. "That's our Earth."

"The Earth?" said Wilbur. "What's it doing off there?"

"Our angle of flight has changed and we've gotten far enough out," said Gil, "so we can see the ball of our Earth away from the sun. When we get to the moon, we'll see the Earth go through different phases—quarter, half and full—just as the moon does."

"Well, what do you know?" said Wilbur. "Remind me to study astronomy some time."

"It's past sunrise in Arizona right now," Gil continued. "Our Earth has been turning right along and you can begin to see the outlines of our continent in that crescent. Wait till we see our Earth like a full moon. That will be like getting a close-up look at a great illuminated globular map!"

"Won't that be something," said Diana. "I can hardly wait!"

Gil turned away from the Earth-side windows, removed his dark glasses, and looked toward the moon.

"We'll be coming in for a landing in a little over an hour," he said. "We've got a lot to do to, get ready. I've already set the automatic cameras to take pictures of the lunar landscape as we approach. Wilbur, you'll have to stand by the television and radio and keep them both in operation. If possible we want to televise our landing back to Earth."

"Great stuff," said Wilbur. "If we can do it... I suppose you want every kind of a record you can get?"

"Yes, our wire recorder has been making a record of everything we've said here," revealed Gil. "It can be transcribed later."

"Why didn't you tell me?" asked Wilbur. "What have I said?"

"You'll find out—eventually," said Gil, if all goes well. If it doesn't, perhaps the next man who lands on the moon may salvage some of our equipment and playoff this wire recorder—

and get a clue as to what happened."

"Don't talk so pessimistic," said Wilbur. "You'll give me high blood pressure."

Gil smiled. "We'll have Diana's written record in our log and your radio reports back to Earth as other means of preserving the events of this trip."

"Well," said Diana. "I'm ready for anything. Bring on the moon..."

Gil switched on the atomic power motors.

"Now what?" asked Wilbur.

"We're coming under the moon's gravitational influence," said Gil. "And we've got to do something about it. Get Schenectady..."

Wilbur opened his transmitter and began sending.

"This is Station Moon. Spaceship *Goodbye, World* calling Experimental Station G. E. Schenectady... This is Wilbur Williams... Come in, please..."

There was a moment of silence and then a booming voice.

"This is Experimental Station G.E. Schenectady acknowledging Hello, Williams... What's new out there?"

"Plenty. We've just entered the moon's field of gravity," Wilbur reported. "Gil Benson's started up the motors and is turning the ship around in the direction we're falling so as to slow up our speed." He motioned to Gil. "I'll let him explain this."

Gil, having completed the operation, stepped before the microphone.

"Hello, Mack...are you still with us?"

"You bet, Benson, and it didn't take any black coffee to keep me awake, either. Everybody's sticking until you report a safe landing."

"Everything's under control so far.

The moon, as you know, has a velocity of attraction of two miles a second. We've overcome that now with our motors and are falling toward the moon at a reduced speed. I'll gradually keep lowering this speed to almost zero. I'm looking for a landing site now."

Mack's booming voice came back from Earth.

"Good boy, Benson. We've arranged a re-broadcast of your moon arrival on every network...biggest hook-up in world history. It's getting close to noon our time and you never saw more excitement...I understand Times Square, New York, is jammed with people. The New York Times has rigged up a big television screen on the side of the Times Building. If reception is good, you can imagine what a thrill your fellow humans are going to get down here on Earth."

"I'M SORRY I'm not going to be there to see it," cut in Wilbur. "Gil had to get back on the job. He's slowing up the ship more and more. We're so close to the moon now that it fills the sky below us. It scares me to look at it. It is the damnedest sight—pardon me—I ever saw. We've got our dark glasses on because it's plenty bright. If there was a man on the moon, I could see him now—but there's not a sign of any kind of life. It's the roughest, wildest, rockiest looking landscape you can possibly picture. Gil says we're only eight thousand miles away. It won't be long now... Here—maybe we can pick this scene up by television...it's worth trying...tell me if it comes through..." Wilbur started the television apparatus in operation. He looked anxiously at Gil Benson who was at the ship's controls. "Everything going okay?"

Gil nodded, his eyes searching the surface of the moon. Diana stood beside him, holding in her hands a large relief map of the moon, especially prepared for this trip. It contained all the prominent mountains, craters, deep valleys, ridges, walls, rills, cracks, great dark areas, strange ray formations, and other surface markings discovered and identified by Earth's astronomers during the history of man's telescopic study of this solitary satellite.

"I wouldn't know where to land," said Diana, bewildered and somewhat terrified.

Gil put his finger on the map above and a little left of center.

"This is the section I intend to aim at," he said. "It's below the great Tycho crater and above that tremendous mountain range called the 'Apennines.' There seems to be a big level plains area in that vicinity which should be ideal for landing. Let's see if we can locate this spot from our present position."

Diana looked with Gil at the rugged features of the moonscape. As they did so, a familiar voice from Earth boomed out.

"Calling Station Moon... Space rocket, *Goodbye, World*... This is Experimental Station G.E. Schenectady... Carl Mack speaking... We're getting you... the television images are coming through... What a panorama... We're cutting in the networks, radio and television...we know you've probably got your hands full but try to keep us advised...whole world standing on end... We're pulling for you to make it... Come in, please... Over..."

Wilbur opened up his transmitter. "Hello, Earth... Glad you're seeing part of what we're seeing...of course it's not like being here—not much... Do you begin to notice the moon's strange coloring? All those dark brown and black stretches? Those seem to be rocks...and those tremendous light streaks, fanning out from different centers. I can't tell, from here, what they are or what causes them... Wait till I ask Gil..."

Wilbur laughed. "Gil says he doesn't know-that no one on Earth does, either...so I guess I'm not so dumb...but, brother, if we land okay, we're sure as hell—I mean—we're certainly going to find out." He turned to look at Gil who was further decreasing the spaceship's velocity of approach. "How close are we now?" he asked. "My body feels a lot heavier than it did."

"Mine, too," said Diana. "It's a strange sensation after feeling like you almost didn't have any weight at all."

"This is about how you'll feel while you are on the moon," said Gil. "We're within a thousand miles of it now. I hope we're getting some good photographs. That view is absolutely stupendous..."

"Never mind the photographs," said Wilbur. "You just get

us down all right. Those are the wickedest looking mountain peaks I ever saw. I'd hate to get hung up on one."

The moon had been so well charted from Earth that it was like following a road map in a car to pick out its lunar landmarks as the spaceship, now descending almost like a huge elevator, dropped down, down, down, being braked at different altitudes by application of atomic power motors, until it was only ten miles above the indescribably scarred and wrinkled surface.

The zero hour for the three Earth passengers on their pioneer voyage through space had now arrived and they shuddered at the thought of settling on so barren and forbidding a terrain.

"If there's a man in the moon, he's crazy," said Wilbur. He spoke into the microphone, "Hello, Earth... Well, this is our big moment. Gil Benson is taking us down for an attempted landing. I'm watching the altimeter... We're down to five...four...three...two miles. I can see Tycho crater from here and it's enormous. There are craters of all sizes all over the place—but there's a big stretch of what looks like smooth volcanic rock beneath us and that's what Gil's heading for. We've passed over the Apennines mountain range...the sharpest peaks I ever saw—they looked like upended ice picks. Now we're down to less than a mile and we're settling very slowly. The power in these motors is certainly wonderful. Amazing. There're some awful cracks in that surface. We just cleared one that looked like the Grand Canyon... Hold everything, folks... This is it! Gil's putting us down..."

America's Number One Playboy was anything but a playboy now. He leveled off the two hundred foot spaceship, inclined its nose slightly toward the moon's surface and cruised slowly downward, keeping his eyes on the terrain ahead. There were ridges and walls of dark evil-looking rock, which would mean disaster if he should land and skid into them. He pressed a button and lowered his retractable landing gear. It dropped noiselessly into place for there was no external air and thus no sound waves to report its operation.

Diana and Wilbur could only look on, helplessly and prayerfully, hoping that Gill might select the right moment and the right spot to bring the great ship in.

"We're skimming the surface now," Wilbur managed in the microphone. "We're going to make contact any second… It looks awfully rough…we're almost touching…here we go…"

There was a jarring impact and a sliding sensation. The landscape reeled crazily. There was a ripping, rending sound in the cabin, then the steel monster rocked to a standstill.

"We're down!" reported Wilbur, excitedly. *"We made it…* Just a minute… Something's happened… I think we've been damaged…something's wrong…it looks like—yes, a window's broken!"

"Our oxygen!" cried Gil. "It's escaping. Quick—I need help!"

CHAPTER SEVEN

THE human creatures on planet Earth had palpitation of the heart.

The sudden cessation of broadcasting from the space rocket, *Goodbye, World* immediately after the crash landing on the moon left everyone, everywhere, in a state of agonized suspense. Those witnessing the spaceship's approach to the moon and actual descent on the screens of their television sets were even more excited. Whatever the damage sustained in landing, the television equipment had not been put out of commission.

An enormous and enthralled crowd in Times Square, New York, and other big centers of population throughout the world where mammoth outdoor television screens had been set up, stood speechless with awe and fear. Before, on the television screen, was the image of a great, jagged wall of rock, which seemed to be but a short distance from the now motionless rocket ship.

A radio announcer's voice broke in. "Ladies and gentlemen, as you know, we have temporarily lost contact with the first space travelers to the moon but we're switching you to Los

Angeles where Professor Crowley, who was to have accompanied Gil Benson on his flight, is standing by in our studios to comment on the progress made. Professor Crowley will tell us what he thinks has happened... Professor Crowley...!"

"Ladies and gentlemen," spoke the Professor's voice. "If a window in the spaceship has been broken, this is extremely serious. The oxygen in the cabin, depending on how big an opening has been made, would naturally escape and since there is no atmosphere on the moon, Gil Benson and his two passengers could not long survive.

"Their salvation would depend upon the speed with which they can affect repairs. I doubt very much if they were wearing the space suits on board when they landed, as they are cumbersome and designed primarily for use on the moon, outside the rocket.

"These space suits carry their own oxygen supply. They may be electrically heated to withstand the cold of the lunar night and they are lead-coated to repulse the destructive cosmic and other rays that would be fatal to human life. Their outer covering is shimmering bright to deflect the sun's rays during the lunar day, which would otherwise produce unbearable heat.

"It would be the greatest possible tragedy if, after having made such a magnificent journey and landing alive on the moon, Gil Benson and his two unexpected passengers should be prevented, by this accident, from exploring the moon and bringing back to us on Earth their first-hand account.

"I'm hoping and praying, as I know you all are, that radio communication will soon be restored and we will learn that they have surmounted this great danger as they have all others thus far."

All work had stopped at MGM's studio. The stars and executives were gathered around their own radio and television sets. Ruth Delano was among them.

"What do you think?" her director, Don Stevens, asked her.

Ruth shook her head. "I don't know. Gil's luck's bound to

run out some time. If he only had his two skilled men with him. That redhead and 'Wee Willie Wilbur' are worse than no one at all!"

"Wilbur's not been doing so badly for an amateur broadcaster," said Director Stevens.

"Anybody would sound good in a situation like that," said MGM's pinup star. "He's in such a dramatic spot, he could recite the alphabet and sound terrific."

"You sound slightly prejudiced against him," kidded her director.

"I know 'Wee Willie Wilbur'," said Ruth, "and just because he's gone to the moon doesn't make him a bigger shot in my eyes."

Director Don Stevens laughed. "How about Miss Fenimore?" he asked.

"Don't mention her," said Ruth. "Gil wouldn't be in the spot he is now if it wasn't for that dame."

"You're just jealous," teased her director. "You'd like to be up there yourself."

"CUT it out!" said Ruth. "I never got a chance to beg Gil not to make this trip. I had a premonition he'd never get back…and I couldn't even reach the poor guy. But that redhead managed somehow. She worked on Wilbur Williams to do it. If they should make it back, I've got a score to settle with her…"

At Schenectady, New York, radio operator Carl Mack of Experimental Station G.E., tried desperately to raise Station Moon on space rocket, *Goodbye, World*. He was having no success.

"Their transmitter still seems to be open and functioning," he reported to anxious G.E. executives and scientists. "I can hear occasional noises as though there is some sort of struggle going on in the cabin. I'm almost certain there's still life there but they must be having a harrowing time."

"It's pretty weird sitting here, looking at that stationary television image," said one of the executives, "and feeling that you're almost there on the moon yourself—and yet not able to help those poor devils in the ship."

"It's twenty minutes now since our last word," said Carl Mack. "I'm sure they'd get back on the air as soon as they could. They know we must be just about dying down here, too. It begins to look very serious."

G.E.'s high frequency operator began sending again.

"Calling Station Moon... Space rocket, *Goodbye, World*... Gil Benson... Come in if you can... Gil Benson!"

*　　*　　*

Gil Benson's first move, in this direst emergency was toward the storeroom, which contained the rocket supplies. He came hurrying back with strips of rubberized sheeting and called on Diana and Wilbur to help him.

The pressurized air in the cabin was rushing out the cabin window.

The three took firm hold of the rubberized sheeting and spread it over the gaping aperture. It took dangerously vital minutes to get it properly in place. When they did, the pressure of the outrushing air held the patch in position but the loss of helium-oxygen had, even so, been extensive.

All three occupants of the spaceship were gasping for breath. The air pressure had dropped to almost half of normal.

"We're in for it," said Gil, his head reeling.

The drop in air pressure had decompressed them too quickly, and a violent reaction set in. Diana and Wilbur were equally affected as they slumped to the floor, twisting and turning in agony.

Gil fought his way back to the instrument board and turned the dial controlling the production and supply of helium-oxygen, on "full." As he did so, he doubled up himself. There was nothing that any of them could do for each other. They had to lie there and sweat it out, not knowing whether any of them would survive the ordeal.

"How long...is this...apt to last?" moaned Wilbur.

"Sometimes...four or five hours," Gil managed. "Hang on!"

*   *   *

It was four hours since any word had been heard from Gil Benson's moon rocket. Newspapers were out with great streaming headlines, declaring that America's intrepid pioneer explorer of space and his two companions were feared lost. It was conjectured that the damage sustained in landing had quickly exhausted their oxygen supply and all had succumbed.

Editorial writers bemoaned the untimely end of such an amazingly successful moon voyage and confidently predicted that Gil Benson had blazed a trail that would soon be followed by establishment of regular scheduled space routes to the moon.

Ironically enough, the television receiver still carried the continuously broadcast image of the lunar landscape, which quite possibly had now become Gil Benson's last resting place. Since all equipment on board was operated by atomic power it was likely that this image would remain visible indefinitely.

*   *   *

Gil Benson was first to recover sufficiently to be able to drag himself to the others. He removed their heavy steel-soled shoes and helped them crawl to bunks where they could make themselves more comfortable.

"The worst is over," he said, putting forth a great effort to reassure them. "You'll be all right in a little while."

Diana and Wilbur watched soberly as Gil, gaining more strength, took a step toward the control board. He had removed his own shoes and was in his stocking feet. His lightness of weight and the weakness of gravity on the moon combined to carry him, in this one step, to the very front of the cabin. In fact, Gil bumped against it as his feet again touched the floor.

Diana and Wilbur, following him with their eyes, were astounded.

"You'll have to be careful when you move around," Gil cautioned. "You'll travel six times as far every step you take. I should have remembered that."

He shuffled himself over, very carefully, in front of the microphone.

"This is Gil Benson," he said. "Hello, Mack...are you there?" He switched on the receiver and waited.

In came a booming voice. "Yes, Benson. For God's sake—are you all right?"

"Just coming out of it...we lost a lot of air. It was pretty bad for a while..."

"How about the damage?"

"Broken window," Gil reported. "Bad oxygen leak. Temporarily repaired. There may be other damage but I haven't been able to look around the ship. I think we're pretty well banged up outside. I can't tell about that until we can get out and have a look."

"Thank heaven you're still there," said Mack. "That's great news back here on Earth. Keep in touch, old man, if you possibly can... I don't want to put through another siege like this..."

"Sorry, Mack," Gil repeated. "I'll try to do better in the future. Got to get some rest... Goodbye now."

Gil turned and eyed his own bunk across the cabin. He calculated carefully and took a short step, landing right beside it.

"Good going," said Wilbur, weakly.

"Oh, boy," said Gil, and stretched himself out. "So we're on the moon... Well, to *hell* with it..."

He dropped off to sleep.

CHAPTER EIGHT

IT WAS six o'clock in the evening, Arizona time, when Gil Benson awoke with a start. Wilbur was standing beside his bunk, shaking him. He looked up, dazedly.

"Where am I?" he asked.

"You're on the moon, you darn fool," said Wilbur. "But you were yelling for help. What was the idea?"

Gil Benson grinned. "I was being chased," he said.

"What by?" asked Wilbur.

"Beautiful women," said Gil. "There were hundreds of them—and they all wanted to kiss me!"

"But they didn't catch you," called Diana, from her bunk across the cabin. "I don't see any lipstick."

"I risked my life getting over to you," said Wilbur. "I was asleep when you yelled, forgot where I was, jumped up, and hit the ceiling…"

Gil laughed as he stood up. "We'll have to get used to walking around here. Since our bodies only weigh one sixth of what they did on Earth, it requires very little exertion to lift them." He looked at his wristwatch. "Here's something funny… The sun will be setting in Arizona in an hour or so, but we'll have about six more Earth days of sunlight here—and it's a good thing. It will give us a chance to get around and explore the moon's surface to see whether or not it really is a dead planet."

"It's not anymore," quipped Wilbur. *We're* here."

Diana sat up. "Yes, and if you two feel like I do, we're good and hungry."

Gil smiled. "Well, we ought to be able to enjoy a real meal this time. Our first dinner on the moon. And we should eat it in style." He looked toward the pantry entrance, then took a step. His body left the floor and he landed easily within a foot of the doorway.

"Come on, you two!" he said. "It's sport… You might as well get accustomed to it."

Diana and Wilbur followed him. They looked like young birds trying their wings. Both piled up against the wall of the cabin. As they picked themselves off the floor, the energy exerted shot them into the air. Gil, watching from the doorway, laughed at their acrobatics.

"Wait till we get outside," he said. "We'll have a track meet and see who can jump the highest…"

He went into the storeroom, presently passing out a card table and folding chairs for them to set up in the cabin. Then he produced a variety of canned foods—the usual well advertised brands.

"What have you got here?" asked Wilbur. "Don't tell me—oh, no, is that Spam?"

"That's Spam," said Gil, handing the cans to Diana who made a half step, landed in the center of the cabin, and set them on the table.

"Well, how do you like that?" griped Wilbur. "I come all the way to the moon to get Spam. I might as well have re-enlisted in the Army."

"You're going to think you did," said Gil, handing him three Army plates, cups, knives, forks, spoons and a can opener. "Give these to Diana."

GIL then turned to the water tank and drew a pitcher full of the cooled liquid, which ran out with excessive slowness. Seated around the table, the three pioneer space travelers eyed one another and laughed.

"This could be a picnic in the country," said Diana. "But hot one prepared by a woman. Every man, if left to his own devices, always eats out of cans."

Gil was applying the can opener to good effect, opening up sweet potatoes, spinach, beets, peaches—and Wilbur's delectable dish "Spam."

"Even the man in the moon ought to go for this," said Gil. "All right, Diana, how about serving us?"

"Delighted!" said Wilbur's redhead.

The three of them made a picture, two men still in evening dress, somewhat ruffled, and the girl in evening gown with the bright red hair and big blue eyes, doling out equal portions of food to them. The trio ate with relish and fell into an excited discussion of the events experienced on what now seemed to have been a dream trip through space.

"It just doesn't seem possible we're actually here," said Wilbur, looking out the windows at the dark lunar rocks that loomed not far from the ship. "Good gosh," he said. "I guess that television set has been operating all this time…"

"It won't hurt anything," said Gil. "We fortunately have ample power—but I'm wondering if they're still getting the image on Earth?"

"I'll find out," said Wilbur. He got up from the table, took a step, and sailed against the instrument board. "If I'm not careful," he said, "I'll knock myself out…"

Diana and Gil laughed. Wilbur turned to the transmitter.

"This is Station Moon calling Experimental Station G.E. Schenectady… Wilbur Williams speaking… Come in… Over…"

He switched on the receiver. A new voice boomed out.

"This is Experimental Station G.E. Schenectady…Fred Denny speaking…I'm relieving Carl Mack… How are things up there?"

"Swell," said Wilbur. "We've just had our first meal on the moon…Spam never tasted so good… Everybody's rested…feeling fine. We haven't been outside yet so we haven't seen any more than you're seeing now, if you're still getting our television image."

"We're still getting it," reported the G.E. operator.

Wilbur snapped off the television set. "Well, you're not getting it now," he said.

"No," laughed Fred Denny. "It just disappeared from the screen. That's pretty quick work. Certainly demonstrates how fast the image travels between the moon and the Earth."

"You must have gotten tired of that scene," said Wilbur. "We'll try to get you some new ones a little later."

"We have a message here for Gil Benson," said Fred Denny. "Professor Crowley wants to know the extent of damage—whether you've carried enough plastic glass for replacement of windows broken."

"How about that, Gil?" asked Wilbur.

Gil judged his distance and stepped lightly to the microphone. "Better let me answer. This is Gil Benson... Tell Professor Crowley I haven't made real survey of damage as yet. I'll give him a complete report later. Ask him to check with Army rocket headquarters at White Sands, New Mexico, and find out if they are far enough along with their experiments to attempt shooting us a radar-controlled rocket containing repair parts, if we need them."

"Ye gods," said Wilbur. "I hope we don't..."

"Okay, Benson," said Fred Denny's voice from Earth. "Will do..."

"Thanks, old man," replied Gil. "It's just possible that we might contact such a rocket with our own Army radar equipment and take over its control when it enters the moon's gravitational field. Have Professor Crowley get me the dope on this, just in case. That's all for now."

"Right you are," said Denny. "I'll have the information for you next time you contact. Good luck..."

Gil switched off the radio.

"Good night," said Wilbur.

"There's not any doubt about our getting back okay, is there?"

"On a trip of this kind," said Gil, "there's always plenty of doubt until you get back..."

Diana smiled. "That doesn't worry me," she said. "Now that I've got something on my stomach." She busied herself with clearing the table, making cautious steps to and from the galley. Wilbur knocked the table down and folded the chairs. He made a grotesque figure, loping through the air.

"I don't think I'll ever get the hang of this," he said.

Gil, who had been studying the small area of lunar landscape, which could be seen through the windows, now turned to his two companions.

"Well, we might as well know the worst," he said. "It's time we were getting outside and seeing what happened to our rocket. Come on. Take off your evening clothes, put on these slacks and I'll help you into your space suit."

He crossed over to the storeroom alcove where the moon suits were hanging and dragged them out carefully, laying them side by side on the cabin floor. They were heavy and contained much equipment.

"Here's what you need to know about these suits," said Gil. "They weighed around six hundred pounds on Earth. I couldn't even lift one of them there. But they're only one sixth as heavy here. You'll be able to navigate in them easily."

"*Navigate* sounds like the right word," said Diana, eyeing the suits apprehensively.

"They carry their own power plant and electric generator," Gil pointed out. "It operates on sun power in the daytime and storage battery during the lunar night. Here it is here…and this is the air conditioning plant. It reprocesses the air you breathe and puts it back into circulation after mixing it with fresh oxygen. This is the suit's lighting system, both internal and external… Here's the cooling and heating equipment…this is the radio and radar apparatus… Here's the place your food is stored for long exploration trips… These motors and controls are to help move arms and fingers. I'll have to show you how to work all these gadgets."

"I'll say you will," said Wilbur. "That suit looks too complicated for me. I'm afraid to get in the darn thing without a can opener."

DRESSED to step out upon the surface of the moon, Earth's three space travelers made a strange appearing sight. Before clamping down their head-pieces and starting the flow of liquid oxygen which they were to breathe while encased in this little air world of their own, Gil produced an American flag on a pointed metal staff and said, "Our first act, when we get out on the moon will be to lay claim to it in the name of the United States of America."

"That's a thrill," said Wilbur. "This ought to make pikers out of the discoverers of the North and South poles. But, say, Gil—how about leaving me the cheese concession?"

"Shut up," said Gil. "This is a solemn occasion. Listen while I give you two a few instructions. The weight of our suits is so great that they'll hold us down so we can walk about, almost as we do on Earth. Remember, there's no atmosphere on the moon, so don't expect to hear any sounds. We can talk to each other, of course, by walkie-talkie. I guess that's all—except we'll have to leave the ship through this special air lock compartment, so the oxygen supply in the cabin won't be affected as we go in and out... Now which one of you wants the honor of being the first to actually set foot on the moon?"

Diana and Wilbur looked at one another.

"That's a real honor," said Hollywood's greatest press agent. "The one who does that will go down in history."

"And that honor belongs to one person," said Diana. "Gil Benson..."

"You said it," echoed Wilbur. "The only honor I want is to be the first to set foot on Earth again."

Gil laughed. "Too bad we can't cover this by television," he said, "but we don't have enough skilled hands to maneuver the equipment. We'll just have to take motion pictures..."

"And I'll do the shooting," volunteered Wilbur. "I'm the best picture-taker of bathing beauties in Hollywood."

"Well, you'll snap some forms here never seen before," said Gil, handing Wilbur the compact movie camera.

"Boy, I've got a great idea," said Wilbur. "We'll make Diana the first pin-up girl on the moon!"

"You stick to the flag-raising ceremony and forget Diana," advised the redhead. "Gil is the star of this event."

They stepped into the air lock compartment and closed the inner door behind them. Gil slid the heavy metal outer door open and shoved out a metal ladder, making contact with the ground, about ten feet below.

He turned and backed out in his cumbersome space suit, feeling one foot at a time for each rung of the ladder beneath him. Diana followed as soon as Gil was clear of the doorway. Wilbur then swung onto the ladder, tripped, and almost fell on her.

"Look out below…" he called. "If I land on you with all this plumbing, it'll be 'Goodbye, baby'."

Reaching the moon's surface, the three stood in a little group and looked around.

The *Goodbye, World* lay with its retractable landing gear smashed, its under belly sunk deep in this fine pumice or volcanic dust which heavily coated everything within sight. It looked as though it had lain undisturbed for ages. Beneath it was blank, wrinkled, rugged rock, which appeared to have been formed originally by lava. This same rock rose above the volcanic ash in fantastic walls and jagged peaks, which cast the blackest of black shadows and gave an uncanny effect to the whole weird landscape.

THE spaceship looked strangely real and life-like against this dead background, resembling a great wounded bird that had fallen in flight. Its dark side was tilted toward the moon's surface with the bright side exposed to the merciless rays of the sun, which beat down through airless space with unrestrained fury. Had not the carefully designed bright-coated suits of the space travelers been conditioned against this relentless heat, they could not have survived even momentary exposure.

At a gesture from Gil, all dropped the shield of dark glass across the window in their headgear and looked toward the sun. It was a frightening spectacle—gigantic shafts of flame in a state of unimaginable gaseous violent turbulence, shining out from a jet black heaven…

Directing their gaze away from this mighty furnace in the sky, they now beheld the Earth from which they had departed about nineteen hours ago.

"Just look at that…" Wilbur exclaimed, his voice being heard by Diana and Gil on their walkie-talkie sets.

The planet of their birth was a tremendous half-moon, eighty times more luminous than the satellite they were on and four times its size. Even as they gazed at it, Earth's continents seemed be swimming slowly across its face, from left to right, in the direction of its rotation. Cloud formations, hovering over parts of the Earth, appeared as bright spots and bodies of water shone with dazzling brilliance.

"What a sight!" cried Diana. "I guess you have to be off the old Earth to really appreciate it."

"When it gets full," said Gil, "it should give us a complete geography lesson. It's still hard to realize that we're looking at the real globe of the world."

It was fascinating and, at the same time startling, to contemplate these new perspectives and new points of view growing out of them. Here was a unique place of vantage, which afforded unrivaled observation of the universe, with sun and stars simultaneously visible in the black corridors of space, and shining with indescribable brightness because there were no dust particles to deflect or absorb light.

"The moon will be headquarters for the astronomers of the future," said Gil. "All scientists and research men will want to conduct their tests from here. I can just imagine how Professor Crowley would be raving if he were with us."

"Please don't bring that up," said Diana. "It makes me feel miserable."

Gil looked about him, then turned to Wilbur.

"Where do you think we should hold this little ceremony?" he asked.

"Well," said Wilbur, "we might as well apply Hollywood technique and look for the best camera angle. I think you should walk out here far enough so we can get your whole spaceship in the background."

"About here?" asked Gil.

Wilbur sighted professionally through the finder of his movie camera, held at the level of his eyes.

"That's swell," he said. "Just right. Sorry we can't get this in sound but you say whatever you think is appropriate and we'll dub in your voice later."

"Okay," said Gil. "Are you ready?"

"Just a minute," directed Wilbur. "We've got to make this dramatic…"

"WE'RE on the moon," said Diana. "Isn't that dramatic enough?"

"No," said Wilbur. "We've got to get the proper sequence. Gil, you step off to one side and let me try to get a shot at the Earth, spinning away, up there. I think it's plenty bright enough to photograph. Then I'll pan down here on this gorgeously desolate moon landscape and come in on a shot of the rocket, lying there like a great, fallen albatross. This sets the stage for the entrance of the hero—the first man on the moon. Too bad we don't have some 'Pomp and Circumstance' music blending in with the 'Stars and Stripes Forever.' Don't forget this when we dub in the sound. It'll be terrific. Then you come marching in. Plant the flag, make your spiel, take a bow, and stand at attention as we finish with the 'Star Spangled Banner.' Brother, that's drama…"

"All right," said Gil, "let's get it over with."

Diana took her stand beside Wilbur to watch this unique movie shot. He raised the camera in position, pointed it at the luminous half moon of Earth, and started shooting. When it came time for Gil Benson's big moment, Wilbur called out, "Okay, Gil—do your stuff…"

America's Number One Playboy, unrecognizable now in this new and spectacular role, lumbered into camera range and jabbed the American flag in a rock crevice. Its folds hung limp because, with no air on the moon there was, of course, no breeze—and Gil, to show the flag, took hold of its upper corner, spreading it momentarily to view.

As he did so, he said, "I, Gil Benson, from the planet, Earth, of the State of Arizona, the United States of America, on this day, as the first man from my planet to set foot on our satellite, do hereby lay claim to the moon and, all its possessions in the name of my sovereign country..."

"Bravo!" cried Diana.

"That was great, Gil, old boy," said Wilbur. "Hollywood will love this."

Gil left the flag in place and came toward them. "Of course this little ceremony is just for the record," he said. "I'll have to file an official claim when we get back to Earth. But it gives you quite a thrill, at that, to think of planting Old Glory up here?"

"Cut it out," said Wilbur, "you're making me homesick."

Gil turned and looked toward their spaceship.

"Speaking of home," he said. "We'd better see what our chances are of getting home."

He led the way in an encirclement of the rocket, examining such damage as had been done with minute care, and satisfying himself that the shell of the rocket was intact. In addition to the crushed landing gear, he found that another section of the plastic glass windows was badly cracked, necessitating replacement. It was not a comfortable feeling to think that breakage of any of these windows while shooting through space might quickly destroy the oxygen content of the cabin and result in their annihilation.

"I can see now," said Gil, "that I slipped up in not bringing enough window replacements with me. I'd hate to have to attempt the return journey with that badly cracked and weakened window surface."

"Maybe we'd better stay on here," said Wilbur. "How long will our food supply last?"

Gil laughed. "About two months, with rationing."

"Well," said Wilbur, "someone else is bound to be up from Earth eventually. Maybe we can hitch-hike a ride back with them."

"You get some of the cutest ideas," said Diana.

"I got here *alive,*" said Wilbur, "and I don't want to go back *dead...*"

GIL'S attention was now being directed to the lunar

landscape.

"How about a little overland jaunt?" he proposed. "I'd like to see some of this moon country."

"It all looks the same to me," said Wilbur. "It would sure make one terrific golf course. What hazards... Oh, boy!"

He pointed to a succession of craters, big and small, interlocking one another with prodigious rock walls and ridges and cracks in the moon's surface in and around them.

They started walking over and about some of the peculiar formations, looking back at intervals to keep their bearings and glimpse their glittering spaceship.

"I think we've done all the exploring we should do, our first time out," Gil said decidedly, after a half hour's slow going. "I'm not sure, even with these protective suits, that we should risk being exposed to the sun much longer, till we know whether or not there'll be any effect. So I'm for returning to the rocket and starting out again tomorrow morning, Arizona time."

"You're the boss," said Wilbur.

The trio turned back toward the location of their spaceship.

"Besides," said Gil, "we should never all of us get out of sight of our rocket home. On any long trip, either you or Diana will have to stay with the ship to guide me back, if I lose my bearings."

"If you lose your bearings," said Wilbur, "I'll lose my mind; don't talk like that."

CHAPTER NINE

AT ITS base on the White Sands Proving Ground, in the desert of New Mexico, the United States Army's moon rocket was poised for its take-off.

Gil Benson's voice was coming in by high frequency radio.

"When do you estimate your rocket will reach the field of the moon's influence?" he was asking.

"Around forty-three hours and twelve minutes after take-off," replied Captain Bruce Elder, Army engineer.

"Then we should be prepared to take over control about that time?"

"Right. We'll follow the rocket's flight and keep you advised. The plastic glass is carefully packed. It should come through unless the rocket is badly damaged."

"Okay. Thanks very much. We're standing by."

With all in readiness for the launching, Professor Crowley withdrew from the rocket site to the radio car where he could watch the take-off and communicate with the "man on the target."

"Check your watch, Gil," said the Professor. "It's Wednesday, two-fifteen here. Ten seconds. Count them off…"

Lt. Col. Harvey had alerted his men assigned to starting the rocket motors and sending the jet-propelled missile on its emergency mission into space.

At a signal from him, the switch was thrown igniting the fuel of liquid oxygen and alcohol. The Army rocket rose slowly from its base as though pulled upward by invisible wires. Then, as it seemed to hang heavily in air—with the fuel fully applied, it took off with a great *swoosh* in a cloud of dust, smoke, and flame, giving forth a thunderous noise.

"There she goes…" cried Professor Crowley. "She's on the way, Gil."

"I could hear it leave," Gil reported from the moon. "That's great. I'll be looking for it…"

"It's a wonderful sight from here," continued Professor Crowley. "It's accelerating at a tremendous rate, trailing a long tail of white flame and smoke. Captain Elder tells me it's up nineteen miles already…thirty…sixty…while I'm talking. It's making a speed of eight thousand, four hundred feet per second…now it's being stepped up…all I can see is a white vapor trail it's thinning out and disappearing the rocket's reached the stratosphere…it's hitting a velocity of three miles a second…that's not good enough as you know…can't get away from the Earth on that…here's the third step…let's see what happens. Four…five…yes, it's jumped to seven… Gil—it's out there in space—it's beyond the Earth's gravitational pull…it's a free projectile now…they're cutting off the motors…it's coasting toward you…if they can keep it on course, it should make it. Here's hoping…"

"You said it," came Gil's voice, from the moon. "Nothing for us to do now but wait. I think I'll go out and see what I can of our surroundings, while I'm putting in time."

Professor Crowley laughed, excitedly. "Wish to hell I was with you!"

"I wish to hell you were, too," said Gil. "I may be an explorer, but I'm no scientist."

WITH the Army's relief rocket on the way to them, the three moon occupants could now relax and give their attention to other matters of absorbing interest close at hand.

"Wilbur," said Gil, "I'm sorry, but you're elected to stay here and keep in touch with Earth by radio—and also with us on the walkie-talkie, in case we need to make contact. Diana and I are going on a little cross country hike."

"That's ducky," said Wilbur. "I come all the way to the moon and I don't see anything but Diana and you and the spaceship."

"Why, Wilbur," said Diana. "Are you tired of looking at me?"

"You're still beautiful, baby," said Wilbur, "but now that I'm on the moon, I don't feel so romantic."

"You can see all the sights next trip," said Gil.

"There isn't going to be any next trip," said Wilbur. "If I get back to the Earth I'm going to chain myself to it."

Diana and Gil laughed as they climbed into their heavy moon suits. Once inside, they continued the conversation by walkie-talkie.

"Goodbye, Wilbur," said Gil. "Don't look so lonely and deserted. We'll give you a running description of what we're seeing and you can pass it on to Earth."

"Okay," said Wilbur. "But I think this is just a frame-up to get you and Diana off by yourselves." He shook a warning finger at them. "I don't want any more of this kissing..."

Diana and Gil looked at one another through the glass windows of their bright metal helmets, with their funny rubberized oxygen noses attached to a tank in front. Then they both howled.

"We don't need a chaperone in these things," said Gil.

"A girl could die an old maid in here," said Diana.

They crossed the cabin to the air lock compartment, lifted ponderous arms to wave Wilbur "goodbye" and stepped inside, closing the door. Hollywood's greatest press agent watched them depart through the window and then returned to keep vigil by the radio set.

"I didn't do myself so much good when I introduced her to Gil," he said to himself. "She's giving me about as much attention as an agent usually gets—*ten per cent...*"

*   *   *

As nearly as Gil could determine, he and Diana were about ten miles from their "home base" in a westerly direction, figured from the sun's position. They had traveled up steep inclines and down into deep recesses, keeping in the black shadow of walls and ridges as much as possible, to escape the almost blinding sunlight. But now they found themselves within a mile of a great crater.

Gazing up the rough rock slope that extended to the crater's rim, Gil cried out in excitement, "Look, Diana—see these bright streaks in the ground? Running down the sides of this slope, from the crater's edge?"

"Yes," said Diana. "It hurts my eyes to look at them. What are they?"

"They're one of astronomy's mysteries," said Gil. "As seen from Earth they extend in straight lines of great brilliance, in all directions from hundreds of different centers—like spokes in a wheel."

"They look like a lot of quicksilver that's been heated and run out from one spot—and frozen all over," said Diana.

"It's not that," said Gil. "And it's not a stain on the under rock surface. It's a substance of some sort... Just see how these lines extend... They aren't broken by any of the landscape. Our astronomers call these streaks 'rays.' Some think they were caused by gases produced by volcanoes. Others think they were brought about by action of meteors. It looks to me like they resulted from a white-hot explosion as meteors hit the moon's surface and formed these craters.

"Could be," said Diana. "They're sure splattered in every direction."

Gil knelt and examined a raised vein of bright material that was fused into the rock surface beneath. Several fragments were lying loose. These he retrieved to take back to Earth as samples.

"You know what, Diana. I know just enough about minerals to hazard a guess...this stuff is what Earth scientists would give their right eye for—it's *Uranium...*"

"Uranium?" Diana repeated.

"Yes...I'm sure of it," said Gil. "I've seen pieces of uranium before. This nickel-white metal you see on all sides is the material that atomic scientists have been using to explode their atomic bombs—it's what's needed to create new power for heat, light, and industry. And, if all these streaks are composed of the same material, then the moon is loaded with it. Absolutely loaded."

"Hey," cut in Wilbur, from the spaceship. "Are you kidding?"

"I'll say I'm not kidding," replied Gil. "This moon's a gold mine. It's so fabulous I don't dare think of it. Here's all the power the Earth will ever need—forever. But, say—if the wrong people get up here and get hold of it—it would be just too bad. They could build their own reacting atomic 'piles' on the moon—put them in rockets and bombard any country on Earth. The United States Army had better get up here quick—and take over. We've got to gain control of the moon for our own protection from any possible enemy force on our planet. And we can't waste any time doing it."

"Shall I pass this news on to Schenectady?" asked Wilbur.

"I should say not," said Gil. "Not a word to Earth about this. It's too hot to broadcast. We'll have to wait and trust to luck on our getting back—so I can personally put this knowledge in the proper hands."

"Ye gods," said Wilbur. "What next?"

"Dinner," said Gil. "We'll be back in two and a half hours. Have the table set and the food laid out..."

"Okay," said Wilbur, "but you hand me a few more shockers like this, and you'll find *me* laid out..."

THE Army radar-guided rocket dispatched from Earth forty-three hours ago was now nearing the moon's gravitational field. In the spaceship, *Goodbye, World* the atmosphere was once more tense. Gil Benson, intent on operation of his Army radar set, sat alert and expectant. Diana and Wilbur held their breaths.

"Have you made contact?" asked Captain Elder's voice from Earth.

"Yes," said Gil.

"Are you ready to take over control?"

"Ready..."

"Count off and take over on ten..."

The count started. At "ten," Gil set his dials and watched the radar screen. A look of exultation crossed his face.

"We've got it..." he announced.

"Good," said Captain Elder's voice. "Here's hoping you bring her in okay. We're all pulling for you..."

"Thanks," said Gil, grimly.

It would be almost five hours yet before the rocket would arrive and this time must be spent in exacting concentration.

"Don't lose that baby now," said Wilbur. "I want to get back to Earth."

*   *   *

"It won't be long now," Gil announced at 3:05 p.m. Friday, Arizona time, forty-eight hours and forty minutes after the Army rocket had left Earth.

"I'm going to try to bring her in for a landing this trip."

He had twice caused the rocket to circle a prescribed area at the height of about a mile overhead, as a test of his control.

"Don't bring it in on top of us," warned Wilbur. "Pick a nice soft spot about a mile away."

"Show me a soft spot on the whole moon," said Gil. "Let's hope she comes in at an angle so she's not too badly broken up."

"I'm praying," said Wilbur, "but don't count on it..."

Diana stood near the temporary rubberized covering of the broken window.

"I'm too numb to pray," she said.

"But I've got my fingers and toes crossed..."

"Here she comes!" Gil cried.

They watched the radar screen in anxious fascination.

"She's down!" he said. "About a half mile from here. Stand by the radio, Wilbur...Diana and I, are going out to see what's happened..."

CHAPTER TEN

IT WAS tremendous news on Earth when word came through from the moon that the Army's radar controlled rocket had landed safely. The peoples of the world were thrilled at the thought that it was not only possible for a man-carrying spaceship to reach the moon but that also a cargo of repair parts could be jet propelled after it. The intimations for the future of interspacial travel, with the moon established as a taking off point for other planets, were exciting beyond description. In a few years—it was freely predicted—humans would be colonizing on the moon and going there on weekend excursions.

Even MGM's pin-up sensation indicated that she might make such a trip in company, of course, with Gil Benson.

"I wouldn't trust myself with anyone else," she said, which was her way of paying tribute.

On Sunday night, Arizona time, with the three space travelers about to round out their first full week on the moon, Gil Benson reported, through G.E.'s Experimental Station at Schenectady, that he had completed all possible repairs. The new plastic glass windows were in place and the crushed landing gear had been stripped from the ship.

"When we get back to Earth," said Gil, "we'll have to come in for a belly landing-but I think we can make it."

Monday morning, Arizona time, an earthly event stole the front-page headlines, for the first time, from Gil Benson's moon adventure. The peoples of the world had their minds forcibly brought back from inter-stellar space to face the shocking and imminent possibility of a Third World War. They stared in horror and dismay at these smashing lines:

WAR WITH RUSSIA INEVITABLE
May come at any Moment, All Countries Prepared to meet Devastating
Undeclared Attack

Fiery opening paragraphs set forth the explosive situation.

Relations between Great Britain and the United States and Russia have reached the breaking point. Europe is ablaze with hatred, revolt, intrigue and countless violent border incidents. The tinderbox of the Balkans needs only one final spark to touch off a war for which the new alignments of Eastern and Western powers have been feverishly and openly preparing.

There is no longer any question that this war cannot be averted. The only question—at what moment will it come?

A state of national emergency has been declared in countries throughout the world, and in England and the United States plans are being rushed for evacuation of big centers of population in anticipation of a rain of death from the skies.

This conflict, which, admittedly, may bring the absolute end of civilization, is being precipitated through the utter failure of the world's diplomats and the delegates of the United Nations Organization to effect a peaceful settlement and adjustment of powerful national differences in economy and ideology.

The Congress of the United States is meeting in special session to draft legislation necessary to putting the country on an immediate overnight, full wartime footing.

It is understood that the Army and Navy air forces are standing by with their long range bombers and rockets prepared to launch an atom bomb attack at the first real outbreak of hostilities...

RADIO Operator Carl Mack, in contact with Gil Benson on the moon, read him these headlines and said, "Better stay up there, old man—it's soon going to be hell on Earth."

"Good night," moaned Hollywood's greatest press agent, "and just after me thinking what a nice safe place the old Earth was..."

The end of the lunar day was approaching. In a few more hours of Earth time the sun would begin to dip below the western horizon. It would be the first sunset that these pioneer space travelers would see from the moon and it would take about thirty times as long as it had on Earth for the upper edge of the sun to disappear for, as Gil had explained, the sun from the moon seems to move only about one-thirtieth as fast.

"This is going to be an interesting spectacle to watch," said Gil. "I'm anxious to get back to Earth with this knowledge of extensive uranium deposits but I don't want to leave here until we've experienced part of a night on the moon and have had a look at the other side."

"You don't really mean it, Gil," said Wilbur. "Isn't this side enough for the first trip? Have a heart."

"I second the motion," said Diana.

Gil smiled. "Oh, I don't intend to land but we'll stick it out here till the other side of the moon is lit up and then we'll fly around the moon on the way home. I want to take as many pictures as we can of its entire surface. We've already got some swell close-ups of the lines of uranium and the formations around us."

"Gil," said Wilbur, soberly, "as your radio man, photographer, master of ceremonies and general all-around flunky, I'm about to stage the first strike on the moon..."

"And I'll walk out with him," threatened Diana.

Gil grinned. "Go ahead," he said. "Take a walk. If you don't want to go with me, I'll pick you up my next trip."

"The strike is over," said Wilbur.

At Gil's suggestion, Diana and Wilbur donned their space suits and left the rocket to watch the sun as it slowly descended beneath the moon's saw-toothed horizon. It shone with all the splendor of noonday until its lower edges began to disappear. Then its light commenced to grow dimmer but the blackness of the sky remained.

THE three Earth visitors could not help but contrast this strange sunset with the settings of this same sun which they had witnessed so many times on their own planet and which had been attended by a magnificent blaze of heavenly reds and golds.

"They wouldn't even give this sunset one star in Hollywood," said Wilbur.

"I agree," said Diana. "It's kind of dismal, if you'd ask me."

There being no air to catch the sunlight, with the last upper edge of the sun now slipping below the horizon, there was no twilight. The instant the sun vanished from view they were plunged into darkness. And now it was only the mammoth half-luminous body of their own Earth above them that cast any light upon the doubly desolate surface of the moon. As they looked upward at their home planet a strange and inexplicable nostalgia seized them. It seemed so near and yet so far away.

"Just an overnight sleeper jump," said Gil, "five years from now."

"Put me to sleep and take me back," said Wilbur. "I don't

care if there is another world war. I'd even re-enlist again. What choice have I got? It's certainly better than this, unless you can find another planet where everything is sweetness and light and everybody loves everybody else and they haven't invented gun powder and atomic bombs yet."

"The moon's got you," said Diana. "You've gone loony."

"If you haven't turned on your heating units," warned Gil, "you'd better do it in a hurry. The temperature's taking a nose dive right now and in a few hours it will be at least two hundred degrees below zero, Centigrade."

"What a place," said Wilbur. "It beats the cool nights in California. I thought I'd freeze there, every time the sun dropped behind the mountains."

"You and me both," said Diana. "But I'll never complain after this."

"Look!" Gil suddenly exclaimed. He pointed in a direction away from the rocket. "I saw something hit the moon…"

Even as he spoke, their heavy metal suits were sprayed with a rain of rock particles. They hit with such force as to dent the suits in several places and the air inside their mobile houses recorded the sound. The surface of the moon shook under their feet.

"It must have been a meteor," cried Gil. "That was a mighty close call…"

"Let's get out of here!" cried Wilbur.

"No," said Gil, "let's investigate. I want to see where it hit."

He turned his suit's searchlight in the direction of the fallen body. "Come on," he said. "Follow me…"

Aided by the bright rays of their searchlights, the three moved away from the vicinity of their spaceship, continuing for about a mile in and around and over the rough and uneven terrain. They finally came to a spot giving evidence of new devastation. A thin vapor was rising from a newly formed crater where the huge heavenly cannon ball had landed. It had crushed the moon surface about it into powdered rock and now, under the glare of their searchlights, they could see thousands of meteor fragments spread out in all directions from its awesome point of contact.

Gil stooped and picked up a piece of the meteor in one hand. It was black and jagged, large enough to have weighed a hundred pounds on Earth.

"THIS is iron," he said. "Perhaps alloyed with a little nickel. It's incredibly hard. If this meteor had been falling toward our Earth, the friction of our atmosphere would have caused it to burn up in space, but here on the moon these shooting stars, with no air to check them, hit the surface. I can see right now that a lot of these craters we've been wondering about have been made by meteors just like this one. Lucky it didn't hit the ship…"

"We'd better get away from here before one does," said Wilbur. "It's even worse at night—you can't see them in time to dodge…"

"Dodge?" said Diana. "How can you dodge when they're going a million miles a second?"

"Not quite that fast," laughed Gil. "But they must be falling somewhere on the moon all the time. If anyone was going to stay up here, he'd have to live in a cave or build underground."

"We might as well go back to Earth and start dodging atom bombs," said Wilbur.

Gil looked down at the large fragment of the meteor he was holding.

"I'm going to take this back to Earth as a specimen," he said. "No doubt many of these craters were also caused by volcanoes now extinct but the surface of the moon has certainly been peppered by ages of meteoric bombardment."

"It makes me feel like ducking my head all the time," said Diana. "I don't think I'm exactly going to enjoy the rest of · my time on the moon."

Gil smiled. "Think of all the countless thunderstorms on Earth and how few people are ever struck by lightning."

"But think of the ones who are," said Wilbur. "Come on,

Gil. We've stayed long enough. Let's go home…"

Gil shook his head. "It will take more than a meteor to chase me off this moon till I finish up what I want to do," he said. "Let's go back to the rocket and get something to eat."

They turned about and their searchlight beams, unrestricted on the airless moon, struck the glittering surface of a portion of the spaceship that was visible.

"Hello, *Goodbye, World*," said Wilbur. "I'm going to change your name. It's soon going to be *Goodbye, Moon*…"

*   *   *

The Earth was a magnificent full moon above them as the first three humans to reach the moon prepared for their take-off. They could see it through the plastic glass windows with the outline of the continents standing out as though sculptured in space. The oceans were brilliant flashing gems and the white glistening polar caps sparkled with dancing rainbow halos. It was a sight far more transcendent than the moon had ever looked from Earth.

"I can darn near see the lights of Broadway," said Wilbur. "With a good telescope, I'll bet we could even read the electric signs and see what pictures were playing."

"I wouldn't want to look," said Diana. "If I saw Ruth Delano's name in lights, it would spoil my trip."

Gil laughed. "You girls certainly love each other, don't you?"

"Like sisters," said Diana.

"Never mind," soothed Wilbur. "If you get back to Earth, you'll be bigger than Ruth Delano ever thought of being. They'll wrap up Hollywood and give it to you."

"I don't want Hollywood," said Diana—and looked sidewise at Gil.

"Cut out that double-talk," said Wilbur. "You hired me to put you over once and I'm going to do it this time. I can't miss. I can see your billing already: 'Diana Fenimore, Entrancing Queen of the Moon, the Original Rocket Girl, the Woman Who

Put Sex in Space—the Sweetheart of the Man in the Moon.' "

Diana looked at herself in the cabin mirror.

"You still think I should wear this evening dress back?" she asked.

"Sure thing," said Wilbur. "It's a terrific gag. We all return to Earth exactly as we left—in evening dress. It will make this moon trip seem just like another premiere."

Gil Benson stepped before the instrument board and placed his hand on the starting lever.

"Better get on the radio," he said to Wilbur, "and get ready to report our trip." He looked at his wristwatch. "We're leaving here, just two weeks to the day that we departed from Earth. It's Monday at nine a.m. Arizona time…have you got Schenectady?"

"Yes," reported Wilbur. "It's just coming in now."

"Hello, up there!" sounded Carl Mack's voice from Earth. "Is this the day?"

"It's the day and the minute," informed Wilbur. "We're just taking off now but Gil wants me to tell you we're not coming straight home. We're going around what you call the dark side of the moon first. Only it's light over there now."

"That's great," said Carl Mack. "The scientists at G.E. have been hoping Gil would do that."

"And his two passengers have been hoping he wouldn't," said Wilbur. "But you know Gil…"

Carl Mack laughed. "You're sunk, Williams. Might as well sit back and enjoy it."

"I'll sit back," said Wilbur, "but I won't enjoy it…"

Gil motioned to Diana and Wilbur.

"I'm starting the atomic rocket motors now," he said. "I'm going to raise this ship horizontally off the moon's surface and ascend to a height of about ten miles, from which altitude I hope to cruise around the moon. This will give us a chance to get excellent photographs and fine observation. Tell Mack I'm not sure how good our radio reception will be on the other side and if he can't get us, not to worry—we'll pick him up again as soon as we come around on the Earth-side, once more, and head toward our own planet."

Wilbur passed on this information.

Gil's hand pressed the starting lever down and the atomic power motors hummed inside the cabin. Momentarily, the huge ship trembled like a great bird coming to life. The moon's surface commenced to fall away, looking weird under the reflected light from the ball of Earth. Gil then pointed the rocket in a westerly direction, following the course taken by the sun in its setting of just an Earth week ago.

"We're making a speed of about fifteen hundred miles an hour," said Gil. "In a little over an hour, we'll be coming into sunlight on the other side of the moon. Then I'm going to slow us down considerably so we can really see what it looks like. This is going to be the most exciting part of the trip to me."

"I can predict right now," said Wilbur, "that the other side will look like a second showing of the same picture. But I'm reconciled. It will only take us a few more hours at the most."

He turned back to the radio and spoke into the microphone.

"Say, Mack—how's the third world war coming, down there?"

THE voice from Earth reached him almost instantly. "Swell. We're getting closer to it every day. Beginning next week, they are starting to evacuate every big industrial and coast city. But that may not be soon enough. The war's apt to be on before you get back."

"That's lovely," said Wilbur. Then, turning aside, he continued, "Gil, did you hear that? Just look up there at that Earth of ours... Can you picture those little insignificant human ants getting ready to kill each other again? If they could only see what a wonderful planet they're living on. How terrific the universe really is... I wonder if it wouldn't change their whole attitude—or would they just get more greedy than ever—and want to grab off a few extra planets for themselves?"

"You're a member of the human race," said Gil. "You

answer that one…"

"Well," said Wilbur, "aren't we already trying to grab off the moon? And when we get that, do you think we'll stop there? We'll be shooting through space, establishing trade routes all over the place…"

"Which wouldn't be a bad idea," said Diana. "And I'd be the first interplanetary saleslady."

"You should settle down," said Wilbur, "and marry—and stay on one Earth—and have children."

Diana's blue eyes went into action for the first time in a long while.

"I may marry," she said. "But, after this, I refuse to stay on one Earth and my children will just have to be born wherever I am at the time."

"That's bad," said Wilbur. "The poor kids won't know where they are—and they'll be citizens of no place."

"They'll be citizens of the universe," Diana rejoined. "Which ought to be good enough for anybody…"

Wilbur eyed her. "Who's loony now?" he asked.

CHAPTER ELEVEN

AS THE spaceship sped over the rough-fringed curvature of the moon, the sun burst upon it, almost without warning. Emerging from darkness into daylight was a momentary shock but not half the shock that was occasioned by Wilbur's discovery that the Earth was no longer in the sky.

"Hey!" he cried. "Our Earth… Where has it gone?"

"It's on the other side of the moon," said Gil. "We're seeing a panorama right this minute that no Earth-bound man ever has seen or can see. So keep your eyes peeled and spot everything you can."

He turned on the automatic cameras, which started making a photographic record.

"It's just as I figured," said Wilbur. "Nothing new or different…"

Traveling at a greatly reduced rate of five hundred miles per hour, excellent observation was possible. The lunar landscape did have a similarity at first but it soon became apparent that it was much more rough and mountainous than the other side. It was still honeycombed with craters of various sizes but these were broken by gigantic towering peaks, many of them looking from the air like the pointed steeples of deserted stone cathedrals.

Diana, surveying this scene, exclaimed, "Talk about the Badlands on Earth. They're not in it with this. I'd hate to have to parachute down from here."

"I'd hate to have you," said Gil.

"Since there's no air, the parachute wouldn't open..."

Wilbur, keeping up a running fire conversation with Carl Mack on Earth, said, "Thank heavens for radio. If it wasn't for hearing your voice, I'd think our planet and everything on it had vanished for good. It's the queerest feeling to be completely out of sight of it."

"Well, we're still here all right," laughed Mack. "But if they begin dropping atomic bombs, you may not have any Earth to come back to..."

"Oh, brother..." said Wilbur. "Don't even suggest that." He glanced through the side windows of the spaceship and a sudden strange flash caught his eye. What he saw all but paralyzed him.

"Gil!" he cried. "Oh, my gosh...look!"

Almost simultaneously there was a similar bright flash on the other side of the ship and Diana, seeing it, cried out, "Oh for heaven's sake! Oh, Gil!"

Startled, Gil Benson, at the rocket's controls, looked right and left.

"Spaceships!" he exclaimed, unbelievingly. "Mammoth ones!"

There was a third brilliant flash through the windows in the sky dome above them.

"Three at least!" cried Wilbur. "At each side and above us.

We're hemmed in—it looks like we're being taken captive…"

These enormous aerial vessels, looking like great pointed silver pencils in flight, were possibly a thousand feet long. Gil realized, in that blood-chilling moment, that he was being forced to proceed on a course determined for him by his space captors.

"Can't you put on a burst of speed and try to get away from them?" asked Wilbur.

"I could if they weren't so close," said Gil. "But we'd be apt to crash into one of them and that would be our finish."

"Where do you suppose they are taking us?"

"I haven't any idea," said Gil. "But it's some place on the moon. We're being forced down. Get word of this back to Earth."

Wilbur turned excitedly to the microphone.

"Hello, Mack," he cried. "Are you there?"

"Right with you," said Carl Mack's voice.

"Mack!" cried Wilbur. "This isn't a gag. This is serious. We're surrounded by spaceships—big ones. There's someone on the moon…" Wilbur paused to look out and down, at outcries from Diana and Gil. "For cryin' out loud," he exclaimed. "Oh, this is terrific… There's an absolutely tremendous hole in the moon…and—oh, my gosh… There's a huge lunar city down inside that crater…"

Carl Mack's excited, incredulous voice came booming in. "Cut it out! What are you drinking up there?"

"No!" insisted Wilbur. "Listen, Mack, carefully. This is on the level. We may not be able to broadcast much longer. These spaceships are as big as the Queen Mary… They're bringing us down for a forced landing… We're only about two miles above the moon now…I can see great round shining buildings…some look like tremendous Quonset huts…! They're all connected by big, long silver tubes—some kind of metal—and they're laid out around the inside walls of this stupendous crater…"

Carl Mack cut in, highly aroused. "We're recording this, Williams. Keep going as long as you can. Can you tell where these spaceships came from…? Do you see any forms of life?"

"I can see them now," Wilbur reported. "They're right

alongside and we're looking through our windows at each other. I don't know where they came from—but they're not human… They're lined up against the windows of their ships, staring at us. They're reddish skinned and their heads are about twice the size of ours, with extra large noses and big eyes…I can't see the rest of them but if they're as big as their heads, they're enormous…"

"What do you suppose they're doing on the moon?" cried Carl Mack.

"That's a mystery, too," said Wilbur. "Though I don't think it's anything good as far as we're concerned. We're down below a mile now and we're being directed toward some tremendous runways in the center of this deep crater, which extends as far as I can see. We're heading toward what looks like a big shiny metal hangar… I guess they intend us to go right down inside that thing!" Wilbur turned, excitedly, to Gil. "What do you think? Isn't that what they are directing us to do?"

Gil nodded, grimly. "Apparently," he said. "That hangar looks like a tremendous train shed. It must be half a mile high and five miles long. Yes—the whole end of it is opening up. We're expected to fly right into it."

Wilbur got back on the radio. "I was right," he cried. "We're coming in now and this could be an enormous wind tunnel we're going into… Looks like it was made of aluminum. There are figures running around in metal suits, something like ours. These spaceships are flying right in with us. There's lots of them in here—all lined up like ships at a dock. I'm sorry, Mack—I've got to sign off."

A square of red lights lit up in the space in front of Gil Benson's descending rocket. By manipulation of controls he set his ship down on the spot indicated. It came to rest with only a slight jar and rocking motion. As he completed the landing, Gil could see the three great aerial vessels gliding beyond to designated plots of their own. The end of the cavernous hangar had closed behind them.

Diana, Wilbur, and Gil looked tensely at one another. *They were prisoners on the moon.*

THE peoples of Earth, terrified at the momentary prospects of another world war, were given a second major fright on receipt of news that the Moon was inhabited. But, more stunning still was the sensational knowledge that Gil Benson and his two space travelers had fallen into the hands of the strange, unknown moon dwellers who appeared to be strongly entrenched on the dark side of the satellite.

Frantic efforts were being made and utmost vigilance maintained to reestablish communication with the now grounded spaceship but the *Goodbye, World's* radio was dead and indications were that it might remain so. The Earth had quite possibly heard the last of Gil Benson and his crew of one man and a girl but, at least, they had managed to forewarn the world that potential danger to Humanity existed on the Moon.

Ruth Delano was so upset that she walked off MGM's lot, refusing to do any more work before the cameras before she had some definite word as to Gil Benson's fate.

"A relief expedition should be organized and sent up to rescue him," she said.

But Professor Crowley, when asked if this might be possible, declared that no other spaceships were available. The Army and Navy could be expected to be of aid in time. However, it would require some months to go into manufacture of the atomic rocket motors as designed by Crowley and Benson. The present jet rockets, operating on liquid oxygen and alcohol, generated sufficient power to project their missiles to the moon but not to lift the additional weight of fuel and supplies necessary for the successful launching of man-carrying projectiles.

"Gil Benson and his two companions will have to extricate themselves if there is any hope of their escaping from the moon under whatever circumstances they may now be facing," said an editorial comment. "This has usually been the price that pioneers in exploration have had to pay for their courage and daring.

"Unfortunately, we on Earth have vast problems of our own to meet and can only give passing thought to this tremendous drama in the sky which, in peaceful times, would have engaged the complete and enthralled attention of every human on this planet.

"As for possible dwellers on the moon, accepting this statement as true, since we have heard nothing from them, we should not view their residence there as constituting any threat to us. Quite naturally, Gil Benson's appearance on the moon might have been regarded by these beings as an invasion, just as we would probably look upon the arrival from space of some strange creatures in a similar projectile. But we should control our fears and our imaginations until and if we receive more detailed information upon which to judge."

*   *   *

Hardly had Gil Benson landed his spaceship in the immense hangar into which it had been forced, than it was surrounded by a small army of short, bigheaded, barrel-chested, two-legged, reddish-hued beings. They clambered up the sides of the rocket, peered grotesquely in the windows and rapped on the door for entrance.

"Maybe we'd better shoot ourselves right now and get it over with..." said Wilbur.

"They won't take any beauty prizes according to our standards," said Gil. "But they've got to be plenty intelligent or they couldn't have a set-up like this."

"They look like a bunch of Mummers I saw in the Mummers' parade at Philadelphia last year," said Diana. "I'm not afraid of them."

Gil looked at her. "You're all right," he said, admiringly. "I'm glad you brought yourself along..."

"I wouldn't miss this for anything on Earth," said Diana. "How do I look, Gil? Maybe those funny eggs out there will go for sex appeal!"

"Good gosh," moaned Wilbur. "Go easy, baby. You don't know what you may be getting yourself in for..."

Diana looked at the bigheaded row of curious red faces staring in through the windows. She smiled at them and waved. They looked startled and then some of them grinned and waved back, revealing large white teeth.

"See," said Diana. "They're not so bad. I think they're almost human. They can laugh." She smiled and waved again.

There was an immediate pounding on the side of the ship.

"You've made a hit," said Wilbur, "but I can't tell what kind yet."

"We'll know as soon as we open the door," said Gil. He crossed the cabin. "I suppose we might as well face it." Then a warning thought struck him. "I wonder about the atmosphere inside their buildings," he said. "They obviously require oxygen but their nostrils and lungs are so large, I'm guessing they're not native to the moon and that they've come from some planet where the air is much thinner than on Earth. If that's the case, maybe it will be too rare for us to breathe."

"I'll find out for you," volunteered Diana.

She motioned to her bigheaded audience, caught their attention, pointed to her nose, and then drew a deep, exaggerated breath, accompanying it with a questioning gesture. The row of big heads grinned and nodded reassurance.

"There you are," said Diana, triumphantly. "The sign language is universal. We understand each other."

"I don't get it," said Gil, thoughtfully. "How do they know we can breathe out there? They've never seen humans before."

The rappings on the spaceship became more insistent.

"Well, there's only one way to tell," said Gil.

Reaching out, he lifted the lock arm from the door and swung it open. He looked down into the upturned features of these strange beings who regarded him with their enormous black eyes. They were all dressed the same in what appeared to be loose-fitting work uniforms of some closely woven bright material. The shape of their big-chested bodies required loose apparel.

"GREETINGS," said Gil, and smiled.

There was an answering chorus of sounds, which the three voyagers from Earth interpreted as a salutation.

"They seem to be friendly," said Wilbur. "But I'd hate to meet any of 'em in a bad dream."

"The trick is not to let them see that you're afraid of them," counseled Diana. She stepped in the rocket's doorway beside Gil and turned her blue eyes on their captors. "Hello, boys," she said. "We're glad to see you. Does anybody speak English?" Then, aside to Gil, she said, "I might as well ask that as anything. You never can tell."

There was a jabber of sounds and many of the weird looking beings pointed to their large, round, bald heads—and then at Diana.

"They've gone for you in a big way," said Gil.

"It's your red hair," said Wilbur. "That's what they're raving about."

"Is it?" asked Diana, pleased. She ran fingers through her long bob of rich, red tresses, and her audience gave the Earthly equivalent of an admiring cheer.

"Apparently," said Gil, "judging from their appearance, hair is a scarce commodity with them—red hair, especially!"

"That's fine," said Diana. "I've always hoped my red hair would be good for something some day."

It was too high above the composition floor of the immense hangar for them to descend without some steps, but when Gil became convinced that they could breathe in this vast interior, he put down the extension ladder. It was grabbed on both sides by their captors who waited expectantly for their exit from the ship.

"Look at their hands," said Wilbur. "How wide they are across. Each one is as big as two of mine together."

"And their legs," said Diana. "How thin and spindly. What funny shapes... Piano legs, narrow hips, beer barrel chests and big heads... I'd say Nature gave them a raw deal."

"Maybe that's what they needed where they came from,"

speculated Wilbur.

Diana prepared to be the first one out of the ship. She turned her back, wrapped her evening gown carefully about her, and stepped on the first rung of the ladder. Wilbur and Gil watched her descend, not without considerable apprehension.

"They ought to go for her legs, too," said Wilbur, "if they know a good pair when they see 'em…"

But the interest of the moon dwellers appeared to be concentrated upon the other end of her anatomy. Large red hands reached out from all sides, at the first opportunity, to touch or stroke her red hair. These beings were treating Diana as though she were some miraculous live doll. She accepted their pawing good-naturedly, and when she reached the floor, motioned to the two remaining occupants of the ship to join her.

"I wonder what they'll do to me," said Wilbur, as he started down.

HIS tuxedo was badly in need of pressing but Hollywood's greatest publicity agent was not the least concerned about that. Gil followed him closely and the two reached the floor, unmolested. They were surrounded by easily half a hundred of these strange beings whose main interest was still centered in Diana.

"You seem to be their Number One Pin-up girl," said Wilbur. "I guess you really said something when you figured they might go for sex appeal."

"We'd better watch our step just the same," warned Gil. "I'm getting a damned uncomfortable feeling that they're just playing with us. There doesn't seem to be any authority here."

But, as Gil spoke, a new group of these strange beings, in much smarter bright attire and carrying peculiar looking weapons that looked as though they might be a form of ray gun, came marching up. The leader was a being about a half-head taller than the usual run of these creatures, and they fell back respectfully as he motioned to Diana, Gil and Wilbur to "fall in" and accompany the squad of guards.

Some of the moon dwellers now began to mount the ladder leading into the spaceship.

"Get down from there," ordered Gil, gesturing. He turned to the leader and appealed to him, by voice and signs, to keep his fellow being out of the rocket.

The leader understood and soberly assigned a guard to stand at the foot of the ladder. He then said something totally incomprehensible, giving Wilbur and Gil a push forward. Diana, for protection, slipped in between the two men and took their arms.

"He's not so susceptible," she whispered. "But I'll go to work on him first chance I get."

The leader fell in behind them and the whole party moved off. They walked at a good swinging gait for perhaps a mile down a long center ramp, passing great spaceships on both sides with their crews busy at work around them. Each moon dweller looked up and stared at Diana as though entranced. Her red hair was proving an object of instantaneous attraction everywhere.

At a command from the leader, his guards made a left turn and escorted the three captive space travelers toward the side of the tremendous hangar, with its high, arched duraluminum roof, half a mile above them!

"This building is unbelievable," Gil remarked to Wilbur. "It dwarfs anything we've got on Earth. I'd like to see the system that manufactures oxygen for this place. And this is only one of the structures. You have to hand it to these round heads. They're damned smart."

"Where do you think they're taking us?" asked Wilbur.

"Probably to meet some high mogul," said Gil.

They were entering a tunnel-like enclosure with guards stationed at regular intervals, each armed with this strange weapon, which had a funnel opening at the end of a gun barrel. Again they seemed to have walked about a mile, passing many intersections, which led to other buildings along the way. The three humans from Earth began to notice a slight shortness of breath. They felt as they had when high in the mountains on Earth.

"It's just as I thought," said Gil.

"The oxygen content is thinner here per cubic inch because these beings don't require as rich a mixture. We can get along if we don't exert ourselves too much."

The wonder of this great moon city began to grow upon the space travelers, so much so that they temporarily lost concern for themselves and their own safety.

"This is a simply colossal engineering feat," admired Gil. "It must have taken years and years for them to have accomplished this. I'm wondering if these metals were mined on the moon or whether they had to be brought from some other planet?"

"Probably dug them up here," said Wilbur. "I can't imagine carrying such a tremendous amount of material on a long haul through space."

FINALLY, the guards turned up a metal stairway and into the lobby of an administrative-looking building. Two guards stood in front of a great steel door. They saluted the leader by extending the right arm in front of them, at an angle over their heads. Then they stepped back and the large door slid noiselessly open, revealing a magnificent circular room containing bright chromium plated furniture and a large semi-circular council table at which sat eleven high officials of whatever government this represented. In the center, flanked five on a side, was seated the ruler. These beings were attired in loose robes of greenish-blue.

Diana, Wilbur, and Gil were marched across and left standing, facing the ruler. The leader saluted, bowed, turned on his heel, and led his guards out. The great door closed behind them.

It was an uncomfortable moment for the three humans from Earth. They looked up and down the formidable row of large, red faces with the big black eyes and distended nostrils. Every head was bald and almost pumpkin shaped.

Diana, standing between Wilbur and Gil, noting again that she was the center of attention, ventured a smile but it brought no answering response here. The ruler spoke to his associates in a succession of sounds that were entirely unfamiliar. Several of them gravely replied.

"They're deciding what to do to us," guessed Wilbur, in a low voice, "and the decision is not going to be good."

"I wish I could understand their language," said Gil. "It would help a lot."

"That will not be necessary," said the ruler. "I will speak your language."

No more thunderstruck and completely dumbfounded humans ever existed than these three voyagers, now so far from Earth. They even doubted their own senses.

"What did you say?" ventured Gil.

The red face of the ruler was impassive. "I said, I would speak your language," he repeated. "You may tell us now what you are doing here on the moon."

All three space travelers, astounded and unnerved, started talking at once.

"It was only a pleasure trip," said Wilbur.

"I just came by accident," said Diana.

"I wanted to see if it could be done," said Gil.

"Who is in command of your party?" asked the ruler.

"I am," Gil declared, taking a step forward.

Eleven pairs of big black eyes focused upon him.

"So that you may not have occasion to lie to me," said the ruler. "I should inform you that we probably know as much or more about your planet and what is taking place there, than you do."

"I can believe that," Gil replied.

"From the little I have seen here."

"Then you may be interested to know," the ruler continued, "that your arrival on the moon has saved us an expedition to your Earth to kidnap some of your men of science who possess your atomic power secret. We expect to obtain such information from you and your associates and from a study of the atomic motors in your spaceship."

Gil's amazement was growing.

"You speak of an expedition to our Earth. Are you implying that you possibly have been there before?"

The impassive face of the ruler relaxed in the suggestion of a smile. "We have been there many times," he said, "in the last two hundred years."

"I don't believe it," said Wilbur, impulsively.

"THEN let me remind you of several mysterious disappearances on Earth," said the ruler. "I will select three of a number that have happened in more recent times which should be within your memory or knowledge. On March 4, 1918, your time, a United States ship of nineteen thousand three hundred tons displacement, left the Barbados, West Indies, with three hundred and nine on board—and has never been heard from since."

"That's right," identified Gil, with a feeling of sudden horror. "That was the U.S.S. Cyclops..."

The ruler nodded. "You have an excellent memory," he said. "On July 13th, in 1923, the Mallory liner *Swiftstar* left the Gulf end of the Panama canal. It was never heard from again. There were thirty-three aboard. And, five years later, in December of 1928, the Danish Cadet Auxiliary ship, *Kobenhavn,* left Montivedeo, Uruguay, bound for Australia. There were sixty aboard. It never arrived."

There was a moment of tense silence and then Gil burst out, "Are you trying to tell us that you are responsible for these disappearances?"

The ruler nodded in affirmation. "You peoples of Earth have occasionally caught a glimpse of us," he said. "But you had difficulty believing your own eyes. Our spaceship maneuvers were witnessed the night of February 9th, 1913, and reported by your Earth astronomer, Professor Chant of Toronto. His findings were published in the 'Journal of the Royal Astronomical Society of Canada,' as collected from observers in many points of your northern United States and Canada."

Gil was listening with fascinated interest. He broke in, "I remember reading of this phenomenon. It was never explained."

"I'm giving you the explanation now," said the ruler. He pressed a button and a drawer in the large semicircular table slid open. From it, he took a sheaf of papers and thumbed through them. "Here is a statement made by your own Earth periodicals concerning the happening," he continued. "It says that 'a strange procession of unknown forms moved across the sky on the night of February 9th. Early in the evening, a luminous body was seen near the horizon, traveling straight across the heavens. Observers noted that the body was composed of three or four parts with a tail to each part. This complex structure moved with a peculiar, majestic deliberation. When it disappeared in the distance, another group emerged from its place of origin. Still a third group followed.' According to one watcher, 'there were probably thirty or thirty-two such bodies. The most peculiar thing about them was that they moved in fours, threes, and twos, abreast of one another. So perfect was this line-up that it seemed almost as if an aerial fleet was maneuvering after rigid drilling. The strange heavenly bodies were observed for almost an hour. Meteors do not move slowly and horizontally across the sky, or in orderly fashion. Careful checks revealed that no human airships had been aloft that night. What things not of this Earth these were, God only knows."

THE ruler put down the paper and looked at Gil. "You have seen us at other times as well. Once on August 27th, 1885, over Bermuda...another occasion in April of 1912, over Chisburg, England...where it was reported that, 'These strange triangular shapes, moving as might a modern autogyro, remained stationary as cloud after cloud passed by them. They finally ascended and moved out to sea, as if intelligently directed. These incidents should be enough to convince you."

"Then this possibly explains something else," said Gil. "Through radar, quite recently, contact has been made with mysterious objects of great size, moving through space on apparently pre-determined courses. Could they have been...?"

The ruler nodded. "With your scientific development, we have had to, be increasingly careful. We have not wanted you to know of our existence or our plans until you were incapable of protecting yourselves. But we have also needed to study the human race. Whenever we have required subjects, we have landed on your oceans near the selected vessels, taken all on board captive, destroyed all trace of the ships, and transported the human cargo direct to the moon or our planet."

"What is your planet?" demanded Gil.

The ruler smiled. "Our name for it would sound, in your language, like 'Erakea.' But you Earth people call it Mars."

"Mars..." exclaimed Wilbur.

"You have often wondered if Mars were inhabited," said the ruler. "Now you know."

"But what are you Martians—excuse me, Erakeans—doing on the moon?" exploded Gil.

The ruler eyed his associates, all of whom turned their heads in his direction, before he replied. "We are preparing to move our population to another planet," he announced.

"You mean you are going to transfer all your Erakeans to the moon?" asked Gil.

The ruler shook his head. "No," he answered. "We are going to take over the Earth."

"But you can't do that," protested Wilbur, impulsively. "We won't let you..."

The ruler and his ten high official associates smiled in unison, as though amused.

"We do not expect you Earth peoples to surrender peacefully—but you cannot help yourselves. We will overwhelm and annihilate you."

This declaration was made as simple statement of fact but it almost froze the blood in the veins of the three humans from Earth.

"But why pick on us?" spoke up Diana. "Why don't you go to some other planet that isn't inhabited?"

The ruler's black eyes fixed upon her. "You will make a fine citizen of Erakea," he said. "We have been trying for years to breed offspring with red haw. It is a symbol of Erakean strength and beauty."

"Oh, I'm not staying here," said Diana, quickly. "I've got a date back on Earth!"

"You are all staying here," announced the ruler, quietly. "You are joining our little colony from Earth."

The stunning force of these words hammered against their consciousness.

They had been kept standing, at almost attention, before these seated officials who were amiable enough in a reserved way, but who extended no human courtesy.

"You don't intend to mix your species with ours, do you?" Wilbur blurted out.

The ruler smiled and nodded. "That experiment is now being conducted. It may be found desirable to preserve a remnant of your best human specimens to combine with ours in order that our future generations may be provided with a more suitable physical organism to live on your Earth."

The frankness of this ruler was appalling.

"You didn't answer Miss Fenimore's question," persisted Gil. "Why did you not select an uninhabited planet to occupy?"

The ruler's reply was direct and startling. "We have scouted every planet within a radius of two hundred million miles of Erakea and your Earth is the one with atmospheric and living conditions most nearly approximating ours."

GIL'S mind now began to encompass the diabolical reason for the Martian's colonization on the moon. This tremendous organization was being set up here as a jumping off base for the launching of a devastating attack upon Earth. It looked to Gil as though the time for this assault was fast approaching.

"But why are you Erakeans leaving your planet?" Gil asked.

"It is not a matter of choice," replied the ruler. "We have known for centuries that we would one day be compelled to abandon Erakea. Despite all our scientific efforts, we have been losing our atmosphere, oxygen, and water. We have built an elaborate system of canals to tap the remaining water from our fast diminishing polar caps. We've tried to encourage vegetation, rich in iron, which gives off oxygen—but the red surface of our planet has rightly indicated to your Earth observers that an oxidation process is taking place and we are losing oxygen much faster than we can replenish it.

"The situation is now critical. In another hundred years, no life such as ours will be possible. The complete transition must be effected within that period."

The three travelers from Earth stood silent and momentarily speechless. The ruler, perceiving this, continued.

"So, you see," he quietly explained, "it is either our extinction or yours—and we prefer it to be yours…"

It was difficult to defy such an attitude. There was no outward belligerency, no external war-like gesture.

"Your planning has been very thorough," Gil finally observed.

The ruler nodded in agreement. "It has been going on for centuries. Our study of your human race has shown us that we had but to wait and you would ultimately almost destroy yourselves. We have seen the great wars rage over the Earth's surface, time and again, in your short modern history. We have been vastly amused that you should have named our planet Mars after the 'God of War,' because of its bright red color, when we have witnessed your carnage on Earth. But, now, we have not much longer to wait. Your Third World War, almost within one generation, is about to break out. This will so weaken you peoples of Earth that our job of conquest will be made easy. You will be incapable of offering any worthy resistance and you will have lost not merely a war—but a planet."

Gil found it difficult to keep his feelings under control. He was humiliated, as a human, to have to concede that these beings from another planet were justified, because of Man's inhumanity to man, in standing by and waiting until Man's own greed and hate and lust for earthly power should accomplish his destruction.

"I'm afraid," he was compelled to admit, "that you Erakeans understand us better than we understand ourselves. It would be useless for me to contend that your plan of conquest is wrong. I agree, knowing what I do now, that if we have another war on Earth, we cannot resist you."

The ruler smiled and nodded. "We are counting on that war," he said.

"Don't be too sure," broke out Wilbur, in a gesture of defiance. "We won't be any pushovers at that. Wait until you run into a few of our atomic bombs…"

The black eyes of the ruler and his ten official associates brightened with interest.

"By the time we go to war with Earth, we will have the atomic bomb secret," said the ruler. "And your entire world will be a helpless target from the moon."

Gil well knew that this would be no idle threat.

"You mean to say, with all your development, you still don't have…?" he started to ask.

The ruler held up his large red hand. "We have advanced far beyond your Earth scientists in the use of gases for fuel and power but we have not yet succeeded in splitting the atom. That is why we are so happy to welcome you and your spaceship, which we learn from Earth broadcasts, is equipped with atomic motors."

Wilbur started to reply again in an antagonistic mood but Gil squeezed his arm.

"Perhaps," he suggested, "if the scientists of our two planets could be brought together, we might help you solve your problems on Mars—I mean, Erakea—so that your population could remain there."

The ruler shook his head. "That has all been considered," he said. "It is too late. We must go ahead with our plan of evacuation. The eleventh hour is already here."

"What's the approximate population of your planet?" asked Gil.

"Our population is not what it once was," said the ruler. "We have had to control our birth rate because of the scarcity of oxygen and water. We now have about two hundred million."

"Why we could stick that number in a corner of Russia," proposed Wilbur. "What's the use of going to war? Come on down and make yourselves at home."

The ruler smiled. "The Russians might not welcome our residence," he said. "We have observed the difficulty that even a comparatively small number of Jews are having, to find a place to peacefully reside. If you Earth peoples are that unfriendly toward one another, we could hardly expect you to permit immigration from a neighboring planet. It will be much easier and simpler to clear the Earth of most humans and, take it over for ourselves."

Diana had been restraining herself with remarkable composure, considering her temperament. "You don't believe in living and let live, do you?" she challenged. "You talk of our killing each other—but is that any worse than what you are planning to do to us?" Her blue eyes had a red glint in them. "I should think you'd be ashamed of yourself."

The ruler and his ten official associates appeared to greatly enjoy this outburst; their smug composure was maddening.

"May I ask," pressed the ruler, in accents directed particularly toward Diana, "what you would do if you were running out of water and oxygen on your planet?"

Diana was nonplused for reply. She started to speak, thought better of it, bit her lip, and then stammered, "W-well, I don't know. I'd probably start looking around..." Her face was reddening. "I mean..." she added, and then gave up entirely.

"Precisely," said the ruler. "You would be compelled to do exactly what we have done. And if you found another world similar to Earth, which would sustain your life, you would begin

133

laying plans to occupy it, even though it was populated. So—why should you blame us?"

THERE seemed no answer, in the larger cosmic sense, to this kind of "survival of the fittest" logic. Diana, Wilbur, and Gil were being reduced to a state of mental and physical helplessness. They were now weary of standing before this strange tribunal and growing more and more apprehensive as to what fate awaited them.

"Then, I guess there's nothing more to say," Diana finally replied. "But I would be interested to know what you intend doing with us."

The ruler smiled. "You will be very useful," he said. "You will be preserved in appreciation for your services to us. And we will permit you to witness our conquest of your Earth at the end of your atomic war."

Diana looked questioningly toward Gil, whose face did not betray his own fears.

"You may have a contempt for the human race," said Gil. "But—if you are expecting us to sell it out, you are badly mistaken."

A hard look came into the black eyes of the ruler. "We will see about that," he said. "You three will step into that side room, please, and remain until your presence is requested."

The ruler pointed to his left and, as he did so, a door, hitherto invisible, opened in the circular wall. A guard stepped through and stood at attention.

The dismissal had an authority about it that couldn't be denied. Without another word, the three humans from Earth took their leave of the Erakean council and marched out of the chamber.

CHAPTER TWELVE

GIL BENSON put a finger to his lips the instant the door of the side room was closed and they found themselves apparently alone. He indicated by his expression that there was probably a mechanism similar to Earth's dictaphone concealed in the walls, ceiling or floor. The three also had the unpleasant feeling that they were being watched by invisible eyes.

There were inviting reclining couches and chairs, upholstered in a greenish blue material, which matched the color of the robes worn by Erakean officials. This room appeared to be a place of waiting for those who desired conference with the ruler or members of his executive staff. On the walls hung chromium-framed, oil painted portraits of Erakeans, with a strange-worded letterings and markings, which seemed to be the dates, under them. The big red heads of these peculiar, important-looking beings, with their abnormally large black eyes, gave the travelers from Earth a feeling that they were imprisoned in some fantastic rogues' gallery.

"I suppose these gentlemen, if you can call them that," said Diana, "are the George Washingtons, Abraham Lincolns, Thomas Edisons and what-have-you's of different countries on their own planet. But just looking at them gives me the creeps."

"I'll bet we're supposed to see these mugs for some reason," said Wilbur. "Maybe they think it will impress us."

"You mean depress us," said Gil, in a guarded tone. "These men of Mars may be nice people, by themselves, but I've had my fill of them right now. I wonder what their women are like?"

"You would!" said Diana. "You've got enough glamour girls on Earth. I have my doubts if you'd like the Erakean variety."

As she spoke, almost as though timed to the remark, an inner door opened and a serving table was wheeled out by two Erakean maids. They were not bald like the men but had black hair which matched their eyes and which they wore in a top knot on their heads. The effect was anything but beautiful as judged by Earth standards.

"Your doubts are confirmed," Gil whispered to Diana.

The Erakean maids, dressed alike in loose fitting lavender gowns, pushed the serving table to a position in front of chairs and arranged the food it contained on silver-colored plates.

They had not as yet looked directly at those they had come to serve.

"If we could get them back to Earth," said Wilbur, "I could sell them to Barnum & Bailey's side show to replace their Ubangis! Boy, could I make a clean-up... 'Women from Mars. Step right up, men, and have a look! Guaranteed to make you love all girls on Earth—or your money back!' "

"You'd better be careful," warned Diana. "Maybe they understand English..."

"I'll try 'em out," said Wilbur. He advanced toward them with friendly gestures. "You're beautiful, babies," he said.

"Hey!" cried Diana. "I don't like that."

The two Erakean women looked up at Hollywood's greatest press agent and gave out sounds that resembled human giggles.

"They may not understand," said Wilbur, "but they get the general idea." He then became more expansive as they stared at him in apparent wonderment. "I'm mad about you. You've got the skin I'd love not to touch; the lips I'd thrill not to kiss; the waist I'd prefer not to hug, and the legs I'd rather not look at... All in all, babies, you're a frightfully delightful mess!"

The two Erakean maids bowed politely as though complimented. Wilbur bowed in return.

"You like that, don't you? I thought you would..."

The maids bowed again. They then indicated that the places were set and the food was ready for eating. Wilbur motioned to Diana and Gil who had been standing back, amused at his antics, despite the serious situation they all faced.

"Come on," he said. "This stuff looks good."

THEY took their seats around the table. The two Erakean maids, now ready to leave, smiled and bowed. The one nearest Wilbur touched him on the shoulder.

"If you want something, just call us," she said.

Hollywood's greatest press agent, in the act of sampling a drink, let it come out his nose and ears.

The two Erakean maids departed with a burst of giggling

sounds.

"I told you to be careful," scolded Diana.

"These Martians are amazing people," said Gil. "I wouldn't be surprised to learn that English is a required language study on Mars in preparation for their invasion. This ought to teach you not to be so funny."

Wilbur was still nursing his windpipe and trying to catch his breath.

"Ye gods," he said. "It's a good thing they had a sense of humor or I'd probably be on my way to the firing squad."

"What makes you think you won't be yet?" said Diana.

The food set before them seemed to be on the order of a vegetable plate and the drink, a new type of fruit juice. The vegetables were not of any recognizable variety but were surprisingly appetizing in flavor.

"They must raise these on the moon," Gil speculated. "Probably in some sort of hot houses. Not bad."

"No meat," said Wilbur. "Maybe that's a good sign. I was afraid, with their big mouths and big teeth, they might be cannibalistic…"

Diana nudged Gil's knee under the table.

"We can't keep up this kidding," she said, in a low voice. "What are we going to do?"

"I'm trying to think," said Gil, almost under his breath. "We're in a terrifically tough spot."

"It's all your fault," accused Wilbur. "Diana and I wanted to go straight back to Earth—but, no—you had to have a look at this side of the moon."

"I'm mighty glad I did," said Gil. "If I hadn't, no one on Earth would have had any warning of the danger they are facing."

"They don't know very much, even now," said Wilbur. "But if we could ever get back, we'd make their hair stand on end."

"We've got to get back," said Gil. "If we don't, it's really going to be Goodbye, World…"

Wilbur looked glum. "What chance do we have of escaping

if the ones they've kidnapped have never been able to get away?"

"That's different," said Gil. "They didn't have any means of getting back. But we've still got our spaceship."

"We'll be lucky if we ever get inside it again," said Wilbur. "We may have what looks like a certain amount of freedom, but I'll guarantee they're covering every move we make. If we get away from this crowd, it'll be a work of genius."

Gil nodded, thoughtfully. "We've got to stick together," he said. "If we let them separate us, we're finished."

"I agree," said Diana. "We'll have to use our wits to keep them from doing it."

"We can't use force, that's certain," said en. "I never felt as helpless in my life. But I'm glad of one thing."

"What's that?" asked Diana.

"I'm glad," said Gill, "that it turned out the way it did and Professor Crowley didn't come with me. His knowledge of atomic fission would be invaluable to these Martians. They can't get too much from me."

"BUT they can get plenty from the study of those atomic power motors," said Wilbur.

"That's true," Gil admitted, "and we'll have to find some way to stop that."

Diana had a sudden thought. "Gil," she said. "If I could fix it so you and Wilbur could make a getaway, would you shoot back to Earth and leave me here?"

"I should say not," Gil declared.

"But wait a minute," persisted Diana. "Just think what it means to Earth for you to get back with a real report. It can be the saving of our planet. I seem to be quite an attraction here. I might be able to wangle it so I could get you and Wilbur back in the spaceship, under some pretext—maybe for a demonstration of some sort…and you could manage to escape."

Gil considered the proposal and shook his head.

"Even if you could," he said, "the spaceship is indoors,

under cover. They certainly would never let us get it outside unless it was manned by their own engineers and we had guns at our backs. Besides, after what I heard the Big Chief say about experiments they are conducting, I don't like the thought of what would happen to you."

"Don't worry about me," said Diana. "I'm going to remain the only redhead on the moon."

"We're living one hell of a movie plot," said Wilbur. "And we can't do anything about it."

The door to the official chamber suddenly opened and a guard stepped in. He pointed to Diana, motioning for her to accompany him.

"Just what I've been expecting," said Gil. "We're going with you."

He took one of Diana's arms and Wilbur the other, as they walked—three abreast—to the door. Another guard stepped in. He said something in Erakean and both guards separated Diana from her two fellow human escorts.

"We go where she goes," Wilbur insisted.

A blast of Erakean language silenced him.

"I think they're swearing at us," he said.

"Better not resist," Diana urged. "It won't get us anywhere."

Gil remonstrated but to no avail. Two other guards appeared. Their round faces had deep-furrowed scowls. They looked savage and threatening as they flanked Diana and made it clear that Wilbur and Gil were to remain where they were. Despite their resolution to stay together, whatever the circumstances, they were being torn apart with ridiculous ease.

"If you get any chance to make a break for it," Diana called. "Don't mind me. I can take care of myself."

The door closed, shutting her from view.

"Damn it to hell…" said Gil.

He took to pacing about the room like an animal caged, and trying frantically to find a way out.

Wilbur sank down in a chair with his head in his hands. "She's a game kid," he said. "She's got more nerve than I have."

"If we could only fight back," raged Gil. "That's what makes it tough."

Wilbur groaned. "If they take over the Earth as easily as they've taken us, there won't be anything to it."

"And they'll do it, too," said Gil, "unless the Earth is warned and prepared. They've spent centuries in figuring out every little move. Before they attack our planet they intend to know just how much resistance we can offer and exactly how to counteract it."

"And here we sit," said Wilbur, "like a couple of stumble-bums, twiddling our thumbs."

"Damn it all to hell..." said Gil.

THE girl from Earth with the blue, blue eyes and the bright red hair was led across the now vacant Administrative Chamber, through a duraluminum tunnel and into a residential type of structure, cylindrical in shape.

She was left by herself in a luxuriously appointed living room, which contained more of the chromium-plated furniture, having the appearance of some of Earth's most ultra-futuristic designs. There was a large oil painting portrait on the wall, which she instantly recognized as a likeness of the ruler. There were no windows in the room—no windows in any of the buildings—yet a soft, evenly distributed light seemed to radiate from the walls, themselves.

But there was one object that caught Diana's particular attention. It stood almost head high from the floor and was about the size and shape of an automatic refrigerator. It contained a white screened panel, about two feet square, set in its upper half and beneath it, what appeared to be a sound box, then two rows of push buttons.

Since she was alone and there was no one to prevent her experimenting, Diana pressed a button that, because of its separate position, she judged must start the operating mechanism. There was a low whirring hum, which died away as the white screen lighted up.

"Let's see," mused Diana. "What next?"

She pressed a button on the first row, and waited. Presently an image began to form on the screen and the face of an Erakean appeared. There was the sound of strange music and the lips of this being were moving.

"My gosh," exclaimed Diana. "I've tuned in on the Frank Sinatra of Mars…"

She listened for a moment to what sounded like the melancholy wail of a heart-broken lover.

"I can't take it," she said, and pressed a button on the second row. The scene immediately vanished and another image slowly faded in. A voice was singing which sounded strangely familiar.

"When the blue of the night, meets the gold of the day…boo-boop-a-doo! Someone…waits…for…" The face of the singer was now clearly visible.

"Bing Crosby!" cried Diana.

The sensation of seeing and hearing him, so close and yet so far away was too much. She burst into tears.

"This is your Old Groaner, Bing Crosby," said the voice. "Coming at you from the golden hills of Hollywood, where one little pull is worth a thousand pushes—or, as I've often said to aspiring boys and girls, 'where there's life, there's Hope. Hi ya, Bob… Are you listenin'?"

Diana, fighting to gain control of herself, suddenly felt a presence in the room. She reached out to push off the button as a large hand stroked her hair. Whirling, Diana found herself caught in the arms of the ruler of Erakean forces on the moon.

"You are beautiful," he said, in excellent English, as he held her.

"I've heard that line before," said Diana. "Let me go…"

"We have waited a long time for someone like you," said the ruler. His big hands had grasped her shoulders in a vice-like grip. He held her powerless at arms' length as his large black eyes enjoyed the sight of her.

"I suppose I should be flattered," Diana said. "But I'm not."

The ruler seemed stung by this remark.

"We are the more advanced race," he said. "If we offer a few of you humans survival, you should be honored to blend your race with ours."

"Are you kidding?" said Diana. She threw back her red head and exploded with laughter.

The ruler stared at her with an expression of outraged pride and bewilderment.

"Excuse me," laughed Diana. "I haven't heard anything so funny for years. Blend our race with yours? Why, we've got monkeys on Earth that are better looking than you are..."

The ruler shook her savagely. "Stop it!" be commanded. "You cannot make fun of me. I won't permit it..."

Diana kept on laughing. "You're a scream," she cried. "You should be a comedian."

Angrily, the man from Mars drew her to him and kissed her. "Do you think that's funny?" he demanded.

Held tight in his embrace, Diana still managed to feign amusement. "*Funny!*" she repeated. "You're getting funnier all the time..."

SHE laughed in his face and this kind of treatment, whether on Earth or on Mars or on the Moon, would have been too much for any romantically inclined human or other type of being.

A torrent of choice Erakean epithets burst from the mouth of the chagrined ruler as he shoved Diana from him. She sat down suddenly in a half reclining chair and lay looking up at him, still convulsed. Her conduct posed a psychological problem of major significance to the man from Mars. There was no humor in this situation for him.

"We know we are not a handsome race," he finally admitted, as he paced up and down. "That is because of the changing environment on our planet. A million years ago, our ancestors were great seven-foot red men. They did not need the lung capacity or the air chambers we require in the brain today, in order to live.

"Nature demands that all life adapt itself to the changing conditions she imposes. We expect to regain, in time, much of our past physical glory, by residence on your Earth. We had hoped, through experimentation, by blending certain Earth types, such as you represent, to greatly shorten the time when we might acquire the stature desired.

"You are the first woman from Earth, in our possession, who has reacted in this manner. But perhaps, after you have been with us for a few years, and when we have taken over the Earth, you will change your attitude."

Diana had listened quietly. "You've got a problem," she said. "But you're not going to solve it through the human race without a terrible fight. You might as well annihilate us all to begin with."

The ruler looked at her as though he respected her counsel.

"We may have to do that," he said. "But your red hair is beautiful. And, since this color is a heritage of our species, I was hoping that a new race..." He broke off and gave a shrug of the shoulders. "Oh, well—in that case, we must be prepared to eliminate you Earth peoples quickly. Only one step remains. We must acquaint ourselves with your method of creating atomic power."

Diana sat upright. "How do you propose to do that?" she asked.

"You and your associates have that knowledge between you," said the ruler. "You will reveal it to us."

"We will die first," Diana declared.

"You will not die," said the ruler. "We will see to that. But we have a serum, similar to yours on Earth, which, when injected, causes one to talk freely and speak the truth. When the time comes, we will assemble our scientists, place them aboard your spaceship, and have you three explain its workings. It will be very simple."

Diana laughed to cover up her own fears.

"I'd like to see you try it," she challenged. "I don't think you've got such a serum—and, if you have, I'll bet it wouldn't work on us."

"It's worked on other humans," said the ruler. "We've always obtained what we wanted to know."

He watched her reaction, closely.

Diana's blue eyes met his black ones. "But you've not always gotten what you wanted," she said.

The ruler stepped to the door and opened it. A guard stood outside. He snapped an order in Erakean.

"We have ways of getting that, too," he said, pointedly, to Diana. "We will see. Go with him..."

Diana advanced toward him, pulling a long strand of red hair from her hair. She handed it to the amazed ruler.

"Here, your Majesty," she said. "Keep this to remember me by..." With this, she walked out the door and fell in alongside the guard as a completely baffled man from Mars gnashed the finest set of teeth on the Moon.

CHAPTER THIRTEEN

WHEN the door opened and Diana Fenimore, former parachute jumper with Buzz Reynolds Flying Circus, walked in on Wilbur Williams and Gil Benson, it was cause for a joyous reunion. She had not been away from them very long but every minute had seemed a small eternity to the two men so vitally interested in her personal safety.

"I've made a meal of my fingernails since you've been gone," said Wilbur, exhibiting his hand. "What happened?"

"I'm still the only redhead on the moon," said Diana.

Both men exclaimed their relief.

"If they'd have touched you, I'd have killed somebody," declared Gil. "I just about went mad in here, waiting and wondering. Where did they take you?"

"To see the ruler...the King...his Nibs...Baldy...you know...the Round-Headed Ringleader. You should have seen his snazzy hangout, it was some dump—complete with a

Martian version of radio-television… They're getting all our Earth broadcasts… I pushed a button and got Mars, myself. Then I tuned in on, guess who—*Bing Crosby.*"

"That means soap operas on the moon," said Wilbur. "You can't even get away from them up here!"

"Cut out the gags," said Gil, impatiently. "I want the lowdown. Why did the Big Chief send for you?"

Diana smiled and rolled her blue eyes.

"It seems he had a crush on me," she said, "but I laughed it out of him. That made him mad so he's decided to destroy the entire human race."

"Good going," said Wilbur. "I suppose that includes me?"

Diana smiled. "You're human, aren't you?"

Wilbur groaned. "I don't know what I am anymore."

Gil wasn't in a humorous mood. "So what's he going to do?" he asked.

"You'll like this," said Diana. "He's going to shoot us full of truth-serum and take us aboard your spaceship with a bunch of scientists and have us spill all we know."

"That won't take me five minutes," said Wilbur.

"He says the stuff is sure fire," Diana continued. "That it will make us talk like sixty and we'll have to give out with whatever information he wants."

Gil did not conceal his grave concern. "If that scheme works," he said, "we're cooked—and so is everyone else on Earth. I'd sooner kill ourselves right now than…"

He didn't finish. The door swung open and a line of guards filed in followed by the burly leader who had first escorted them from the spaceship terminal to this administration center.

"Hello," said Wilbur. "This is where we came in."

"And this is where we go out," said Gil.

The leader motioned to them to accompany the guards and they left the side room, re-entering the large chamber. The council of eleven Erakeans had re-convened and seated beside the ruler were five new and important appearing men from Mars, attired in bluish green, light-fitting uniforms with red stripes over their shoulders.

Diana, Wilbur, and Gil were required to face the ruler as before, but this time the guards lined up behind them and stood at attention.

IT IS the decision of the court of Erakea, on the moon," pronounced the ruler, "that your lives will be spared so long as you cooperate with us. Word has just been received from Earth that war is a certainty within the next twenty-four hours. This means that we must proceed at once with our own plans of conquest and it is necessary that we obtain, without delay, the atomic knowledge you possess.

"You are being returned to your spaceship, accompanied by our five greatest scientists and myself. To make certain you will give us the desired information, you will now each submit to an injection of truth serum which, by the time you reach the space depot, will have taken effect."

So speaking, the ruler pressed a button, a door opened, and out walked two Erakeans pushing a portable medical cabinet. They were followed by a distinguished looking man of Mars whom the ruler introduced as the medical chief of staff. His two assistants prepared the syringes and handed him number one. All Erakeans were watching this ceremony with great and tense interest.

"I will take the lady first," said this dignitary in perfect English. His hands were encased in Earth's equivalent of rubber gloves.

Gil stepped forward. "Is this absolutely necessary?" he protested. "This young woman has no information of value to you. Why make her go through this?"

The ruler smiled, showing his set of large white teeth. "This serum will not permanently affect the mind," he reassured. "It does not put you to sleep or make you semi-conscious as your Earth formula does. You simply will feel like talking and telling what you know."

The two assistants stepped to the side ·of Diana, took her

left arm and dabbed a medicated piece of gauze-like material on the inside of the arm, below the elbow. Diana turned her head away as the doctor deftly inserted the needle and injected the serum. He handed the empty syringe to one of his assistants, took a loaded one in exchange, and turned to Wilbur.

"You're next," he said.

"Why don't you have me swear on a Bible?" said Wilbur. "I'll tell the truth just as quickly that way."

"Give me your arm," ordered the doctor.

"You're wasting a shot on me," Wilbur continued. "I'm a press agent—and we never tell the truth." He got jabbed just the same. "Okay," he said. "You've stuck the needle in—but you're not going to like what I play back to you."

The doctor, with an annoyed gesture, took up his third and last hypodermic syringe and looked at Gil Benson.

"How long does this effect last?" Gil asked.

"About an hour of your time," said the doctor.

Gil held out his arm. "Shoot," he said, "and get it over with."

With the injections completed, Diana, Wilbur, and Gil were marched quickly outside where a large bus-like vehicle, six wheels on a side, was waiting with a driver. There were wide running boards upon which the guards stood after the three Earth captives, the five scientists, the ruler and his ten official associates had been placed aboard. They were then whisked noiselessly and speedily, by a different tunneled highway route, to the great space terminal.

IT WAS a welcome sight to catch a glimpse, once again, of the only object on the Moon which was familiar and which had a tie with Earth.

They dismounted from the motor vehicle, under guard, and advanced toward the spaceship, followed by the group of notables. A large crowd of curious Erakeans, who had evidently learned of their forthcoming appearance, surrounded the rocket. The guards made a lane for the official party and the three captives from Earth. They all drew up at the foot of the extension ladder leading into the spaceship. The ruler then addressed Diana, Wilbur, and Gil.

"In a short time you will be ready to respond to the questionings of our scientists. You will be unable to refuse any request we may make for information on any subject with which you are familiar. We desire a demonstration of the operation of your atomic power motor and an explanation of its working principles. While we are waiting for the serum to take effect, my ten associates are going to make a tour of the interior."

The guard, who had been on duty, protecting the entrance to the spaceship, stepped aside to allow the long robed figures of the stately Erakeans to mount the ladder and enter the rocket.

Diana was again the center of attention with Erakeans crowding close to her and some boldly reaching out to touch her red hair. She suddenly turned to the ruler and with her blue, blue eyes registering profound admiration, cried out, "I've got to say it. I've been thinking over what you said to me. I see now it's the only way out for your race and ours, too. After this next war, the atomic bombs won't leave enough of us alive to make a real human race. We're going to need new blood, new stock, new vitality…"

The large black eyes of the ruler were expanding with delight and excitement.

"Diana," Gil broke in. "Have you gone…?"

"No, Gil!" she cried. "You'll see it, too, in time. These Martians have a lot to give us. They can save our human race from extinction. I, for one, will be glad to offer myself as a co-creator of the coming new race… I'm thrilled at the thought and I'm sure other Earth women will be, too, when the time comes…"

There was a stir among high Erakean officials who could understand English.

"Babe," exclaimed Wilbur. "You don't mean it… It's this serum…"

The ruler smiled and shook his head. "The serum does not

persuade against one's will," he said. "It just releases the truth and real convictions of the individual. This fair creature from your Earth has simply awakened, as I had hoped, to the cosmic point of view…"

"That's it," cried Diana, with a rapturous enthusiasm. She impulsively threw her arms around the ruler's neck and kissed him on the cheek.

There was a chorus of ecstatic sounds from the lips of the assembled Erakeans, similar in nature to the reaction of an Earth movie audience during a romantic clinch. The ruler, his red face flushed a brighter red, was immensely pleased. He said something in Erakean to his fellow beings, referring intimately to the feminine object of their admiration, and all big heads nodded in warm approval.

"You will never regret your great decision," he declared to Diana.

The ten official associates, having completed their inspection of the rocket's interior, were now descending the ladder and making way for the ruler and Erakean scientists to take over proceedings. The ruler turned to a stunned and glowering Gil Benson, and said, "My associates and I will now precede you into your ship."

"Very well," said Gil.

"Oh, no," protested Diana. "On our Earth, it's a common courtesy for ladies to be first…"

The ruler laughed affably and made a gracious gesture. "It shall be so here," he said.

Diana pulled up her evening gown above her knees, revealing the prettiest legs ever seen on the Moon, or on Mars, for that matter, and started up the ladder.

"Come on, Gil. Come on, Wilbur," she called.

Wonderingly, her two fellow humans began to ascend after her.

"Wait," called the ruler.

Diana turned at the top of the ladder and looked down, smilingly. "That's all right," she directed. "You're next…come on up…"

THE ruler motioned to the five Erakean scientists who lined up behind him. He followed on the footsteps of Gil Diana stood on the little platform just outside the entrance to the ship. Wilbur, trailing her, let loose a blast of feeling, in a low voice.

"You're a hell of a human, you are!"

"Get in there and shut up!" hissed Diana.

Gil, next, was equally furious. "Damn you…" he said. "I'll never…"

"Get inside," Diana ordered.

Gil gave her a curious, uncomprehending glance as he entered the spaceship. The ruler of all Erakean forces on the Moon had now reached the little landing opposite the doorway. Beneath him, on different rungs of the ladder, were two of his planet's finest scientists and three waiting on the ground level to ascend.

"Greetings to *Goodbye, World*," said Diana.

The ruler paused and bowed. He liked the little ceremony she was making of this occasion. But he didn't like what she did next. She gave him an unexpected tremendous push, which toppled him from the ladder and caused him to land on the scientist under him, breaking his grip so that the two of them fell upon the second scientist and all three bounced upon the three waiting below.

Above them, a redhead from Earth, galvanized into action, stepped into the doorway, then reached out and pulled the steel door of the spaceship shut. There was consternation and pandemonium among the Erakeans.

Inside the spaceship, Diana cried out, "Give it the power, Gil, quick! Get us out of here…"

Gil hesitated. "But the roof…" he said.

"To hell with the roof—let's go!" cried Diana.

Gil jumped for the starting lever and shoved it down. The atomic motors came on with a roar. The ship lifted horizontally, slowly, at first.

Diana looked anxiously out the windows. "Hurry, Gil...they're running to their own spaceships. They're going to chase us..."

"I can't help it," said Gil. "I've got to get the nose up." He worked the elevating levers. "No telling what..."

The half-mile high ceiling of the spaceship terminal was needed for Gil to maneuver his rocket into position. He passed over scores of Martian aerial vessels, docked below. Beneath him all was wild commotion.

"Well, here goes," he said, grimly, and turned the power full on.

There was a blinding flash and the terminal disappeared. Their rocket had cut through the duraluminum roof as a sharp knife slitting through tin foil. They were out in space above the Moon, rising perpendicularly and hanging on to handgrips near the instrument board as their lightweight bodies, removed from the pressurized air balance of the Martian's moon city, now had a tendency to float about the cabin.

"California, here I come!" shouted Wilbur, excitedly. "Diana, you're wonderful... Marvelous!"

Gil, busy at the controls, gave vent to his own appreciation. "You're the damnedest woman I ever met."

"Thanks," said Diana.

"How did you ever think of this?" Gil asked.

"That was easy," Diana laughed. "I rehearsed for the part before we left Earth. Don't you remember what happened to Ruth Delano?"

"You're a great actress, baby," complimented Wilbur. "And you'll never play a greater role than you did just now. You had Gil and me fooled—and what you did to those Martians, they'll never get over."

"You can bet on that," said Gil. "And, if they catch us again, I hate to think what they'll do to us."

"What do you think of their chances?" asked Diana.

"We've got more power," said Gil. "We should be able to keep ahead of them till we get to the Earth's upper atmosphere. We'll have to slow up then and take our time getting down to avoid friction which could burn us up."

"Then they might catch up to us on the last lap?" said Diana.

"It's possible," said Gil. "They've probably had a great deal of experience slipping in and out of the Earth's atmosphere— and there's where I'm handicapped."

"Oh, well," Diana said. "We've gone through so much now—I'm not going to worry till it happens."

Gil looked at her, admiringly. "I could go for you," he said, "in a terrific way…"

"You could?" said Wilbur. "Well, what do you know—so could I…"

Diana looked both pleased and startled. "You're both kidding," she said.

"Not me," declared Wilbur. "If you want to know the truth, I lit a torch for you the first time I saw you. I said to myself, 'Wilbur, old man, she's your dish. So you might as well know it, I'm head over heels, baby. You've got me on the hook and I don't want off."

"But I wasn't even fishing," Diana protested.

"Your eyes were doing something," said Wilbur. "And so was your red hair…and your figure, your legs, if you don't mind…"

"Why, Wilbur," said Diana.

"Okay," rejoined Gil. "If you're telling her how you feel, then I have the same right. I thought you were cute and amusing the first time I met you—but when you made that parachute jump on my ranch, I put you down in my book in the Number One Spot.

You've been there ever since…"

"OH, GIL!" cried Diana, impulsively.

"That's just a line," accused Wilbur. "He's handed that out to at least a dozen of his glamour girls. How do you suppose he keeps them all dangling? They all think they're *it*…"

"That may be your opinion," said Gil. "But it's not true. I haven't played any favorites up to now."

Hollywood's greatest press agent was getting more aroused.

"You're not going to take my girl away from me," he cried.

Diana's blue eyes flashed. "I'm not your girl," she declared.

"We'll settle this right now," said Gil. "Diana, do you or do you not love Wilbur?"

"You don't have to answer that here," Wilbur warned.

Diana hesitated. "I've got to answer it," she said. "I'm sorry, Wilbur, I'm very fond of you, but I don't—"

"There you are," Gil persisted. "If that's your answer then I have one more question, Diana—how do you feel toward me?"

"I'm crazy about you and you know it," Diana replied at once.

Gil turned from the controls, grabbed her in his arms, and kissed her.

Wilbur moved away, forlorn and heartsick.

"It's that damn truth serum," he said. "But I'm not giving her up yet. When Gil gets back to Earth and sees Ruth Delano, he'll probably feel differently."

Looking glumly out the windows, Wilbur suddenly sighted something.

"Here they come…" he cried.

He pointed and Diana and Gil saw, glistening in the sunlight, a great fleet of aerial vessels, flying in formation. They looked like small silver bullets at their distance.

"The case is on," said Gil. "And they're making greater speed than I thought they could. They'll be able to hear our broadcasts but since they're on our trail, it won't make any difference. Get on the radio, Wilbur. Make contact with Earth and tell them what's happened."

All personal feelings were swallowed up in the common emergency.

CHAPTER FOURTEEN

TIME is only the measuring stick between events whether they occur on Earth, on the moon, or in the vast reaches of space.

In the seven hours since no word had been received from Gil Benson and his two companions, much had happened on

Mankind's spinning planet. Sporadic fighting had broken out in Korea and Alaska. It was unofficial, as yet, but battle-scarred Earth was reeling under the initial impact of another world war.

Diplomats, who had exchanged millions of words of charges and countercharges, now abandoned their oratory, grabbed up their brief cases containing worthless copies of peace documents, and rushed for cover. They had failed, utterly, to reconcile the antagonistic differences of age-old economic interests and savage racial prejudices.

Man's only way of winning an argument with finality was to resort to brute force. His whole bloody evolution could be traced through his weapons of destruction from his bare fists, to a rock, to a club, to a slingshot, to a bow and arrow, to a lance, to a sword, to gunpowder, to a blunder-buss, to a cannon, to a rifle, to a machine gun, to poison gas, to a rocket, and—finally—to the atomic bomb. But atomic warfare had not actually, as yet, been tried. Power-lustful leaders believed that now, at last, Man possessed the destructive means for a merciless aggressor to conquer the entire human race and forever enslave the world.

This was the bright, happy picture confronting all humans as contact was again made, through Schenectady's high frequency station, with three distant travelers from Earth.

"Hello, up there," greeted Radio Operator Carl Mack. "Are we glad to hear from you. Where are you? What happened?"

"Plenty," Wilbur reported. "We made a lucky escape, but they're hot on our trail."

"Who's on your trail?"

"Martians…"

"Martians? Don't give us that Orson Welles' stuff…"

"On the level. Here, Gil wants to talk to you…"

Gil's voice came through the loud speaker. "Hello, Mack. I've got to talk fast. Get this—our planet's in danger. We're going to lose it, sure as hell, if we're not careful. These Martians are out to take us over… We know too much and they're trying their damndest to keep us from getting back to Earth alive… If we don't make it, I want the World to know what it's up against…"

"Okay," said Carl's voice. "So what do you want me to do?"

"Get on the short wave and line up the leaders of all the countries. Have them listen in...give us the networks...get everybody on the radio...notify the newspapers... We've got a message that will rock the world..."

Carl's voice came back from Earth.

"The world's rocked enough now.

We're in a terrible turmoil here. *The war's on!*"

Gil's voice came in like a pistol shot. *"No....!* That can't be... We mustn't fight! Do what I tell you, Mack. Let me talk to those war-makers. Unless they call off this war, the Earth is doomed..."

"I'll do the best I can," Carl promised. "But I'm afraid it's too late... I'll report back."

"Good boy. Hurry it up! We can't tell how long we'll be here..."

THE leaders in the different countries of Earth were quite annoyed and disturbed at the emergency summons and urgent pleas from radio stations in the United States to listen in on the special broadcast emanating from the Earth's first spaceship; now returning from the Moon and pursued, according to fantastic reports, by a rocket fleet of war-minded Martians.

Enemies of the United States were disposed to consider this communication as an ingenious ruse of some sort but when the same plea was issued through diplomatic channels, a more sober view was taken of the matter. Within an hour after Gil Benson's urgent request had reached Earth, the world's greatest radio audience awaited his message.

"Okay, Gil," reported Carl Mack. "The world is yours..."

"Thanks, old man," said Gil.

The scene on the spaceship was tense. All three occupants were keyed to a high state of excitement.

"Hello, Earth," said the man known best to the world as 'America's Number One Playboy.' "This is Gil Benson speaking to you from spaceship '*Goodbye, World,*' enroute back to Earth

155

from the Moon.

"I have requested this chance to talk to you, my fellow humans, so that I could warn you of a very terrible and a very real danger. The armed forces of another planet—the planet you've known as Mars—are organized and ready to attack the Earth...

"This is no hoax. This is not another 'War of the Worlds' broadcast—*this is the real thing*...

"The Martians have been preparing to take over our planet for the past two hundred years. They have the most modern weapons and they are thoroughly entrenched on the other side of the Moon.

"There is only one thing that is holding them up. We have the atomic bomb and they haven't.

"They are waiting for us to destroy ourselves with it—and if you humans are damned fools enough not to stop fighting at once and unite to face this common enemy from space—we'll lose our planet to the Martians...

"As I'm speaking to you, I can look through the windows of my spaceship and see a fleet of at least fifty Martian aerial dreadnoughts following me. So far, thanks to atomic power, I've been able to stay ahead of them. I frankly don't know what will happen when I have to feel my way down through the Earth's atmosphere.

"I appeal to you world leaders, to the heads of the Army and Navy and Air Forces of every country, no matter how opposed, to call off this war at once, adjust your differences, forget your grievances—and pool all resources toward meeting the greatest crisis in all of Earth's history.

"It is not too late to save yourselves if you will. The greatest immediate blow you can deal the Martians is to put an end to this war—and stop destroying yourselves...

"What can any aggressor nation or nations hope to gain if, by conquering the world, they lose a planet? And if you leaders are unmoved by my warning and my plea, then I appeal to you, my fellow humans, in the name of what may be left of ordinary humanity and decency and love of whatever freedom you possess, to rise up and see to it that there shall be no more war.

"These words I speak to you are being heard simultaneously by Martians through their own type of radio equipment, both on the Moon and on Mars. They know that I am returning to Earth with information of the utmost importance and they will do everything possible to prevent my arrival.

"My spaceship is unarmed while their huge, man-carrying rockets are heavily gunned. This may, therefore, by my one and only message to you, so I beg you to heed it. This is Gil Benson, now signing off from spaceship, *Goodbye, World.*"

HIS voice had scarcely died out of the ether than the repercussion of what he had said began to be felt everywhere on Earth. Millions of excited humans all over the world scanned the skies with the hope of glimpsing the returning spaceship and terrorized at the prospects of seeing an invading Martian fleet.

Carl Mack, contacting Gil from Schenectady, asked, "Have you any idea where you're going to land?"

"I'm aiming for the Eastern seaboard," Gil replied. "Want to get to Washington right away and report my findings. Better alert all the airports—Boston, Philadelphia, New York, and Washington. I'll come down at the one most handy, if it's at all possible."

On board the *"Goodbye, World"* the situation was desperate. Approaching, as it was, the Earth's atmosphere, the Martian aerial dreadnoughts dived to the attack.

"This is it," Gil cried. "Hang on! Get yourselves set! I've got to slow us up. If we hit the Earth's atmosphere at this speed, we're goners…"

Diana and Wilbur groped their way to their bunks and strapped themselves in. Gil buckled himself to the control board.

"This may black you out," he warned. "But I've got to do it…"

Then he pushed the starting lever. The atomic power came

on and the ship's downward plunge was checked with a jolt. Blood drained from the heads of all three occupants and, momentarily, they lost consciousness. As they came to, they heard Gil shouting.

"Look...look, quick... Look at that..." He pointed out the window just as a great flaming mass shot past.

"What's that?" gasped Wilbur.

"It's one of their ships!" exclaimed Gil. "Here comes another..."

A second flying meteor-like object went by the window...and yet another...

"That's what might have happened to us," Gil cried, "if we hadn't slowed up just in time. But there's plenty more coming and they're wise. They won't make the same mistake."

Martian aerial dreadnoughts loomed up through the Earth's moonless night, their jet-style motors shooting out a blaze of illumination behind them. Gil switched off the lights in his ship in an attempt to avoid detection, also rapidly reducing the velocity as they entered denser and denser atmosphere.

They were down now to a ten mile height above the Earth's surface. In the distance, Diana caught sight of a large area dotted with lights.

"What's that down there?" she asked.

"That," recognized Wilbur, "is little old New York..."

Suddenly criss-crossing Martian searchlights, which fanned the skies, caught them in their full glare. They were immediately struck by a shell, which hit amidships beneath the cabin floor, shaking the rocket violently. It began to fall, half out of control.

"I can't make any airport," Gil cried. "I'll have to set her down wherever I can..."

"Don't land in the ocean," cried Wilbur. "I can't swim..."

"Oh, for a parachute," said Diana.

THE Martian aerial vessel that had scored the lucky hit, circled and nosed down for a second attack. As it did so, three high altitude United States Army jet-propulsion pursuit planes flashed through its searchlight beams, firing point-blank.

Diana, Wilbur, and Gil gave a yell of delight.

"Who says they can take our planet?" said Wilbur.

There was a great flaming explosion and the Martian dreadnought of the skies went plummeting down past the *"Goodbye, World"* to plunge into the ocean, five miles off Rockaway Beach.

The joy of the three space travelers was unbounded.

"They've had enough!" cried Diana. "They're turning back to the Moon…"

In almost no time, the Martian aerial fleet reached an altitude beyond the capacity of Army planes to follow. But they were then fired upon by coastal defense rocket guns, radar operated. One of these salvos found its target and a second Martian aerial battlewagon burst into flames and dived, miles further out, into the sea.

Gil Benson meanwhile was struggling with his damaged ship. They passed dangerously close above New York's towering skyscrapers with Gil unable to control its direction, and settled low over the Hudson, skimming the Palisades, missing rooftops and sliding finally down into the flat swampland of New Jersey.

"We made it!" said Gil. "We're back again on good old Mother Earth…"

"Home, sweet home…" said Wilbur.

"And one sweet landing," said Diana.

But Gil did not hear her. He had slumped, exhausted, at the controls.

CHAPTER FIFTEEN

NEWSPAPER headlines, in morning extras, piled sensation on sensation in telling the incredible but true story of the first human adventure in space. Great black type fairly shouted:

GIL BENSON'S SPACE SHIP LANDS IN JERSEY MEADOWS

THREE OCCUPANTS SHAKEN; UNHURT AFTER
MOON VOYAGE

ARMY PLANES FIGHT OFF MARTIAN SPACE ARMADA

WORLD WAR OFF!

EARTH PEOPLES PREPARE TO REPEL SPACE
INVASION

Diana, Wilbur, and Gil, rescued from the swamp by excited residents of New Jersey and then rescued from the admiring residents by the police, were taken into New York and put up at the Waldorf-Astoria.

America's Number One Playboy was photographed as he entered America's Number One Hotel. He and his two companions, one a stunning redhead, all attired in evening dress, looked as though they were getting in from a dizzy night's round of New York hot spots. The photographers who met them chortled in high glee and fired away. Then the reporters took over and did some firing of their own.

"Tell us about the Martians."

"What do they look like?"

"When are they going to attack us?"

"How did they capture you?"

"What did they do to you?"

"How did you escape?"

"Sorry, boys," said Gil, "but you'll have to wait till I give my official report to Washington. However, I can say that we own our lives to Miss Fenimore."

"No, no, Gil," protested Diana. *"Please…"*

"How come?" queried reporters.

Gil shook his head. "Guess that will have to wait till later, too."

"Gil's dead on his feet," explained Wilbur. "He's got to get some sleep and get on to Washington. We're all of us all in. Let us go, boys, till we freshen up. We can't think straight."

Three worn-out space travelers walked, glassy-eyed, to the elevator and got off at their floor.

"I'm almost afraid to go to sleep," said Wilbur. "I might dream I was back on the moon…"

Diana stopped at her door. "Goodbye, boys," she said. "It was nice knowing you."

"Be seeing you after my nightmare," called Wilbur.

"Maybe," said Diana, stepping inside and closing the door.

Wilbur looked at Gil. "What did she mean by that?"

Gil laughed, wearily, as he entered his own room. "I don't know and I don't care. Let's get to bed…"

BY LATE afternoon, when Gil Benson had left word that he might be "disturbed," the lobby of the Waldorf-Astoria was filled with a crowd of newspaper reporters, photographers, scientists, government officials, radio executives, theatrical managers, motion picture producers, booking agents, autograph seekers, hero-worshippers, the idly curious—and Ruth Delano, MGM's pin-up sensation, who had just arrived by special chartered plane from Hollywood, to see "her man from the moon."

"Are you and Mr. Benson engaged?" asked an enterprising reporter.

"I prefer to let Mr. Benson answer that question," Miss Delano replied.

She was stunning in a smart traveling suit, extremely figure-revealing; while her vivid black hair was caught up in a new and exciting coiffure.

"You look very photogenic today," said one of the cameramen.

"I hope so," said Ruth. "I was afraid you boys wouldn't look at a girl unless she'd been to the moon…"

There was a sudden stir in the lobby. A young woman with bright red hair, attired in a black-as-night evening gown with half moon and stars design, had just emerged from an elevator.

"There's the Moon-girl now!" cried someone.

There was a rush in her direction and Ruth. Delano was pushed along with the crowd. The two women came face to face.

"Well," greeted Ruth, "if it doesn't sound like an old bromide—fancy meeting you here."

"You've saved me from making the same original remark," said Diana.

Newspapermen pushed in as photographers sighted their cameras.

"Listen, Miss Fenimore— Kling Features wants your life story," called a syndicate man. "Don't talk. We'll give you fifty thousand for it."

A booking agent elbowed in, his glasses hanging over one ear. "Hold everything, Miss Fenimore, till you see me. Whatever they offer, I'll get you double…"

"Business seems to be pretty rushing," remarked Ruth, icily.

"I have nothing to say," declined Diana, to those pressing her. "I'm not interested."

"Not so fast, girlie. You can't high hat us," said a reporter. "You're the hottest glamour girl on Earth and you know it. You can have the world with two fences around it and we can help you get it. So just give, girlie—with the intimate details of your trip to the Moon—and we'll plaster it on the front pages."

Diana, looking greatly distressed and a little panicky, sought a way of escape.

"This is your first experience with a crowd of admirers, isn't it, dearie?" said MGM's pin-up star. "Maybe you'd like to have me handle your press conference?"

Two daggers appeared in Diana's blue eyes. "I'd like to have you mind your own business," she said.

A howl of delight went up from the newspapermen. If they couldn't get one story, they'd get another.

"Well…" cracked an old-timer. "Gil Benson's two flames are getting hot. Would you ladies like to put on boxing gloves?"

Ruth Delano relished the scene she had made for herself. "Miss Fenimore is extremely ungrateful," she purred. "I realize she is under a strain and I only meant to help her."

"Let me out of here, please," said Diana. "I have an appointment. There's nothing I can say. You'll have to see Mr. Benson."

"Oh, no… We've heard that one before!" came a chorus of protests. "Benson said you saved his life. We want the story. How'd you do it?"

Ruth Delano laughed. "She saved Gil's life? Don't you believe it. Gil's a perfect gentleman. He's just made up a yarn to save that redhead's face. I haven't forgotten how she threw me out of the rocket, slammed the door as I tried to get back in—and then the thing took off. If you want a real story, boys, let her explain how that happened."

"Yeah, Miss Delano, you've got something there," replied a reporter. "You mean—the whole thing was premeditated?"

Ruth eyed Diana. "Could be," she said. "I've thought so from the start. And Buzz Reynolds—he's the head of that Flying Circus that she used to be with—he says it would be just like her to pull a stunt like that."

It is said that a redhead can take only so much without blowing its top. Diana blew hers.

"All right," she raged. "So I deliberately started the rocket! So I risked Gil Benson's life and Wilbur's and my own! So I did it just to make a name for myself… So we got to the Moon and back again alive, anyway. So you're jealous and trying to make me look bad. So what are you going to do about it?"

Ruth Delano had reached the climax of her scene.

"I don't have to do anything about it, dearie," she soothed. "You've just done it to yourself."

Diana made a desperate break for it and fought her way through the crowd, calling on the aid of two house detectives to get her to the street and a taxicab. She was followed by a string of photographers who photographed her in flight, but she left newspapermen and all at the curb, wildly entreating her to "make a statement for the press."

*   *   *

Wilbur Williams awakened with his telephone bell tinkling. He reached over sleepily and took the receiver off the hook. He had arranged, after four p.m., to have all calls for Gil Benson or Diana routed to him, as their representative.

"This is me," he said. "Who are you?"

"Wilbur, dear," said a feminine voice. "How are you, darling?"

Wilbur was waking up. "Do my eyes deceive me or is this Miss Delano of MGM? And when did you get in—and what could possibly have brought you to New York?"

The voice on the wire was syrupy. "Now, Wilbur, don't be so naive, which you're not. There are ten thousand people down here in the lobby, more or less, waiting to see Gil. The best I could do was get the management to let me put through the first phone call. I must see him right away…"

"Excuse me a minute," said Wilbur. "The valet's just here with some new clothes for Gil and me. I don't think Gil's awake yet. Give me ten minutes and come up to the reception room on this floor. I'll get you in to see him."

"Wilbur!" cried Ruth. "You're an angel…"

"No," said Hollywood's greatest press agent. "I'm a devil— and I wish you luck…"

Five minutes later, Gil Benson was awakened by a rap on his door.

"Who's there?" he called.

"The Other Man from the Moon…" said a voice.

Gil looked around the hotel room to get his bearings. Then he got up drunkenly and opened the door. Wilbur came in, completely outfitted in his new street clothes, a dapper gray suit, blue shirt, and red tie. He handed a suit to Gil.

"Pretty good fit for ordering over the phone," he said. "I hope I got the right sizes for you."

Gil broke the box open and laid out the clothes.

"I feel like I'm about half here," he said. "It's hard to believe we've really been to the Moon—and that Martians are more than a bad dream. Did you get me a Pullman for Washington tonight?"

"Yeah, I got it," said Wilbur. "How long do you expect to be there?"

"I'll fly back tomorrow night. Jerry Torrence ought to be here by that time to take charge of digging our ship out of that swamp. Say—don't forget to pick up our Moon photographs. Are they going to have them developed and printed so I can take them to Washington with me?"

"That's what the studio said," Wilbur reported. "They put all their other orders aside and have the whole force working on it."

Gil stepped into his new trousers. "I guess these are going to be all right," he said. "The way I feel now, I'm through with formal clothes for life."

"Me, too," said Wilbur. "I wouldn't even be buried in evening dress."

There was the sound of a telephone bell ringing and ringing, down the hall.

"You're getting lots of calls," said Wilbur. "But I'm not there to answer them."

Gil laughed. "That's okay," he said. "There are very few people I want to see, anyway."

Wilbur had been waiting for this opening. "There's one person I imagine you'd like to see," he suggested, "if you could..."

"Who's that?" Gil asked.

"Ruth Delano, she's in the reception room, on this floor, right now."

GIL'S face lighted. "She is?" He stuffed his shirt inside his trousers. "Well, bring her in. What are you waiting for?"

"For you to get your pants on," Wilbur said, grinning.

"Wait," called Gil as Wilbur went for the door. "Did you wake Diana?"

"Not yet," said Wilbur. "I thought I'd let her sleep for

awhile. The poor kid was more beat up than we were."

Gil looked at his wristwatch. "You'll have to get her up. Didn't you date Saks to send over some new clothes for her to select from, at four-thirty?"

"Oh," said Wilbur. "Oh, yes... Don't worry about that, Gil. I'll take care of it...I'll send in Miss Delano right away."

Hollywood's greatest press agent hurried out as Gil turned toward the full-length mirror and put on his tie.

MGM's pin-up sensation was pacing impatiently up and down the small reception room, just off the elevator bays.

"That's a pretty long ten minutes," she said to Wilbur, when he appeared.

"I had to wait until Gil got dressed," he said. "After all..." Wilbur straightened a fancy handkerchief in his suit coat pocket. "We've both got on new outfits. How do you think I look?"

"That's beside the point," said Ruth. "How do you think I look?"

Wilbur gave her the critical onceover.

"I could kiss you myself," he said, "if I had the time. No kidding, Miss Delano—I think you're just what Gil Benson ordered."

"That's all I wanted to hear," said Ruth. "Where is he?"

Wilbur pointed down the hall.

"He's in Twenty-seven-eleven."

"What a number," said Ruth.

"He sure is!" said Wilbur.

MGM's pin-up sensation took her perfect figure in Gil's direction. Wilbur followed, admiring her rear view.

"If she only had red hair," he said to himself. "But, I guess there's only one Diana..."

*   *   *

There was a lady-like tap on Gil Benson's door.

"Come in," he said.

The door swung open and, framed in it, was the life-sized,

flesh-and-blood picture of Hollywood's most glamorous pin-up girl. She stood there for a moment to let her one-man-audience ogle her form.

"Ruth!" said Gil. "It's wonderful to see you..."

"Oh, Gil, my darling..." She pushed the door shut behind her and rushed into his arms.

They kissed and she clung to him. "I've been so worried about you. I've lost five pounds..."

Gil laughed. "I had to go to the Moon to get you to do that? You're better looking than ever."

"You mean you don't miss the five pounds, Darling?"

Gil encircled her waist. "Just a trifle," he said. "I believe I can hug you a little tighter..."

She kissed him again and left a nice smudge of lipstick. Gil stroked her hair.

"Oh, oh! Don't touch! I can't put that up myself—and if we're photographed together..."

Gil eyed her. "Are you acting or do you really mean it?"

"Why, of course I mean it. Do you think I'd have flown clear across the country just to see you...stopped production and everything...if I didn't love you...?"

Gil spoke slowly. "Yes," he said. "I believe you would..."

Ruth sat down on the arm of a chair, her face registering pain.

"Why, Gil...how can you say that? I naturally want to look my best when I'm with you, dear...but I still have my public. I can't forget that...and since you're so much in the limelight at present...we mustn't be caught off guard."

"No, of course not," said Gil. "We should have a make-up man here to fix your lips after each kiss...and a hair-dresser to comb your hair...and a dressmaker to be sure I haven't wrinkled your dress every time I put my arm around you. I don't think I like that kind of romance."

"Now, Gil, darling," pleaded Ruth. "I didn't mean it the way it sounded. If you don't mind the way I look in public, why just forget my hair, my lips, everything..."

She offered herself to be kissed.

Gil took her in his arms and placed a hand on her hair. She shuddered and drew back.

"You see?" he said. "It's no good. It would never work. You're absolutely right—you can't forget your public."

Ruth burst into tears. "Gil, you're being cruel... Now look what you're making me do... You say I don't love you...that I'm just after publicity... How can you say that after the way that redhead has acted? She's the one who's come between us... Of all the shameless, cheap, brazen things for a girl to do! I've got a reputation—my name means something. Our marriage would be the talk of the country...I do love you, Gil...I do, I do..."

GIL looked at her, unmoved. "You love the idea of the publicity our amalgamation would bring—but, for us, it wouldn't be a marriage—it would be a business proposition."

There was a sudden excited rap on the door. Ruth nervously ran to the mirror and commenced to dab at her face.

"Who is it?" asked Gil.

The door opened. "It's me," said Wilbur. He had a sealed envelope in his hand. "The people from Saks are here but Diana's not in her room. I found this envelope addressed to you." Wilbur sighted Ruth wiping the tearstains from her face. "Excuse me, Miss Delano—but I thought this might be something important..."

"Don't mind me..." snapped Ruth. "Especially if it has anything to do with Miss Fenimore."

Gil slit the envelope open and took out a note.

"Damn it to hell," he said.

Ruth stared at him, wonderingly. "What's the matter?" asked Wilbur, "anything wrong?"

"There's plenty wrong," said Gil, restraining his feelings with difficulty. "I'm going to read you this, Ruth, because it makes you eat your own words about a certain party." He fixed his eyes on the note and continued. " 'Dear Gil: This is your show.

I butted in on it at the start and now I'm running out on it at the end. This wasn't a circus stunt-it was a real scientific achievement. I hope I haven't spoiled it for you...Diana.' "

There was a moment of painful silence.

Ruth stood up. "If I had her wrong, Gil, I'm terribly sorry. Of course, that could be a grandstand play..."

Gil's jaws tightened. "Goodbye, Ruth," he said. "Your public is waiting..."

MGM's pin-up sensation went out the door.

"Wilbur," said Gil. "You find Diana for me or I'll break every bone in your head."

Wilbur looked at Gil, disconsolately. "I've only got one," he said, "and it's one solid piece..."

GIL BENSON flew back from Washington after a day closeted with the President, the cabinet, high military officials, scientists, and representatives of all foreign countries. The confidential report he gave them of his experiences on the Moon, substantiated by remarkable aerial photographs, particularly of the Martians' Moon City, profoundly impressed his hearers and produced immediate action toward setting up every possible defense against attack from space.

"I recommend," Gil Benson had told them, "the establishment of terminal stations in space at a height of above five hundred miles above the Earth, where a state of equilibrium exists, enabling such great floating islands to revolve perpetually around our planet. These great platforms will act as tiny Earthbound satellites.

"If we place these in space at equal distances around the Earth, each platform or terminal possibly three miles in diameter, we can use them to dock our huge spaceships in the coming traffic between the Moon and other planets. We can also store atomic bomb rockets there, as launching sites for repelling any attempted space invasion.

"These terminals would circle indefinitely in frictionless, weightless, and airless space. Once established, it is going to be necessary for the united people of our world to invade our side of the Moon and either make friends with the Martians or drive them off. Otherwise, because of their own desperate situation, they will prove an increasing menace.

"This will be particularly true, if and when they learn how to create atomic power, because of the great quantity of Uranium on the Moon. We must get there before they gain this knowledge and control the Moon and its Uranium deposits for ourselves. If we don't, gentlemen, with no pun intended, it will be 'Goodbye, World...' "

SCIENTISTS who had already been planning and designing such terminal stations, highly approved of Gil Benson's recommendations, as did those engaged in atomic research.

But Gil, with the world clamoring for an opportunity to honor him, had but one thought in mind, once he had left Washington. Arriving back at the Waldorf, he went immediately to the room of Wilbur Williams, whom he found with three telephones installed and talking on two of them at once.

"Hello, Gil," greeted Wilbur. "How'd you make out...? Just a minute..." Then into one of the phones: "No, Mr. Benson wouldn't be interested. He's not endorsing anything." He looked up at Gil. "It's been this way ever since you've been gone. You could make millions and I have to turn it all down." He spoke into the other phone, "No, it's not enough—I'll only let Miss Fenimore make one 'Moon Picture.' And she's got to get ten thousand a week..."

Gil broke in. "Get off that damn phone!" he shouted. "Listen to me! Have you located Diana?"

Wilbur hung up and all three phones started ringing. He took all receivers off and dropped them on the floor.

"No, Gil—I'm sick. I've got Burns and Pinkerton both trying to trace her. They turned up the cab driver who took her from the hotel. He said he let her out at Macy's...and a girl in the Women's Ready-to-Wear said she waited on her, sold her a gray suit and she changed right there. The dick said, since she appears to be hiding out, that she may have dyed her hair."

"If she's dyed her hair, I'll kill her," said Gil.

"I wouldn't like it, either," said Wilbur.

The two men looked at each other. Gil eyed Wilbur with sudden suspicion.

"See here," he said. "You're not, by any chance, behind Diana's run-out?"

"Me?" said Hollywood's greatest press agent. "I should say not."

"Let's not kid each other," said Gil. *"You love her, too!"*

"I don't need any truth serums to admit that," said Wilbur.

There followed an awkward moment.

"Well," said Gil, where do we go from here?"

Wilbur shrugged his shoulders, helplessly.

The phones were making strange, protesting noises with the receivers still on the floor. He reached down and picked two of them up, placing one to each ear.

"State your business," he said.

"What's the matter? Why don't you answer your phone?" said an angry voice.

"Hollywood calling," said an operator.

"I'll take Hollywood," said Wilbur, and dropped the other receiver. "Who's calling?"

"Ruth Delano—calling Gil Benson," said the operator.

"Tell her I'm not here," said Gil. "I'm going out and look for Diana myself."

Wilbur held up his hand. "Take it easy…" he warned. "You'll get yourself a lot of publicity you don't want. I told the papers Diana had a nervous breakdown and is in a private sanitarium for a few days." He spoke into the phone. "Put Miss Delano on…"

"I won't talk to her," Gil insisted.

"Hello, Gil?" said Ruth's voice.

"No," replied Wilbur, "it's me."

"Oh, hello, Willie. I've got to speak to Gil right away. It's very important…"

Wilbur looked at Gil who shook his head. "He's very busy right now. He wants to know—can I take the message?"

"No," said Ruth. "But tell him I've got some information about that redhead."

"YOU'VE wha...?" cried Wilbur. He put his hand over the mouthpiece. "She says she knows something about Diana. You'd better get on the line."

"She's kidding," said Gil, "just to get to talk to me." But he took the receiver. "Hello," he said.

"Hello—hello, Gil. Are you still sore at me?"

"You calling long distance to find that out?"

There was a pause—and a sob on the phone. "No—I was just calling to find out if you knew the whereabouts of Miss Fenimore...?"

Gil drew in a deep breath. "Not yet," he said.

"Well, I do," Ruth replied. "I ran into her at the airport when I was taking off. She was with Buzz Reynolds. They were flying somewhere in his plane."

Gil had held the receiver from his ear so that Wilbur could get this same information.

"Well, I'm a son-of-a-gun..." said Wilbur. "What do you know about that?"

"Ruth, I don't know how to thank you," said Gil. "You're swell."

"Wait!" cried Wilbur. "Don't let her hang up. I want to speak to her..."

Gil handed over the receiver.

"Say, Ruth," said Hollywood's greatest press agent. "You told me, some time ago, you'd let me do your publicity... I'd like to see you when I get back to Hollywood. How about dinner at Sardi's...just us two?"

"Why, Wilbur—I think that would be nice," said Ruth.

"After all," said Wilbur. "I want to impress you that you're going out with somebody important. I was the second man on the Moon."

Ruth laughed loudly. "I can hardly wait," she said, "and I mean it."

She hung up and Wilbur sat looking off into space. "She doesn't have red hair," he said. "But then, I guess a guy like me can't have everything." He looked around. "Hey, Gil," he called; "Well, I'll be damned... He's gone!"

*   *   *

Buzz Reynolds had a wife and two kids and a summer place on a bluff overlooking Lake Michigan. He also had his own private airfield.

It was early morning when he heard the motor of a high-speed plane circling overhead and coming in for a landing. Buzz kicked his feet into some slippers, pulled a sweater over his pajamas, and went outside.

"Must be some airman in trouble," he said to his wife.

Walking out back, Reynolds saw a handsome appearing man in a new suit of clothes striding toward him.

"Hello, Reynolds," he greeted. "I know she's here, so don't try to cover up. Trot her out..."

"Who are you talking about?" stalled Reynolds.

"Your redhead parachute jumper," said Gil Benson. "I might have suspected you'd be after her."

Buzz Reynolds was short and stocky. He buttoned his sweater around him to keep out the cool morning breeze.

"I didn't go after her," he protested. "She phoned me long distance; begged me to come and get her. She was crying...she's a swell kid...what else could I do?"

"That's okay," said Gil. "But I want to talk to her."

"She's not up yet," said Reynolds. "And you're not going to take her away from me now. She's going back with me next season... She's cooked up one of the most sensational parachute jumping stunts ever pulled... We're going to have a rocket built and shoot her up in it to a height of ten miles... Then it breaks open and she makes a parachute drop-in a space suit."

Gil laughed. "That was her idea?" he asked.

"Honest to God!" swore Reynolds.

"I wouldn't let her do a thing that dangerous," said Gil.

"And just what have you got to say about it?" said a voice.

Gil Benson looked around into a pair of blue, blue eyes.

"Thank God!" he exclaimed.

"For what?" asked Diana.

"That you didn't dye that red hair..."

"I thought you weren't up yet," said Reynolds.

"I can't ever stay in bed when I hear a plane," said Diana.

"If you don't mind," said Gil, pointedly. "Miss Fenimore and I are going to take a nice morning walk in your woods."

Reynolds grinned. "And if you don't mind," he replied. "I'm going to get back under the covers. It's damned chilly out here."

The first man and woman from Earth to land on the Moon walked slowly down the path into the woods. Nature was just waking. The birds of the forest were singing their morning songs.

"I've always liked red hair," Gil said, as the blue eyes looked up at him. "And, while I'm not a Martian, I'd greatly appreciate your aid in conducting a little experiment."

Diana smiled. "What kind?" she asked.

"I need a wife and a home," Gil proposed. "And I'd like to see if, in time, there might be some little redheads to go with it."

There was the light of the morning sun in Diana's blue eyes.

"I think, Mr. Benson, that I could devote myself to that experiment with great enthusiasm..."

The Moon and the Martians seemed very far away in that moment—and the Earth seemed very sweet.

America's Number One Bachelor had surrendered his title.

THE END

If you've enjoyed this book, you will not want to miss these terrific titles...

ARMCHAIR MYSTERY-CRIME DOUBLE NOVELS, $12.95 each

B-16   **KISS AND KILL** by Richard Deming
         THE DEAD STAND-IN by Frank Kane

B-17   **DANGEROUS LADY** by Octavus Roy Cohen
         ONE HOUR LATE by William O'Farrell

B-18   **LOVE ME AND DIE!** by Day Keene
         YOU'LL GET YOURS by Thomas Wills

B-19   **EVERYBODY'S WATCHING ME** by Mickey Spillane
         A BULLET FOR CINDERELLA by John D. MacDonald

B-20   **WILD OATS** by Harry Whittington
         MAKE WAY FOR MURDER by A. A. Marcus

B-21   **THE ART STUDIO MURDERS** by Edward Ronns
         THE CASE OF JENNIE BRICE by Mary Roberts Rinehart

B-22   **THE LUSTFUL APE** by Bruno Fisher
         KISS THE BABE GOODBYE by Bob McKnight

B-23   **SARATOGA MANTRAP** by Dexter St. Claire
         CLASSIFICATION: HOMICIDE by Jonathan Craig

ARMCHAIR SCI-FI & HORROR DOUBLE NOVELS, $12.95 each

E-5   **THE IDOLS OF WULD** by Milton Lesser
         PLANET OF THE DAMNED by Harry Harrison

E-6   **BETWEEN WORLDS** by Garret Smith
         PLANET OF THE DEAD by Rog Phillips

E-7   **DAUGHTER OF THOR** by Edmond Hamilton
         TALENTS, INCORPORATED by Murray Leinster

E-8   **ALL ABOARD FOR THE MOON** by Harold M. Sherman
         THE METAL EMPEROR by Raymond A. Palmer

E-9   **DEATH HUNT** by Robert Gilbert
         THE BEST MADE PLANS by Everett B. Cole

E-10   **GIANT KILLER** by Dwight V. Swain
         GOLDEN AMAZONS OF VENUS by John Murray Reynolds

ARMCHAIR SCI-FI & HORROR GEMS SERIES, $12.95 each

G-21   **SCIENCE FICTION GEMS, Vol. Eleven**
         Gordon R. Dickson and others

G-22   **HORROR GEMS, Vol. Eleven**
         Thorp McClusky and others

If you've enjoyed this book, you will not want to miss these terrific titles…

ARMCHAIR SCI-FI & MYSTERY CLASSICS, $12.95 each

C-40   **MODEL FOR MURDER**
by Stephen Marlowe

C-41   **PRELUDE TO MURDER**
by Sterling Noel

C-42   **DEAD WEIGHT**
by Frank Kane

C-43   **A DAME CALLED MURDER**
by Milton Ozaki

C-44   **THE GREATEST ADVENTURE**
by John Taine

C-45   **THE EXILE OF TIME**
by Ray Cummings

C-46   **STORM OVER WARLOCK**
by Andre Norton

C-47   **MAN OF MANY MINDS**
by E. Everett Evans

C-48   **THE GODS OF MARS**
by Edgar Rice Burroughs

C-49   **BRIGANDS OF THE MOON**
by Ray Cummings

C-50   **SPACE HOUNDS OF IPC**
by E. E. "Doc" Smith

C-51   **THE LANI PEOPLE**
J. F. Bone

C-52   **THE MOON POOL**
by A. Merritt

C-53   **IN THE DAYS OF THE COMET**
by H. G. Wells

C-54   **TRIPLANETARY**
C. C. Doc Smith

HUMANITY ON THE BRINK OF TOTAL DESTRUCTION

From out of Earth's forgotten past sprang a terrible menace to all mankind. Sweeping down from the black void of outer space came an invading horde known as the Rif. The Rif was led by a monstrous machine made of metal, standing higher than the tallest skyscraper. This monstrosity was known simply as "The Metal Emperor." Though metal it was, encased in its giant skull was the brain of a human—a malicious brain with evil intent, thousands of years old. Its plan was simple: exterminate the human race! With Earth's leadership incapacitated, it was up to a lowly engineer and a beautiful mistress with a fantastic mind-probing device to save Earth from total destruction.

"The Metal Emperor" was written by Ray Palmer, longtime editor of magazines like Amazing Stories, Fantastic Adventures, and Other Worlds. *It appeared in the November 1955 issue of* Imaginative Tales. *It was his last published work of fiction.*

CAST OF CHARACTERS

JAC AZAD
He was merely a third tier engineer; but because of his ruler's apathy he was thrown into the role of his planet's savior.

KAY LIN
Companion and mistress of the current ruler of Mekka, one whom the whole city looked upon as irresistible.

HUGH SPEAR
This space soldier was a squat man for a Mekkan, but as broad at the shoulders as two normal men—and perhaps as strong.

JILL LANG
By trade she was a lion tamer, unafraid of the wildest jungle cat; but a speeding levitor sled gave her a real case of the jitters.

MAZHART
He was the heart of the Mazarind clan and ruler of Mekka by popular vote, but how strong of a ruler was he really?

THE METAL EMPEROR
He was al- powerful and all wise—and stood nearly a mile in height over the mainland!

THE METAL EMPEROR

By
RAYMOND A. PALMER

ARMCHAIR FICTION
PO Box 4369, Medford, Oregon 97504

*The original text of this novel was first
published by Greenleaf Publishing Company*

Armchair Edition, Copyright 2016 by Gregory J. Luce
All Rights Reserved

*For more information about Armchair Books and products, visit our
website at…*

www.armchairfiction.com

Or email us at…

armchairfiction@yahoo.com

CHAPTER ONE

"OPEN hatches and drop the uranium bombs into the crater!"

The red warning signal flashed on the control panel of the giant spaceship, and the Rif captain clutched his fingers about the microphone.

Having said the words, he turned to stare at the television screen before him, and at the scene depicted upon its glowing surface. Red flame and black smoke almost obscured the view, but through rifts in them could be seen the glowing crater of the volcano—two miles below. And now, plainly visible in the screen, were the rapidly diminishing diameters of the uranium bombs as they fell toward the center of the crater. There was no explosion as they dropped into the seething lava, for these were bombs only in the sense of their shape to guide the tons of pure uranium into the crater's mouth. Actually they were only "food" for the volcano's vitals, to create a chain reaction in its atomically digestive bowels that would eventually build up to an atomic explosion beyond all belief in its violence as a whole volcano exploded and destroyed the greatest city on all the Earth.

The warning light on the control panel of the spaceship dimmed and went out. The deed was done.

A strange metallic-sounding voice, awesome in its deep rumbling, sounded now in the control room. The captain listened.

"Good! I have seen. Now drop your agents into the city environs itself, and set them about their duties. And when you have done that, signal the transports to descend and disembark their armies according to plan."

"Yes, Sire," said the Rif captain, respectfully. "It shall be done. Earth will know again, after these many thousands of years, the heavy tread of the Rif, and of your, metal majesty, the Emperor of Mu…" The captain raised his hand in a symbolic salute, then spoke once more into the microphone.

"Agents parachute… And when you have made your way into the city tunnels under cover of darkness, await the signal for the planned sabotage. And above all, destroy the governmental heads as planned. Mazhart must die—yet seem to live."

The Rif captain leaned back, a grim smile on his lips. And far out in the void, in the largest spaceship of all, awaiting the moment to descend to the planet and take up his rule, sat the Metal Emperor, who was not smiling at all.

THE home planet of the Rif was a strange world, secret and impenetrable to all but the more foolhardy of traders, those who failed to note how few of them returned. Strangest of all the many dark and secret places of that planet was the Golden Dome of Nalenq, the hidden city of the jungles where the green webs of the spider folk kept all mankind from the forest paths.

In that golden dome lived the Metal Emperor, who was worshipped not only as an emperor and supreme ruler, but as a god. Not human was he, but metal, and gigantic. He had always existed, first (according to his own word), on a planet called Earth, many thousands of years gone, when it was a youthful planet and filled with a great science and a great civilization. Mu had been the name of the civilization, and there the Rif had lived, although none remembered except the Emperor. Long ago, to escape a disaster that overwhelmed Mu, the Rifians had escaped, in spaceships, led by their Emperor. Now, with the Rif planet insufficient in its resources to build such a civilization as had existed on Earth, the Emperor was going back. Agents, sent back to Earth, had reported it once more habitable, and in fact, possessing a great new civilization. Not more than a hundred years previously, the instruments of Rif had recorded strange emanations from Earth, which had stirred the Metal Emperor to action. There was life on Earth! It was now possible to return to the home planet.

But the strange emanations had turned out to be powerful echoes, the result of a long-ago war wherein atomic energy had been employed. It had almost wiped out that civilization. But the emperor's spies had discovered that an even newer civilization had risen from the ashes—a new civilization tremendously advanced in science. If the scientific knowledge of this civilization was allowed to grow and prosper, it might soon thwart any plans by the emperor to invade and conquer. So the deed had to be done now or never. And the Metal Emperor had prepared carefully. Key to the situation was the capitol city, Mekka, and its chained volcano, with its national atomic reactor providing unlimited power. Destroy that, and the planet would fall. And once fallen, the Rif would again take up their abode on their ancient home, and the Metal Emperor would rule, as he had ruled ages before.

Sitting in his spaceship, the Emperor reflected on the results of his opening skirmish. He'd sent a fleet of invading warships, and in a great space battle, they had been repulsed. The armadas of the Rif, accustomed to much raiding in their own System, had gone forth from the planet of war, had descended upon Mekka—and had lost the battle! No infant civilization, this!

The huge warships of the Rif had been driven off, and although the defenders of Mekka had never known the origin of the attackers, they had somehow been alerted. In any future attack, the Metal Emperor knew one thing— Mekka had to be destroyed, with its central power plant, to ground and render impotent her air fleet and her armies. This, now, was the vital attack. If successful, Earth would be helpless. And it would succeed—for the volcano had been primed! Nothing on Earth could halt the holocaust that would follow.

Also, when his armies gained a foothold one Earth, they would fight with a ferocity beyond imagination, for after the first defeat, the Metal Emperor had crushed the lives out of many generals, many chieftains, many famous warriors, upon the altars of his wrath. They would die rather than retreat once more, knowing full well the fate that defeat would bring to them.

Many were the younger Rifs who grumbled at the ancient cruelty of the Metal Emperor, for they felt that in this day of the machine, such dark and evil things should not be. But their grumbling went unheard, or was heard and caused their deaths.

CHAPTER TWO

MEKKA! The mechanical city! Mazhart, heart of the Mazarind clan, ruler of Mekka by popular vote, stood combing his curly black beard before the great round mirror that was not a mirror, but the polished receptor plate of his private penetrating ray and central command installation. Turning his sleek head to admire his noble and truly handsome appearance, he wondered if any thought him too young to rule a great city? But was not Mekka queen of the world under his rule? Was not peace a thing of years' duration since the repulse of the mysterious Rif from outer space, some undiscovered planet away? Were they not alerted and ready for any repetition? And was it not all his work, his alert foresight, his support of the scientists who had made Mekka great?

Satisfied, he put away the comb, turned from the big mirror—and found himself facing an individual who had entered without sound. He retreated one step in complete amazement, for this man was no one he knew, yet he was as familiar as the image in his own mirror! In fact, it *was* himself, to all practical purposes; the same eagle eye bright above the straight nose, the same luxurious red lips, the same strong cheekbones, the same curling black beard. Himself, even to the shining black metal-cloth fitting sleekly over the muscled shoulders, accentuating the powerful thighs with inwoven gems in patterns of the Mazarind flower, the gentian. Identical, from top to toe, it was evident the man had made his way in here by impersonating Mazhart.

The only detectable difference lay in the needle-ray he carried in his hand, the tiny opening in the blunt muzzle staring at Mazhart like a hypnotic eye. Mazhart reached backward for the toggle switch of his mirror ray. At least the thing would automatically connect him with the central exchange and the operator would observe and take action...

KAY Lin, current favorite of the ruler of Mekka city, was a woman built on a generous pattern. Her skin was that translucent milk-white found only in certain red-haired types. Her hair, a bright copper made more vivid with a dye, lay in generous masses of ringlets about a strong but shapely throat. Big-framed but graceful, her body was sleekly covered with that layer of velvet-soft flesh which is the possession of the most feminine of women when in perfect health and the flower of their youth. And Kay Lin was boisterously healthy, and likewise young enough to delight any eyes.

Just now she was intent upon her own beauty, repeated before her in a mirror similar to Mazhart's—for it was a gift from him, and was equipment denied any but the most favored people in the city. She had just awakened, and sat clad only in a filmy sleeping garment, which she had slipped to her shoulders so that it lay in a soft cloud over the proud arches of her hips, leaving her unbelievably beautifully formed breasts completely bare.

The huge machine, of which the mirror was only the visible part, was supported between the beaks of two great red metal birds. The controls were concealed by the metal feathers, of which they were a part. Beneath the floor the great dynamos hummed a silent song of waiting power. For Mekka was a city of rays, and nearly every moment of the inhabitants' active day was taken up in some use or other of the myriad of wavelengths at their disposal. Nothing was done but by the means of rays. There were the stimulating pleasure rays; the beams that gave them instant vision into any distance of the city built in and at the base of the mountain; the healing rays which gave them the very life-force itself.

Kay Lin's installation was peculiar in but one respect: it was in continual connection with Mazhart's home over a fixed beam, requiring no focus adjustment, so that but a flip of a switch gave them instant contact with each other, a contact that, because of the pleasure rays, was sometimes very interesting indeed.

But now, at this instant, Mazhart's startled hand, unconsciously moving in a habitual way, flipped the switch connecting him to his beloved, Kay Lin, rather than the switch alongside, which would have connected him to the central command. On such little errors do the lives of men sometimes depend.

Yet, it was not Kay Lin's face that appeared in the mirror, but the back of her head—for in that same instant a young and muscular young man had burst open the door and plunged into her boudoir, and she had swung about.

Her striking eyes (tinted by a dye injection to a more startling shade of blue best calculated to contrast with her white skin and copper hair) fixed in fascinated and not unpleased surprise upon the intruder's rugged face. His whole bearing was that of intense preoccupation, or repressed excitement.

Neither of them saw the repeated image of Mazhart and his double, nor the deadly needle ray half concealed in the double's hand. Neither of them noticed the hiss of the discharge, nor the body of one of them slumping out of view within the mirror-screen—and with good reason, for Kay Lin had her back to the mirror, while the young man had his eyes implacably chained upon the beauty of Kay Lin.

ALLOWING herself the proper long instant of surprised immobility, Kay Lin reached embarrassedly for her dressing gown, pulling it loosely about her nude shoulders, nor noticed that her elbow struck the feathers of the great red bird, switching off contact with Mazhart. And, which she carefully failed to conceal aught but her shoulders, she covertly reached for another feather and depressed it. An invisible beam sprang from the floor upward into the face of the young man, holding him motionless. And instead of Mazhart's death-scene upon the mirror, there now appeared the thought images of the young man, laid bare by the probing power of the forbidden mental ray.

Kay Lin turned aside from him so that she might watch both the young man and his thoughts, as they flashed across the mirror's bright surface. She turned up the power to a forbidden strength, fixing rigid control upon him. Such power was permitted officially only to the police during emergencies. But Kay Lin knew she would be immune from criticism. Caught like a fly in a trap, his inner self was but a waiting comfit box for Kay Lin to open at her leisure.

She turned away and began to comb her coppery hair as she suggested question after question, violating all the ethics of polite society by prying open the very soul of the young man. On her lips was a mocking smile. Did not the man deserve what he was getting, bursting in thus upon her privacy? And she deliberately suggested questions to which the answers would be most embarrassing, and her eyes lighted with extreme interest at some of the answers. As she watched, she grew desirous to know who he actually was.

"Who are you...and why are you here?" asked Kay Lin.

Helplessly his mind began to tell her his story, as it had happened to him, in actual picturization on the screen...

Kay Lin, who now learned he was Jac Azad, Engineer of the Third Tier of the Thermal Patrol, saw him glide upon a levitor sled toward his Post in the offices directly beneath the Vulcana. Suddenly he jerked back the drive lever. The sled dropped to its runners with a screech of steel upon stone, ran across the polished floor for yards among the fantastic mechanisms of the Grot of the Magic Hands.

This was a section of underground factories, directly connected to the power outlets of the Vulcana, where endless aisles of machines toiled and built a steady flow of fabrications from numberless materials. Boxes, barrels, decorative fabrics on great looms, metal sheets bent swiftly into all manner of shapes—being stacked or woven or assembled, and without a workman in sight. Every visible operation, however, was performed by a pair of life-like floating hands apparently unsupported by any material means.

These hands were really metal, under automatic magnetic force control, so built that the whole vast space seemed inhabited by invisible workmen, tireless and infinitely accurate, whose hands alone could be seen. It was an illusion contrived by the inventor of the basic machine at work there, a machine whose moving parts conquered friction by floating in powerful supporting magnetic fields; fields manipulated in predetermined patterns by an extension of the principle by which a television beam is manipulated within the tube to form an image. The moving metal parts passed through intricate magnetic field patterns of weaving or construction whose design was itself a science and a trade among the men of Mekka.

But Jac Azad stood only for an instant watching the awesome mystery of the creating hands. To him it was no mystery, but a somewhat outmoded robot factory. More interesting was a spurt of almost invisible vapor from a crevice in the polished stone walls. That insignificant spurt of vapor had caused every nerve of his body to scream an alarm of peril.

JAC stood watching it until his eyes adjusted to the dim lights, then he put his hands to his head with a groan of despair. Newly formed, high in the wall face, the angry crack angled across the mirror—bright polished rock! He would be sent to the jungles along with most of his comrades of the Thermal Patrol for this. Only negligence or worse could have allowed such a disaster.

He leaped back to the sled more swiftly than he had gotten off, a vicious warrior's oath crackling from his lips (and Kay Lin, watching his image on her mirror, put her shapely hands to her ears), and the levitor sled sped away. A second later and a mile away, it settled beside a big red alarm box. Jac pulled the great general alarm lever. Then he began trundling out the rolls of woven metal hose before the repair robots even stirred from their wall niches. Within minutes a score of the mechanical statue-like metal men had moved ponderously to help him, and his immediate superior, a dark-browed young giant named Dee Atzin, arrived to take charge.

"I'll take over, Jac. You get up to the main observation lab and run a ray tracer to the source of this thing. If that crack is clear through to the Can itself, instead of just a burst pipe near the mains, it not only means we are out of a berth on the Patrol, it means that all Mekka is in peril. Get going, and give me that hose. Trace that fissure, then go to the Mazarind. We've caught a Rif spy, and there is no doubt this is some of their work."

Dee Atzin turned away to direct the placing and bolting of the pressure plates to the rocks of the wall, and the pumping of the liquid thermal plastic into the fissure. This was a compound designed to harden in heat, remain liquid at normal temperature. Filling the fissure with the cement would only temporarily restrain the terrible forces that had caused the fissure.

On the screen Kay Lin saw Jac's mind leap a bridge of time now, back to the surprise attack of the Rif forces from space. She herself had not been concerned then in affairs of government, being in the southern hemisphere at a famous school for beauty culture. She had only a hazy knowledge of the attack, and she did not know how narrowly the Air Force of Mekka had averted disaster for them all. But she learned now.

As Jac's sled raced away toward the main laboratory under the fires of the Vulcana, his mind was busily matching bits of memory from that time with certain similarities of today's conditions, coming to the suspicion that this was not just sabotage, but the beginning of a new and more dangerous attack. His mind went back to those former battles, and with them to a young and lovely lieutenant of Women's Air Force Reserve, the beautiful Freya Velt.

KAY Lin, in spite of the fact she realized this was a situation of gravity, could not help being womanly, and more, could not resist this chance to lay bare the inner secrets of this young man's mind in relation to the pretty girl whose face kept flitting across the screen, intermingled with his racing thoughts. She flicked a second small beam to his motionless head, suggesting further thought concerning the girl. Jac's mind automatically and helplessly furnished the fact that the girl had died in the war.

A twinge of unexpected jealousy burned for an instant in Kay Lin's intense blue eyes, then was repressed. Why should she care who this young man had loved? Also, he was not as young as he looked, she noted, in more ways than one. Not only had he seen action during the war with Rifia, it was obvious that he had been quite in love with the dashing Amazon of the Air Force. Not the sort of love of a Mazarind for a courtesan, but a tender, vital love…

Kay Lin brushed her unexpected reaction aside, noting that her heart was disposed to take unwonted interest in this young man with something of self-scorn; watched while the images on the screen ran over the high points of his war career. She glimpsed a score of savage space battles, Jac's one-man fighter plunging and rearing with the terrible concussions of space bombs, his eyes blinded with the unchecked fires of atomic fission sweeping over the ships of his comrades.

All this while she held him in hypnotic subjection with her powerful neural ray, her natural instincts getting a sensual satisfaction out of so holding the fiery inner man here before her mind's eye, to do with as she wished. But at last she released him, but not before she had impressed upon him an unforgettable hypnotic compulsion to see her as she wished to be seen, a command she had used before with telling and entertaining effect.

As he relaxed, the tension of the subjecting flow of neural electricity subsiding, his own body taking charge again with its own energies, she knew that he was telling her the truth. The Vulcana, the great central-heating and power plant of the frigid underground factory portion of Mekka, was about to blow up because of a secretly administered dose of fissionable material into the great outer cone of the fire. And he had come to her as the quickest way to Mazhart.

Somehow she was not in the least flattered that he had done so...

CHAPTER THREE

JAC Azad, coming out of the mental bondage that had been so complete, suddenly realized time was passing while he was engaged in an endless mental dalliance with this sex-minded female. He stood half-angrily on his feet, even though he saw her now as actually fine-charactered as well as superbly bodied.

"You should be flogged with a length of cables. There is no time for this sort of thing. Send for Mazhart at once, or I'll go to his home, even if it means death under these conditions."

Kay Lin only smiled seductively, mockingly. "The great one will arrive here very shortly, Jac Azad, as he does every day—in about twenty swings of the pendulum of the clock there on the wall. I could not hurry him. I could not stop him. He is as regular as the magnetic flow of the time cable. And usually about as exciting. He comes and goes, Jac, with somewhat the same inexorable unconcern for the wishes of others that the sea exhibits in her tides. Make yourself comfortable, you have only to wait. I am not as dense as you think; I understand the urgency of the situation. But I could not help but to take advantage of an opportunity ordinarily denied me—that of seeing exactly what makes a man tick inside. Most men are so bashful about the springs of ego, you know."

Jac sat, his eyes watching the great golden pendulum of the clock on the wall. Its swing was halted, then released, by impulses from a central source along a cable. The thing stopped and swung, stopped and swung, with maddening deliberation. Yet, in spite of his boiling anxiety, he could not keep his eyes upon the pendulum and off the sleek perfection of Kay Lin's physical opulence, still far from concealed in any way by the draping of her nightdress. He could not help noting how her breasts rose and fell, rose and fell, in perfect cadence with the pendulum, but he did note the gleam in her eye as she so timed her respiration to attract his attention. Kay Lin had violated the ethics of the period mightily when she had held his mind open with her illegally powerful ray, when she had peered beneath his defenses into the secrets of his past. Not yet could he release his mind from its magnetic contact with hers. The burning sensuous images she had allowed to alternate back and forth between them still burned upon the now violent-hued curtains of his thought. This sensuous woman had impregnated all his inner self with a consciousness of her vital femaleness.

Suddenly he associated the swing of the pendulum with her breathing. "Even in the face of annihilation for the whole city you cannot help being a woman, can you, Kay Lin?"

"You are welcome to the same privilege, if you wish to retaliate, Jac," she said, smiling suggestively. "You can use the ray on me."

"I wonder! If that is a promise, I will call upon you at some future date to fulfill it. I am sure there is no other mind whose memories would prove more diverting..."

At his answer, which could be construed as an insult, she began an angry retort, but at that instant a terrific lurch and shudder of the very floor beneath their feet cut short their half-angry, half-fascinated conversation. Shortly after came a blast of ear-painful sound. A fragile vase crashed from a niche to the floor at Jac's feet.

Following the shock of the explosion, there came a repeated thrum and twang as of great bow strings, sounds that told Jac the street patrols were firing the great rifles mounted at the street intersections. There was fighting in the very street outside Kay Lin's door...

SECONDS went by while they stared at each other, held by sheer surprise. Then Kay Lin, a poem of sudden swift motion, sprang for the opened door, reached it just in time to crash into a tall bearded form. The man staggered and would have fallen, but she embraced him with a cry of relief. He leaned upon her weakly, his boldly carved face now dull with shock, stained with dark dust from some near explosion.

"Someone threw a hand bomb at your gate, Kay. Stupid Rif, trying to assassinate me! If they only realized that no one else in charge could make as many plunders as I, they could have remained alive. The street patrol has become alerted and is firing on their hiding places."

Kay Lin asked swiftly, "What makes you think it is the Rif, Mazhart? There hasn't been a Rif caught in the city for years."

The big man sank weakly on a divan and Kay Lin wiped the dust from his face with the soft fabric of her nightdress.

"I think I know a Rif when I see one, Kay," he murmured, leaning back, his eyes shooting repeatedly to Jac, as if not sure whether to recognize him or castigate him. "They plotted to kill me here. We have caught a few of their spies today."

"It is more than a plot against your life, Sire," said Jac. "If that was a Rif bomb, the two events are linked. It is a step in a plan to annihilate the city, for the Vulcana is about to burst!"

The man put his two hands to the divan, pushed himself forward, and peered at Jac as if the place was dark, which it was not.

"Just who are you, and how do you know the Vulcana is not her usual complacent self? And too, what are you doing in this particular boudoir at a time an attempt is made upon my life? It seems a bit opportune, to me!"

"There is no time for such petty thinking, Mazhart. The Vulcana has been sabotaged. Fissionable material has been dumped in from the stratosphere, unobserved. She is going up—just when can be known only to those who dropped the materials. By my observations, I give her about ten hours to complete eruption. That I am a member of the Thermal Patrol should be passport enough at this time to your concubine's bedroom—if that is necessary to reach you..."

"Couldn't you bring your business to my offices?"

"You weren't there; and everyone knows where else you are most likely to be."

The famous Mazarind stood up ponderously, his hands pressed to his temples, his face averted. Jac decided he was an over-rated stuffed shirt, but hoped that his impression was due to the state of shock in which the concussion had left the ruler. He seemed to be in the grip of complex emotions, endeavoring to concentrate while he grappled with the natural anger at the attempt made upon his person and the fact that his dignity had been ripped at the seams. He glared about suddenly like a great bear looking for someone to blame everything upon.

"You Thermal troops have let the Vulcana get out of hand, then you come to me with a tale of an attack. Why, the Rif have not dared to show their faces in Mekka since their defeat."

Jac noted Mazhart was contradicting his earlier statement, but ignored this. "There is no time for blame or any action but evacuation. It is too late to stop the culmination of the chain reaction now building up within the fire center. Please pull yourself together, Sire! The life of all our people is at stake, and you alone can give the order for a council meeting to order an evacuation."

THE big man sank as if bemused to the divan. Jac gestured to Kay Lin with a meaningful expression. She understood, smoothed the ruler's brow with one velvet palm while she clucked motheringly into his ear. He relaxed upon the divan and after long minutes of silence during which neither moved, murmured: "Kay, call the offices and command an immediate meeting of the officers of state. Make it imperative that all attend."

Jac stepped forward angrily. "Mazarind...that would play directly into their hands! You couldn't give a worse order if you were working for them. The council must be held by way of ray central as expeditiously as possible, and openly and for all to hear, or not at all! You could call more than half of them to a death that is undeniably waiting for them, by your own experience. The Rif are in the city in force; didn't that bomb and the fighting you hear outside tell you that?"

The huge man stared at Jac almost venomously. Seemingly his mind tried in vain to reason out what to do with this creature who kept telling his important self what not to do. His eyes drifted to the sidearm that Jac nervously fingered, and at last he roared out: "What would you have me do, you oracle of wisdom?"

"Connect the central command with Thermal headquarters under Vulcana. Let them give a general report to each officer in the city. Call a vote for evacuation or try to put out the chain reaction now building within the cone, whichever is most feasible. Abide then by that vote, swiftly, with everyone alerted to the danger and its nature. Do it now, not when it is too late!"

After another precious minute of apparently labored thought, the flushed and angry face relaxed reluctantly. Mazhart sighed.

"Do it his way, Kay Lin. I seem to have lost my wits, it's true. Set things in motion for me. I can't seem to think at all."

Kay Lin went to her ray controls and did as she was bid. In a few short moments Jac was coupled to nearly every ray beam in the city, his voice going out to every important mind in Mekka. Mazhart had given him the needed permission to explain the sudden crisis.

"People of Mekka, we face annihilation in short hours! The Vulcana has been tampered with, and our heating plant has become an atom fission pile. Just what ingredients were dumped into the cone by a new plot of the Rif, we don't know, or canceling out their work would be simple."

In a low voice, Mazhart, whose form showed on the sending screen just behind Jac's, murmured: "Explain what has to be done, how they should conduct themselves. I don't trust myself to speak now."

"As you all know, ordinarily our volcano is a source of heat and power in these normally frigid manufacturing excavations of ours, and is not difficult to control. But when the fires within the great central cone we call the 'Can' are made explosive by the addition of chain reaction materials of an unknown nature, then we can only experiment, hoping to strike the right damping combinations. Until we bring the increasing pressures of the Vulcana under our control again, it would be wisest for our city to be evacuated. Quietly, without panic, without looting or disorder, leave the city by the routes nearest to each of you. Do not all crowd onto the stem toward Old Philadelphia, nor rush into the trains for the forests—but each of you go as normally as possible to the nearest long route exit and leave Mekka. We will try to bring the Vulcana under control. If we fail, we will have only to build a new and greater Mekka. But if you remain in your homes, or if you disobey and cause riots that block off exits, it means that many of us will die in the holocaust of fire that is coming to Mekka. Now go. You have perhaps twelve hours, perhaps eight. Be careful and goodbye."

JAC'S voice rang with a sad command, and he waved his hand with a finality of dismissal. Kay Lin cut the switch that connected her beam to the central command beam.

Mazhart, ruler of the doomed city, leader of his family, sat with a curious air of frustration, as if he would not have allowed the broadcast had he seen how to prevent it. He had not said a word to the people.

Jac spoke to him with an incisive, clear-cut scorn, "Now the Rif will attack, when the people get beyond the city's fixed installations of guns and rays. What do you plan to do to protect them then?"

The man stirred, his face twisted in an enigmatic smile. "Such emergencies are provided for in Central Command staff training. They have certain plans ready to put into instant action. It will be attended to without special orders."

"It might be effective," answered Jac, "to gather a group of volunteer fighting men and be ready to counterattack when the Rif show their hand. This thing is well planned, and it is quite likely that ordinary methods will not suffice. I know where such men can be found. I have some ideas where the Rif may lay in wait to massacre our people. We might be able to scotch the Rif snake before it bites us seriously."

Mazhart eyed the young man who seemed so experienced a hand at straggle and death. "Where has one so young seen action before?"

Kay Lin answered for him. "This seemingly youthful person is a veteran of the former war with the Rif, having been in every major engagement. He piloted his own fighter jet in the last two great battles. Not only that, he was Halvor's chief aide in the counterattack that was not expected to succeed, but did. To its success we owe the life of every person in Mekka. Yet what little publicity, what pitiful reward the people of Mekka gave to the men who accomplished it that you do not even know them!"

Mazhart nodded with an irritated motion of his hand. "I see. There is some reason and excuse in your proffering a Mazarind your advice, then." Mazhart took a pad from his pocket, scribbled upon it, tore off a slip of the tough plastic, gave it to Jac. "There is an emergency commission as captain of volunteer forces—whatever their number— that you are able to gather. Go ahead and make your attempt to foil the Rif plot. I am first going to see that the Mazarind clan reaches safety, and then make sure everything is being done to damp out the atomic fires you say have broken out in the Vulcana. I know something about atomics, and I have never heard of a pile that could not be damped."

"But the Vulcana is not a pile; it is merely a vast fire in the rocks, fed by natural coal deposits. It has been primed with fissionable materials, and it is not equipped with built-in barriers, not intended for the necessity that has arisen. We can dump in cadmium, yes, but we can't get proper distribution in the irregularly shaped fire chambers of the Vulcana. You can't halt that chain reaction, and I am sure Mekka is doomed. If I had been in charge of the Rif forces, the materials I would have used would have been completely unstoppable under the given conditions."

JAC turned away from the obviously confused leader, stared for an instant at Kay Lin, who stood with her lips parted as if to speak, but said nothing. Then he went out the door on the dead run, clutching his emergency powers in his hand. He wondered if he could find anyone calm enough to listen to him or to care how many emergency powers had been given to him.

"A capable young squirt," growled Mazhart to Kay Lin, "but somehow I detest him."

"One dislikes people for no reason, sometimes," murmured Kay Lin, turning away to hide a sudden telltale flush. In her heart she knew exactly why Mazhart disliked Jac Azad, knew that he sensed her own emotions toward the young man. Too, Jac had been none too polite to the ruler. She could not help feeling that Mazhart was showing himself an incompetent in an emergency, as well as a heartless sort of creature. He seemed worried only about the loss of power and prestige, and not about the people. She sighed, for a moment all thought of her own peril banished from her mind by a sudden realization that in grasping for fame and wealth by taking up with Mazarind, she had only gained notoriety and had lost her own self-respect. But now, there was something she must do or lose even more. What did this man intend for her, if Mekka truly perished?

She seated herself before the mirror that was so much more than a mirror. She flicked the decorative feather that was the switch, turned the metal ornament that was the focus control, and the beam suddenly licked out upon Mazhart, freezing him in an instant to subjection to her will, just as it had Jac Azad.

As she scanned his inner, hidden thoughts, a terrible series of scenes from an alien mind stole nightmarishly across the mirror. Kay Lin probed deeper, in a fog of horror that piled terror upon terror in her mind as she knew him for an interloper in the body of her own Mazhart! Rage began to burn over the horror within her. How long had this thing been posing as the ruler? Just who and what this monster was became clear to her at last, penetrating her benumbed understanding, and her rage flamed into a frenzy—a bright anger that moved her hand to the head of the great metal bird and pulled it down with a savage triumph. A lambent ray licked out over the man, a flame no more intense than her own flaming anger, spread and grew over the false Mazhart's face and limbs. His body became for an instant transparent as molten glass, and as swiftly melted away. There was left of the Rif spy only a bad smell and some wisps of ash of the metal fabric of his clothing. Kay Lin's hands sank trembling to her lap.

"Mazhart is dead!" she moaned. "Mekka comes leaderless to her doom, and I…what comes for me without Mazhart?"

As she sat there—dejection personified, far more beautiful than usual—her mirror glowed slightly and its whispering, metallic-sounding voice came to her from an imposed enemy ray. It mocked her softly.

"We have fooled you, Kay Lin! He, whom you loved and now have murdered, was the real Mazhart. There was no substitution or impersonation! By reading my imposed ray instead of Mazhart's thoughts, you have seen in his mind what I placed there for you to see. How does it feel to be a murderess, to have killed the one you loved? What a patriot, what intelligence, how proud of yourself you must feel!"

For an instant Kay Lin was held in rigid horror, realization surging through her. Then she sprang with a scream to her feet and plunged out of the room, unable to bear the self-accusation of her conscience. She had been tricked by one of the oldest of thought-mirror deceits, the substitution of thought, and her only excuse was that she had forgotten to expect enemy tampering here in the heart of Mekka. It had not occurred to her she could be so completely fooled as to commit murder! She ran sobbing down the aisles of her home, in mental agony.

And behind her, on the polished surface of the mirror, a monstrous metal form loomed for an instant, peering after her, something which, had she seen it, would have stayed her horror, but piled something even worse upon it. And through the room the humorless chuckle of the Metal Emperor echoed in rasping tones.

CHAPTER FOUR

JAC Azad, coming into the city terminals in his levitor sled, found them filled with hurrying Mekkans. It was evident that panic flight was in their minds, and that orderly evacuation was going to be hard to achieve. Sleds darted hither and thither, or turned on their tracks as drivers remembered some valuable left behind—in a place considered immutable and time-proof, but now to be thought of as evanescent, to be gone on the morrow. Jac sped above the growing turmoil, in the express levels, where only official conveyances on special errands and the regular freight carriers were permitted.

He was on his way to a rallying place of his own. It was a club, membered by veterans of the Rif war, and older warriors who had lived through the wars of the beginning of Mekka, after the great war that had destroyed the old civilization. As he went, the sorrow-to-be, the gathering weighty peril for each of these handsome men and lovely women below him, for each chubby angelic babe, for each gangling youngster, was like an increasing pain in Jac's chest as full realization of the doom of Mekka came to him. A far-off shudder ran through the rocks at regular intervals, and Jac knew, if the others did not, that that shuddering was the shock waves of the increasing atomic reaction building up in the Vulcana's fiery heart. Interspersing this almost inaudible but increasingly fearful shudder of the rocks was a far-off intermittent twang and thrum and twang again of the big mounted rifles, fighting off some attack in one of the city tubes. Jac suspected that this warfare in the distance was the feint attack, designed to draw off the defense of the doomed city to some point that would leave the nerve center of the city undefended. The real attack would come only when such feints had been successful, and after the exploding Vulcana had destroyed the factories and the city's fighting potential, its fixed installations.

"Without a whisper of warning the bloody Rif have got this far toward the death of us all!" Jac cursed to himself. "This damned Mazhart is probably the greatest fool ever to hold the helm of Mekka, or of any other city. He has probably been keeping all warnings quiet on the assumption that they were the prattle of alarmists seeking to discredit his regime."

THE trickle of early evacuees grew rapidly as Jac's sled sped across the city. A steady stream of vehicles flickered beneath his own and beneath these, along the footways, more and more people were hurrying, carrying bundles of necessaries, wrapped in rich tapestries and other fabrics they considered indispensable to their future. As this throng grew in turmoil, Jac realized that not all of them would reach a rendezvous with some vehicle of some friend or relative. This growing conviction that the city could never be evacuated in the short time left was made more certain by a sudden shock and a splitting of the rock wall that cracked with a noise like thunder, throwing out a cloud of burning gas that flickered and went out.

It was this incident that made him see the scene that drew his speeding sled to a stop and a dive toward the tunnel floor. Here the walkways along the side were filled with hurrying figures. The sudden flare of brilliant red light from the gases emitted by the volcanic crack had given Jac a glimpse of a scene on the walkway; struggling figures about one central figure playing about with a bright wand. It was a weapon from which the surrounding figures leaped back, only to come in again. Jac halted his sled just above the heads of the group. There were a half-dozen dark-clad men, and in the center, one silver-clad young woman. Her legs were cased in scaled metal hose, her hair a mass of tossing midnight about her tense, anger-flushed face. She was breathing hard, but the wand in her hand pulsed with electric flame. Jac recognized it as an animal trainer's defense weapon, harmless but numbing in its effects. Jac called down.

"What's the trouble, lion-tamer? Can I be of any help?" The men glanced up, aware of him now. One slunk away into the shadows and took to his heels, another tugged at a gun in his short coat. But Jac flicked his own needle-ray from its holster and showed the man its muzzle. He dropped his hands to his sides, stood irresolute. As he turned away, the others joined him, and they hurried off, leaving the woman standing, alone. The wand of ruddy flame in her hand was no brighter than her grateful eyes and flushed face as she turned her head upward to Jac.

"Can I come aboard, soldier? They wanted me to accompany them to a place of safety. Safety, with them, hah! I think not."

HER voice was a clear, sharp contralto. Jac could imagine it cracking with command as she put a monster of the jungle through its paces for the entertainment of a crowd of thrill-seekers. He lowered the sled to her side. She stepped aboard lithe and supple, and her strength of hand as she seized the fore rail to settle in her seat gave Jac a queer thrill of admiration such as no female had ever aroused. It was very odd to admire a woman for strength and agility, and at the same time feel drawn by the softer feminine qualities so apparent on her flower-petal cheeks, in her deep midnight eyes.

"What is the matter with the Vulcana soldier? Is it as bad as the announcers made out?"

"It's worse," growled Jac, rocketing the sled up through the speeding traffic and forward again at full speed. The animal trainer gave a gasp at his daring, and Jac smiled.

"Don't tell me that a levitor sled can thrill you?"

"I don't mind the biggest cat out of Africa, but speed gives me butterflies. What do you mean, it's worse? Is the city really going to be filled with lava?"

Jac waved below. "Plenty of those people hurrying to get passage out of the city aren't going to make it. What is your name?"

"It wouldn't mean a thing to you; it's a stage name. You may have seen my billing as 'Armora, the Fearless'. My real name is Jill Lang. My family has been on the stage for generations, and I was born on the road. My father was Lou Lang, the greatest stunt flier who ever thrilled a crowd by risking his neck. But the jets got him in the end. You can't stick at that game when your nerves begin to slow up, and he did. He was killed in an exhibition flight over Chicago."

"I remember him," said Jac. "I was there with Darreg with the Space Patrol during the Rif war."

"You knew Darreg? I knew him when I was a kid. He used to visit our tent on the Midway."

"I knew him the way a pilot knows a general, from a respectful distance. That's different from being dandled on his knee."

"He and Dad used to talk ships until all hours. I use to fall asleep at their feet, like a dog."

"So we have mutual friends, Miss Lang. I'm called Jac, which is short for Jac-alin. My mother wanted a girl. My family name is Azad, the north branch. But the family money in the western clans has something to do with my need for a job. I inherited none of it. So I make a living with the Thermal Patrol, engineer third tier on the official papers."

"You should be on duty at the Vulcana. Are you deserting in the face of danger? They'll have you shot."

Jac flushed a little at the sudden scorn in her face. Her voice had chilled instantly to distant impersonality.

"I'm on a special mission, Miss Lang. It might be wiser if you remained at the Club on the chance you can get a hop out of the city. I am going to pick up some buddies and take a shot at the people back of this."

Her face changed again, this time to a warm interest and curiosity. Her voice slid down the scale to a husky note of apology. "Couldn't I go along? I can shoot, and I'm not exactly a coward..."

JAC set the sled down before the great sleeping stone dragon, which was the symbol of the veteran's organization. It was an apt symbol, for these men were for the most part pilots of the fiery-breathed war-jets, and in time of trouble would come out of civilian life to take, their place as riders of the flaming coffins that jets in wartime so often become.

As Jac came in the round hole of the doorway, made to resemble the entrance port of a big space liner, a chorus of cries greeted him.

"Here he is now, the great Mazarind's chief counselor!"

"Yeah, here he is. That spiel he made left out the most important part—how did the Vulcana get that way? And why isn't Jac Azad at his post?

"Talk, Azad! You've got some explaining to do!"

The men were gathered around the centrally located newscaster, a large spherical screen that sat like a bubble of light in the middle of the lobby. It was the meeting place of the famous warriors of Mekka. Every man who had achieved any notice for courage in battle was invited to join, though any veteran who had been in battle was eligible. There were about two-score men gathered about the screen, within which the figure of the city's chief coordinator was visible. He was giving orders to some force of police in action, and this was one of the few emergency channels opened now to provide the central command with supplementary forces.

The veterans gathered were waiting for an assignment in the expected attack by the forces behind the eruption. The borings beneath the clubhouse contained a full complement of fast ships, both sport and regular battle planes, owned by the members. The poorest of them, like Jac, owned levitor sleds for getting about the city, the richest owned as high as twenty planes of all kinds, from sport-jets to full-armored battle craft—and they were all very proud of the privilege given the club to own such fighting ships. They were really an auxiliary reserve organization, subsidized by the government to keep them ready for military action.

The full membership of the club was over five hundred, two hundred and more of whom were quartered in the club building itself. Jac Wondered where the rest were, till the man at the spherical screens shifted the view and he saw the space over Vulcana, two miles up, was filled with fighting planes, while lancing down from space came huge troop-bearing spacecraft, their fore-jets blasting as they slowed to landing speed. The vast cone of the Vulcana made the scene lurid even in the darkness with an intermittent blast of fiery rocks, and a steady flare of flaming gases, reaching a half-mile into the air. It was a terrific scene and Jac could only mumble to the many questions being thrown at him.

"Special mission. I'm here to pick up a volunteer force. It's too late for the Thermal Patrol to do anything with the Vulcana. She's going to blow in a few hours."

"What's the mission, Jac? I might volunteer." Hugh Spear, a man who had seen action in the same outfit with him, spoke up. He was a squat man for a Mekkan, but as broad as two of Jac.

"I had figured the Rif might be holed up in the new construction under the north slope. There are a lot of dwelling chambers built and no one even guards them. The whole place is empty except for the automatic borers and a few oilers who stay there to keep an eye on the machinery. I figured we might bottle them up before they come down on the city. But this landing on the South slopes of the cone makes me wonder if I was right."

"You're right, and you don't know it. I hadn't thought of the new borings! They are waiting till we swarm up to repel the surface attack, then they'll come out and mow down the city forces. It makes sense. Let's go take a look anyway. No one's going to send for us till they run into something they can't handle, and everything's under control so far except the broken heart of the Vulcana."

THERE was a terrific tension in the room as the veterans watched the Rif forces disembarking under fire, disappearing into openings in the side of the vast slope of the south shoulders of the Vulcana.

"They must know to the second when the Vulcana is due to blow, otherwise they would never trust an army to those tunnels," said Spear.

"If we could hold 'em there, delay them, the Vulcana might do us a favor and take care of them," Jac muttered to Spear.

Jill Lang spoke up, "Jac, where is our fleet? They are making that landing with only a token resistance. There aren't a thousand fighters in the air."

"Probably out in space fighting off the main force of the Rif. These transports have made a circle around the main engagement, perhaps unobserved by the main fleet. It's up to us to handle them until the fleet returns. You never know, in battle, just where and why everything takes place. You have to do a lot of guessing, and when you guess wrong, you get killed."

"You mean our fleet hasn't maintained contact? Doesn't anyone know where they are?"

"Sure, the brass in Central Command know where everyone is, but they don't tell every non-combatant and reserve pilot the details. We may never learn the true details of the very battles we are going to engage in during the next few hours. That's war, Jill."

Spear, who had been waiting for the answer to a message, was approached by a uniformed attendant of the club who handed him an armload of equipment. There were two rifles, the deadly needle-ray rifles of Mekka, good up to five miles of scope vision. There were two suits of metal-cloth designed to shed the most dangerous emanations and everything except a direct hit with rays, and there were a score of tiny and various instruments some of which even Jac did not understand.

"Come on, Jac, let's take a look at the north borings," Spear shouted, setting off on a dead run for the escalator down into the hangar chambers beneath.

As Jac followed Spear, he noticed that Jill was running at his side. At his questioning look she murmured, "You didn't say goodbye so I figured you expected to take me along."

"Oh no! This is dangerous Jill! You had better stay here and cadge a ride out of the city. If we do run into Rif in the borings, we may not get back again."

"Nonsense. I'm a good pilot, and if you want to use those two rifles, someone will have to handle the levitor wheel."

Spear's armored fighter was no mere jet job, but had both jets and an interplanetary drive—an etheric vortice engine such as is usually used only in the large ships for long space flights. It had also an auxiliary levitor drive and lifter for surface work on any planet.

CHAPTER FIVE

AS the trio clambered into the stubby, nearly cylindrical and unwinged ship, Spear flashed a beam into the club's coordinator chamber, requesting a tractor ray to follow their flight in case their deductions as to the location of the Rif forces were accurate and they were attacked and overwhelmed by superior numbers and could not return or report. Then he set the autopilot of the levitor drive, which device kept a ship centered in a boring, making it impossible to crash the walls. Without it all swift flight in the great subterranean factory network that was the life-blood of Mekka would have been impossible. As the ship lifted to the center channel of the main tunnel through the center of the Mekkan industrial area, it continually shifted aside with a disturbing suddenness to let pass the unending stream of traffic caused by the evacuation.

They sped across the emptying city. The sense of sorrow at all these people abandoning loved homes was constant and painful as they watched the milling throngs in the walkways boarding the passenger levitor platforms or making last minute purchases in the still operating provision automats. They were a beautiful people, light-hearted even in the face of the imminent fiery death about to consume the city, and there were tears in Jill Lang's dark eyes as she watched them pass beneath; knowing that surely many of them would soon pass into the limbo of the past unless the luck of Mekka were tremendous. For with the forces of the Rif circling the southern half of the city, the main exits to the southward were already closed. The east and western ways would soon be closed, and unless the northern ways remained open, many of the people of the underground portion of Mekka would be bottled up in the doomed borings. Strangely, the reason for building the manufacturing portion of the city underground, a lesson learned in the Atomic War, was now proving to be erroneous and disastrous, by reason of the sabotaging of the Vulcana. The danger now was from within, not without.

The ship swung now into the empty north borings, where lay the partially finished new manufacturing areas, which were not yet connected at the extremities with the regular network of tunnels. When finished, they had been planned to form a complete underground suburb of Mekka. The great new transport platforms lay unfinished all along the wide tunnel floors, giving a chaotic appearance to the scene. Tools and equipment lay scattered in all directions. Here and there a small service light burned over some throbbing machine keeping pressure in the airlines or pumping fuel to the temporary turbines. These tunnels were the safest in Mekka right now, as there were no heat pipes or power lines installed and no connection made to the vast inferno of the Vulcana.

"Jac and Jill went up the hill to fetch a pail of water," said Jill, as if to herself.

Jac flashed her a glance. It had not occurred to him how their names jingled in the old rhyme. It gave him an odd thrill of kinship with this lean whiplash of feminine courage and too much ability to be perfectly feminine. She would make someone a perfect mate. One would never have to coddle her; she could take care of herself.

SUDDENLY a voice out of nowhere whispered in his ear. "Oh no you don't, Jac Azad. You won't have to think of such things!"

With these words his brain whirled dizzily and a hypnotic pressure on his senses brought him a completely overwhelming realization of the proxy presence of Kay Lin. He realized she had been keeping contact with him since he had left her chambers, and the thought of this famous beauty, one whom the whole city looked upon as irresistible, had fastened her desires upon him was a sensation of delight and anticipation of transports to come—an anticipation which Jac knew was being suggested by Kay Lin's mind within his own, but which was no less irresistible in absorbing vistas of future passion because of that.

In answer to a suggestion by Kay Lin, he took the slip of vellum from his pocket on which Mazhart had written. Scanning it, he gave an exclamation of rage. For it was an order for his arrest as a spy, signed with both Mazhart's signature and a tiny mark beneath that he recognized as the old Rif symbol.

He did not hear Kay Lin's sigh of infinite relief as he scanned the paper. She knew now she had been right in killing the spy. It *hadn't* been Mazhart.

Jac turned to Jill to find she had been watching his sudden plunge into hypnotic absorption.

"Now who was that? Venus herself, by the look on your face."

"Just a friend," murmured Jac, his voice shaking a little.

"She would like to be more than a friend, and she has equipment only possessed by specially privileged persons, to be able to follow and reach you here. Who is she?"

For some unaccountable reason, Jac felt defiant. "It was Kay Lin, the mistress of the ruler, Mazhart."

"Just a friend, eh?" murmured Jill, sensing his defiance.

He flushed. "I met her today for the first time, trying to get word to Mazhart that the Vulcana was about to blow up. I couldn't find him at his office, so I paid a social call on the most logical place to find him."

Jill looked knowingly at him and there was an exaggerated soothing note in her voice. "And she was impressed with the handsome soldier. Say no more. I understand."

"No you don't," said Jac angrily. "I…"

Jill turned her attention to a map of the city that Hugh Spear had produced. Spear reached across and put his finger on the place where they were now. She nodded. Jac turned back to the side port, watching for some sign of Rif occupation. But the innumerable openings into the future dwellings of the workers were empty of any signs of life.

Spear, with his better vision from the transparent nose of the ship, saw something amiss in the dark tunnel, shot gas into the fore-jets, settling the ship to the rocky floor.

Quickly he rose from his seat at the controls and took one step toward the side port. At that instant a ray bolt slashed through the armor of the cabin and bisected the nose of the ship with a great splash of molten metal. If he had not risen, he would have been very dead now. Swiftly he bent over the control panel, pulled back the levitor lever, and turned on the fore jets. The ship lifted and shot backward just as two more flaming bolts of energy split the air where the ship had been settled. Jac admired his quick decision. The ordinary man would have risen off the ground with a forward motion and been caught like a clay pigeon.

SPEAR flew the ship backward at full speed, then suddenly darted sideways and up a black tunnel without a light. He had shut off the dim cabin light in the meanwhile. As he set the darkened ship down on the rock again, a feat itself done in the dark only by the sharpest of flyer's instinct, Jill read off a communicator tape.

"Our tracer ray contact has seen the attack upon us. The operator assures us forces will be dispatched immediately to handle whatever was hidden there—and commanding us to return to the club of the Sleeping Dragon."

"How about that?" asked Spear of both companions. "Do we run back home now that danger appears?"

"Let's look around first and see what we can learn about their numbers," answered Jac. "It could be an imposed message and our tracer ray shorted out. But if it was, it wouldn't send us back. It just doesn't make sense."

"Everything in Mekka is mixed up—the Vulcana exploding is in itself an impossibility, but it is happening. The Rif must have been a long time preparing this coup."

"I say we scout this section on foot. We can keep out of sight…look around till we learn something."

Jac turned to Jill. "You stay with the ship. We'll look over the borings in this section."

"No you don't! I'm going along. Hide the ship in one of the empty chambers."

They slid the weightless ship within one of the empty dwelling chambers which still did not have its partitions installed, and closed the rough temporary wooden door on it. Then they set off on foot toward the section from which they had been fired upon.

They ascended a stairway and were advancing along a railed balcony overlooking a great central chamber such as all dwellings contain, when a racket beneath them gave them pause. They stood, silent and alert, only to hear the noise of wheels and the hiss of high-powered levitors—the steady burtle and murmur of a great force of men and equipment getting underway. Then they came into view.

There were great sleds loaded down with the heaviest type of ray cannon, manned and ready to fire—at least a hundred floated slowly by beneath them, followed by a number twice as great of one man sleds equipped with deadly needle-ray rifles mounted on swivels.

"We are too late," whispered Jac. "They are departing to attack the city from the north."

"They will run smack into our Sleeping Dragons," said Spear, "Let's hope they are not asleep now…"

"If we could figure some way to muddle them up here as they gather to leave…" whispered Jill Lang.

There was little need of any effort to keep quiet. The rush and crush of the force beneath them drowned the place with echo upon echo of footsteps on the rock of the floor, with the jangle of loose chain against anchored cannon and the lighter ring of side weapons against harness buckle.

CHAPTER SIX

THERE was a deadly air of brutal, serious intent to kill in that gathering force, bedded here for no one knew how long, waiting for things to ripen in the city to the south. There was a sickening efficiency in the speed of their going in the grim-lipped set faces, like masks of death in the dim lights from the sleds' control panels.

"Get back in the tunnel," ordered Jac suddenly. Jill obeyed, but stood watching as he raised the weapon he carried, sighted at the high center arch of the domed chamber. Beside him, Spear raised a similar weapon and the two rifles hissed venomously together. From overhead the report of the explosive bullets was deafening, and down upon the entrance out of which the procession of man and weapons was coming, fragments of rock as big as men's heads rained down. Nothing of a size sufficient to more than worry them, but still, as Jill had suggested, enough to "muddle them."

Again they fired, this time at the key point of the arch over the entryway, and the double charge of explosive pellets knocked a fragment of rock loose weighing at least a ton. It dropped down upon a heavy levitor sled, tipped it over on its side and blocking the whole doorway with its weight. With which success, Jack and Hugh darted back from the railed edge of the balcony and sprinted up the passage behind, brushing against Jill as they passed, but not seeing her. She ran after them, but they were but misleading echoes of footsteps overhead, where they bounded up the stairways. These stairways were but narrow emergency borings, to be sealed up after the place was finished, useful only during construction before the levitor passages and usual means of getting about were installed. All Mekka buildings used a levitor beam for elevators, making anything placed in a vertical boring weightless so that it could be floated up or down. It was this that made their flight sensible, as nothing bigger than one man could follow up these narrow stairways. At the top they knelt, and Jill, panting after, nearly got herself shot before they remembered her.

"Well, we muddled 'em up all right! Now they will hunt us down like rats through these warrens, and your friends will arrive just in time to bury us." Jill was quite certain about it, and Spear laughed grimly.

"We're in no danger. They won't change plans for that, won't send more than a few men after us. We've only delayed them for seconds, but those seconds may be just what is needed to throw them out of stride when the Dragons hit 'em."

As if in answer to his words there came a terrific hiss and sputter as of a gigantic fuse suddenly lit, and after it came a concussion, shuddering deafeningly about then as the air tore apart in the pressure. This was followed by a steady series of shocks as the ray rifles of some heavily armored craft went into action, splitting the rocks of the cavern with sudden heat.

How the encounter between their Sleeping Dragons and the concealed Rif forces came out, they were not to learn, for as they turned to make their way to the front walls of the boring to see the battle outside through some airshaft or opening, a sudden light broke out upon them, a sugar-sweet female voice said mockingly:

"Ah, we have caught the spies who fired upon our caravan of death."

They could see nothing put the blinding brightness of the spot of light directed upon them, but Jac threw up his rifle and let go a bolt at the light itself. The rifle was knocked from his grasp by a force beam even as it discharged. The pellet only shattered the roof overhead, letting down a rain of rock dust over the scene.

SPEAR dropped his own weapon, realizing there was no sense getting killed when no resistance was possible. Jac stood wringing his painful hands, burning with the shock of the force ray. Jill merely smiled at the blinding light; she had faced so many spotlights it seemed quite natural.

The voice directed them to march ahead, and presently they brought up before a wide door of rough wood. It was opened and they stepped through to find half a hundred women. Jac realized these were wives and sweethearts of the Rif forces, who expected to wait there until Mekka was destroyed, then join in the looting and celebrations afterward.

The woman who had captured them stood well behind them, still with her hand light and force beam pistol, and motioned them onward across the room. They were locked into a small dark closet, and left to listen to the chatter of the Rif camp-followers.

Jac uttered a muffled curse. "Captured by women!"

"We're still alive." Jill's voice was light, half-laughing, half-bitter.

"But better dead. Now we'll be taken back to the Rif cities even if they are defeated, and spend the rest of our lives working as slaves for people we detest."

Spear sat down against the wall, unlatched his empty weapon belt, and made himself comfortable. Jac bent to the tiny slit of light from the doorway, peering for a chink to look out at the Rif women. Jill shoved him aside.

"No need your watching those creatures! I'll do it for you."

"It is just as well you do," muttered Jac, sitting down beside Spear. "It would be a sad fate indeed if I were to fall in love with one of them."

"I wouldn't put it past you," said Jill, grimacing.

In the closet, the air grew humid, almost unbearable. Jill kept her eye glued to the slit of the door; Spear and Jac sat motionless, waiting for whatever unpleasantness was in store for them. Jill occasionally gave little sounds of disgust.

Then a broad broom of rays swept hissing across the scene outside. The women screamed and ran. The sound of their feet thudding off down the passages was all that was left of them. Jill gave a cry of delight, and for the faintest fraction of an instant their own bodies felt the intolerable pain of that ray before it followed the fleeing women. Someone had pierced the defenses of the place with a neural wave, generating maddening impulses of an unbearable pain in the bodies of all it touched.

The husky, throaty voice of Kay Lin came to Jac's inner ear, murmuring: "I have found you, Jac Azad. A prisoner of the Rif camp women, I am surprised and disappointed." The faint tinge of mockery in her tones caused Jac to flush in the darkness, but he only grinned at the invisible woman. He knew his own face must be looking out of her mirror in her boudoir. He could imagine her quite clearly, sitting there as if the whole city was not aboil with chaotic activity, fleeing citizens, rumbling fires beneath, marching armies and strafing planes.

"Did your patrol run off and leave you?" whispered Jac, curious as to how it happened the Mazarind had not seen that she was safely out of the city by now.

KAY Lin made a split-second decision and lied. "Believe it or not, Jac Azad, our ruler seems to have done just that. No one knows where he has gone or how to reach him. His family will have to exile him to save the reputation of the Mazarind Clan. Mazhart is no longer the heart of the clan, if I read the cards right."

"Kay Lin, if we could get out of this closet, we could join you. Together we might find a way to strike at these Rif armies, or at least make a sensible exit ourselves before the Vulcana consumes the empty city."

"It is far from empty. There is a pitched battle going on in the western tunnels, and the Vulcana tremors mount steadily on the dials in the seismograph office. The city is calmly evacuating otherwise, and a large part of the Rif invasion force has been sealed off from the city blasting down the western doors. The openings remaining are where the battle is taking place."

"The real danger, then, is the Vulcana itself. Find out exactly when the Rif technician expect her to let go with the big blast. You can find it out if you look into a few Rif minds with your pretty plaything. They must have been briefed on how long a time they have to loot the city."

"I have already done that, and more, Jac Azad. The time is about one hour from this instant, and they are frantically trying to get out of the city themselves. But the battle has blasted down so many gates; a lot of them aren't going to get away in time."

"Good!" cried Jac, at which Jill and Spear shook him, thinking he was asleep and dreaming.

"There's nothing good about this hole, wake up!" cried Spear into Jac's ear.

"I'm awake," said Jac. "Hold still a minute. I'm in contact with Kay Lin. She is working to release us, and she will come for us. The Vulcana is due to blow up in an hour."

Even as he spoke, a heat ray began eating at the doorway. The wood flared, blackened, fell to ash. Within moments they were free and racing down the passage outside.

"Make your way toward my place along the main routes. I will start out in my own private plane to pick you up," ordered Kay Lin in Jac's ear. "Then we will leave this madness behind us and seek calmer climes for our future."

As the ray left them, Spear grinned at Jac. "It's right handy to have so many women worried about you…eh Jac?"

Jac only looked serious. "I don't feel that we should run away and leave Mekka just because the whole place is doomed to go up in smoke."

Jill spoke up. "There won't be time for more than that, Jac. We can die nobly running around like ants on a crushed anthill, or we can get out and be sensible. After all, you've got to think of your girlfriend!" There was derision in her voice, and again Jac flushed.

They set out on foot, running along the corridors toward the place they had hidden the plane. They found it efficiently sabotaged by the Rif women or soldiers. It was useless to anyone now.

THEY went on down the avenues of darkness toward the inhabited portion of the city. Somewhere they hoped Kay Lin would run into them. It was their only chance of escaping from the endless warrens of the factory-city. The whole under-rock was now shuddering deeply, constantly, with an increasing reverberation which they realized was the atomic explosions in the far-off crater building up to a climax as the various materials deposited by the Rif reached their critical mass and fissioned.

"Part of that concussion," panted Spear, running heavily beside his lighter-bodied companions, "is probably bombs by our own forces seeking to bottle up the Rif by blowing down the cavern roofs. If they can get 'em sealed off in time, they will be destroyed by their own deviltry. That will be justice!"

"I can't run away while our outfit is still fighting, Hugh. We've got to get to the front and report. They will need us. Once out of the city in Kay Lin's ship, we've got to stick close and fight with the rest to the last second."

"We can't do a thing without a ship, man. We'll have to take over Kay Lin's ship by force, if she insists on running to a lover's rendezvous with you."

Jac's face set in grim lines as the long gray sport ship of the rich woman settled to the cavern floor in the center of the now deserted North highway. They ran up to the ship, but the entry port—a curiously shaped door resembling a shield with four points on top remained closed. In their ears they could hear her voice over the ray with which she was checking them.

"Oh no you don't, you two patriots…you are too fiery for me. I want none of your last ditch heroism. If you come aboard, it will be on your word of honor to take my orders. I have a plan of my own, and information you are unaware of. You're not setting me afoot in the forest outside the city while you run off to fight a war that was lost before it started."

She had taken a look at their thoughts from habitual caution and surprised their just-formed plan to take over her ship. Jac frowned and Spear grinned.

"Okay, sister, you win. Open the door and we'll behave like little lambs."

With which promise, Kay Lin swung the door wide and they stepped into the upholstered sleekness of her richly emblazoned sport flyer. Gray leather seats, polished wood paneling, a multiplicity of gleaming gadgets, and beyond the glass paneling between the pilot's seat and the cabin, Kay Lin's lushly lovely face a little grim. She did not open the heavy glass panel between the cabin and herself, but motioned them to seats and took off, screaming away from Mekka Industrial City up the exact center of the tunnel. Behind them the narrowing perspective of the great bore suddenly gleamed with a light brighter than the sun, and the ship lurched as a blast of air struck them from the rear. Fire and heat rays shot past the ports. The ship became hot as a furnace inside from the sudden blast of the distant explosion—and each of them knew that Mekka was no more, even as they plunged out of the bore and flashed across the smoking ruined city outside.

"If you two had had your way, we would have been back there just in time to get the full force of that," came Kay Lin's voice.

But Jac and Spear and Jill were not listening. Instead they were staring down at a rapidly vanishing scene behind them. There, towering many hundreds of feet into the air, smashing buildings with grotesque metal arms, and ponderous metal legs was a figure that was so like a man that it staggered their imaginations.

"A robot giant…" exclaimed Jill.

"Something new for the Rif," said Spear. "It will be hard to stop things like that, but they can't have many of them."

CHAPTER SEVEN

KAY Lin's voice came to them…as they zoomed out of sight of the city over the mountain and out beyond, over the silent forest that covered the area between the city and the sea. "That is the only one and it is not a robot, not exactly."

"What do you mean, Kay Lin?" asked Jac. "How can it be not 'exactly' a robot?"

"That is the Metal Emperor, the ruler of the Rif, and it is not a robot, because it has a human mind."

"A human mind," breathed Spear. "How can that be?"

"It is metal, but in its skull case is a brain, an ancient brain many thousands of years old."

"But the size of that head," cried Jill. "Surely, it need not be that large to house a human brain."

"It needs to be that large to house this human brain," said Kay Lin. "I know, for I probed it with my 'pretty plaything,' as you called it."

The speedy ship was now over the ocean, flashing forward at top speed. Kay Lin set the automatic controls, then stepped into the cabin with them.

"It is a long story," she said, sitting down on a leather-covered divan. "If you'll be patient, I'll tell you about it, and what we intend to do."

"But where are we going?" asked Jac. "Why flee in terror over the sea, this way?"

"Listen…and I will explain. In order that you might understand, I will have to go back to the very beginning.

First, Mazhart was murdered by a spy, whom I later killed myself, when he came to my apartment, no doubt to do what he could to aid the invasion and try to track down more of the Mazarind Clan." Kay Lin glossed over the real truth of her experience, which still caused her some perturbation in spite of the fact she had been justified in her action. "In my search immediately afterward for the Mazarind, I checked back on the recording tape of my television mirror and saw a picture of that great metal monster you saw back in outer Mekka. Somehow it had been directing the spy to me, and managed to get a message to him over my own apparatus when I was not looking..." A bit of a flush stole over Kay Lin's face at the bit of fiction she was weaving into her otherwise truthful story, but she went on without otherwise betraying the fact.

"I traced the signal back, and I found this Metal Emperor, as the Rif call him, approaching Earth in a massive space ship. I pried into his mind, just as I did into yours, but not with the compulsion that can be achieved over a mere human mind. I did it secretly, and I learned an amazing story.

"A long time ago, many thousands of years before our present civilization, the Rif were inhabitants of Earth."

JAC Azad gasped. "Inhabitants of Earth! How could that be?"

"It is true, nonetheless," Kay Lin went on. "They were a highly mechanized race, living on a continent that has come down to us in legend as Mu, in what is now the Pacific Ocean, which is where we are heading..."

"But why?" interrupted Spear.

"Never mind that now, suffice it to say that we are not just fleeing in terror, but have a definite objective in view.

But to go on, this Rifian civilization was a vastly mechanical one, and then, just as they really are now, they were enslaved to their machines. In fact, their ruler was a machine, with a human brain, grown greatly by its defeat of death and age through its separation from a physical body, just as that monster you saw destroying Mekka."

"Just as, you say?" asked Jac, sensing her implied meaning.

"Exactly. The ancient Rif were ruled by a Metal Emperor, but there were more than one of these giant robots. A whole race of them existed then, and the humans were but the merest slaves and would eventually have been entirely eliminated. But a great disaster struck this planet, a disaster that sank the continent of Mu into the depths. But it was not a disaster that came too suddenly. It was prepared for, and one great spaceship escaped, bearing one of the metal giants and his crew of human Rif slaves. It had been planned that each of the giant robots would escape in a separate ship, with his slaves, then when Earth was habitable once more, they would return. When I probed the mind of the Metal Emperor, I found that he had been the sole survivor. None of the other ships reached their pre-planned destination, and he was marooned for thousands of years by the damaging of his spaceship, and the difficulty of reconstructing his mechanical civilization. There was a revolt of the slaves, and on their new world, two factions sprang up. For centuries they waged wars, and finally the Metal Emperor triumphed. Then he built up his civilization again, and finally, was able to send scouts to Earth to determine if it was once more habitable, because Earth is a far superior planet, and he wished to return.

"And so he found it. And so he planned to come back. His first attack was repulsed, through underestimating our mechanical status, largely because our own atomic war had forced our true mechanical civilization underground, where he failed to find it in its proper perspective. Now, in his second attack, he has succeeded. The Metal Emperor has returned to the planet of his birth, bringing his Rif slaves with him, and it is his intent to wipe Earth clean of its present population and resume once more what he considers his rightful place as supreme and sole ruler."

"It is incredible," said Jac. "But we saw him, and your story must be true. And because it is, there seems little hope for Earth now. With Mekka destroyed the other smaller cities will fall. There seems nothing we can do."

"At least not here," said Spear. "Why are we plunging out over the ocean to nowhere? I say we must go back and fight, no matter how hopeless it seems. Even if we escape, the Metal Emperor and his Rif slaves will eventually seek us out, and that will be our end. I, for one, do not set so much store by a period of dalliance at love, as by an honorable death. We must go back, Jac. I am surprised that you would even consider the proposition of Kay Lin, no matter what her physical charm. Are you a traitor for so small a cause as a bit of perfumed flesh?"

"Stay!" said Kay Lin's voice harshly. "Don't condemn my flesh before you know my mind! It is true that I was Mazhart's mistress, but I am also as human as you and no traitor—nor so dishonorable as you seem to think. We will continue to our destination."

"And that is what?" asked Jill, a dangerous light flaring into her dark eyes.

KAY Lin eyed her almost hostilely. "A small deserted island paradise in the southern Pacific, if you must know," she said stiffly.

"I thought so!" said Spear harshly. "And I do condemn you!"

"Thank you," said Kay Lin. "And you, Jac Azad? Do you also condemn my heart without even so much as a hearing?"

Up from his subconscious came the hypnotic compulsion that still governed him in respect to his thoughts about Kay Lin. "No, Kay Lin, I do not. I will listen to you, if you will speak. After you have spoken we shall see."

"Then listen, all of you. With my 'pretty plaything' I managed to pry one very interesting bit of information from the Metal Emperor's mind, a piece of information I have already given you—that there were originally more than one of these robot giants. As I thought about that, I began to wonder if the Metal Emperor was really the original ruler of Mu, or if he was simply a lesser one. And I wondered about all the others, whether they had actually died in space unable to reach their destination. And I remembered the ancient legends of Mu, which predict that one day she will rise again. They couldn't have come from this particular metal giant, out of contact with Earth, so I reasoned that not all of them left their home planet, and likewise, not all of them died, or their memory would have died with them. So, with my ray, I sought an answer to the secret. Deep down in the depths of the Pacific I found it."

Jac and his two comrades stared at her. "What did you find?" they asked in unison.

She smiled tantalizingly at them. "I found the *real* Metal Emperor. And I got the *real* story. Believe it or not, that ancient civilization of metal giants still exists, on the bottom of the Pacific, miles beneath the surface, a race of immortal metal men, with enormous human brains, wise beyond all belief, perfectly aware of the life on the surface, but content to remain where they are. But because of the weakness of my transmitting ray, I could not contact them. So, that is why we make this trip. In this ship I have an exact duplicate of the 'plaything' of my boudoir, and with it I hope to contact that Metal Emperor and enlist his help."

Jac and Spear and Jill sat stunned. The enormity of the facts that Kay Lin had related to them were almost beyond belief, but yet they must be true.

"Kay Lin," said Spear, "I must apologize. You are an infinitely clever and brilliant woman, to go along with your great beauty. And I must confess that you have discovered the only way we can defeat the Rif and restore Mekka and all Earth to its former glory. But are you sure you can contact the Metal Emperor, and if you do, will he help us?"

Kay Lin looked at him. "Even the Metal Emperor has a human brain. And being human, I feel sure that I can do to him as I have done to many others. Perhaps my peculiar fleshly charms may have some practical use after all."

Jill Lang looked at Kay Lin a bit strangely, but then she spoke, "Perhaps what you have said is not all egotism. In any other case, I would hope so; but in this, I am all for you. But I wonder if the Metal Emperor will be anywhere near the big bowl of mush that is Jac Azad?"

Jac flushed, turned to her, about to give an angry retort, when he saw her smile. Instead he grinned sheepishly. "I would expect such a remark from a lion-tamer."

Now it was Jill's turn to flush, and Kay Lin turned a lingering glance upon Jac Azad that left him quite flustered.

CHAPTER EIGHT

HOURS later Kay Lin set the ship down on a coral islet in the vast desert of shining water that was the Pacific. Here, she said, the Pacific rolled over the ancient continent of Mu, and far below, forever free of ordinary men's probing adventurings, was a mechanical civilization that had never before been equaled throughout the entirety of the cosmos, a race of mechanical giants, living a life forever bulwarked against interference, impervious to outside influence, and content to remain in its impregnable fortress of water.

The three other Mekkans watched anxiously as Kay Lin set her apparatus into action, sending its probing rays down into the dark, swirling waters; down, down until, many miles deep and as seen on the polished mirror, not even fish were visible, only perpetual blackness, lighted by her rays. At last a tremendous scene burst into view. Here was a city! A tremendous bulking city of imperishable metal, and in it were moving figures, giant figures—metal men!

"It's true…" exclaimed Jill. "And I am proud to be a woman, if only to be able to share the glory of your achievement in conjecturing the truth and having the mental ability to find it, Kay Lin."

Kay Lin flashed her a quick glance of appreciation, then turned back to her control panel. As she flicked lever after lever, at last on the mirror a single great building was focused, and finally, a great room inside that building. And there, sitting on a great throne in an attitude of meditation, was a metal giant fully a mile tall, and with a brain almost unbelievable in its sheer vastness of size. And Kay Lin spoke to it.

"Emperor of ancient Mu," she said, her tones soft and cooing, like a dove's. "Listen to me. I am Kay Lin, one of the surface people who live and love and die far above your realm. I have come to you for help, and to give you a piece of information of great importance to you."

The giant figure on the throne stirred and looked about, then its great mechanical eyes looked upward, peering through the metal of the building's roof, up through the water with a form of x-ray vision, and into the little flyer in which the four Mekkans sat. But he did not speak. It was obvious that for the moment that he was content to merely listen.

"From a distant planet, a member of your own mechanical race—who escaped thousands of years ago from the holocaust that you yourself escaped from in another way, by preparing a city that could survive on the bottom of the ocean—has returned to Earth. He is at this very moment waging a war of extermination on the surface people—my people. It is in his mind to take back the planet of his birth, and to rule it as the sole emperor, for he does not know that you survive, and your companions along with you. His mind is poisoned by his contact with the rays of outer space, and he is no longer of a sane mind. When he learns of you, as he eventually will, he will undoubtedly make war upon you. He is a great danger to you if he is allowed to consolidate his position here on Earth. Look for yourself, and you will see that I speak the truth..."

And now, Kay Lin's rays reached out across the surface of Earth, and brought the smoking ruin of Mekka onto her mirror, and there in the midst of it, the other-world Metal Emperor.

DOWN below, the gigantic metal man rose slowly to his feet, staring upward at the scene. Then, like the rumble of Earth's largest volcano itself, his voice came to them.

"I have seen, beautiful woman of the surface. And I will help you. I come now. Await me."

The shining surface of Kay Lin's mirror became dark, and nothing she could do could bring back the picture of the metal city on the ocean floor far below.

"We shall never see it again..." said Kay Lin with conviction. "The true Metal Emperor knows now, and he will maintain his impregnability against interference. It must be a great mind that he possesses, indeed, to live for eternity in those dark depths, meditating on things beyond mere fleshly scope."

"I believe you are right," said Spear, almost reverently. "We are fortunate above all surface people, to have seen what we have seen."

"Let us watch the sea outside the port," said Kay Lin. "It should not be long before the Metal Emperor emerges."

They crowded to the side ports and stared out over the glistening ocean that extended seemingly to a fading blue infinity. For long moments it remained an unbroken surface, and then a white line of surf appeared far out, as though a reef was there, but there had been no reef previously. It approached now, nearer to shore and a dark object began rising out of it. It advanced swiftly, ever rising, and stepping in what were obviously half-mile strides, and soon the whole head loomed up above the water, then tremendous shoulders, gigantic torso, and at last the stunning reality of towering columnar legs. The Metal Emperor loomed high into the sky, fully a mile or more in height, and at last stood in the shallow water a thousand feet away from the island. As they watched in awe a huge hand reached out, grasped their ship gently in tremendous metal fingers, and lifted them aloft. Then, with a stride as gentle as waves, with a lofting, lilting motion, the Metal Emperor began wading, following the Shallows, so that always he was able to hold the flyer above water, even though at times his head was nearly submerged.

The wind whistled about the flyer, and Spear marveled, "We could not have flown this fast!"

"We shall be back in Mekka before we know it," said Jill.

IN LESS than four hours the shoreline of ancient America appeared. And a few minutes later, the gigantic pall of smoke that was the erupting Vulcana became visible. Here the Metal Emperor set the tiny flyer free, simply by opening his palm and allowing Kay Lin to lift the ship off as from a landing field. Then he strode on—purposefully and grimly. Kay Lin followed as fast as she could in the flyer.

They were yet far away when the two metal giants met. But Kay Lin picked up the scene on her television mirror, and the battle that followed kept them all in silence and in complete awe, stunned beyond speaking by the enormity of it all. It seemed unbelievable, yet it was happening before them.

From the beginning it was very obvious that the giant from the depths of sunken Mu was far superior in strength and mental ability, and as the duel went on, the Metal Emperor led its adversary skillfully away from the city and into the depths of the forest; and there he proceeded to batter the invading emperor of the Rif into a shapeless pile of metal. Yet he carefully avoided damage to the head itself, and finally, when he wrested it from the body, he set it down carefully in the forest floor, and turned back to the city.

Now his huge voice came to them in the ship. "What is the matter with the volcano?"

"It has been sabotaged with radioactive materials, so that it is a gigantic fissioning pile. It will have to be damped."

The giant turned now to the volcano, and his focus of vision seemed intent on it, staring out into it with his great lenses. Finally he seemed to nod a bit. Then he strode off into the distance.

"Where is he going?" asked Jill.

"I suspect he has some plan in mind," answered Jac. "I believe in some way he has analyzed what is necessary to dampen the Vulcana, and is perhaps going off to find the materials he needs."

Kay Lin followed the Metal Emperor with her rays and on the mirror. They saw him stoop finally and wrest the top off a stony outcropping, one of a group of small mountains in the Appalachian chain. Then he came striding back.

AT length he stood almost astride the Vulcana, its flames and smoke billowing between his legs, and its lava flowing past his feet. Then he lifted the huge boulder on high and with tremendous force, jammed it down into the crater. It disappeared in the depths, and almost instantly the crimson glow that lighted the smoky sky began to dim. The brilliant white fire glowing from the now choked openings of the tunnels of Mekka changed to a dull red, then a gray, and finally turned black. The atomic fire was going out.

Then, as the four watched, struck dumb with awe, the Metal Emperor strode back to the forest, and almost tenderly picked up the head of the outlaw Rifian Emperor. For a moment he held it up, looking into its eye pieces, then he tucked it under his arm and began striding toward the sea.

"He's going back to his under-ocean city," said Kay Lin. "We must thank him."

She turned to her apparatus and pressed several different switches, then she spoke into the microphone, "Thank you, Emperor of Mu. We shall never forget you…"

The answer came, rumbling through the sky like the thunder of the gods. "I hear, beautiful one. And if ever you need me again, you need but call. It will be my pleasure."

And then, as they watched, the giant metal figure waded out into the water, ever deeper, until finally nothing remained but a tremendous wave that washed away and was gone.

Spear turned to Jill Lang. "You haven't got a chance in the world with Jac Azad," he said. "Even the Metal Emperor has fallen for her like a ton of bricks. So, if you don't mind, how about concentrating on something you can get?"

Jill looked at Kay Lin, then turned to Spear. "What makes you think I ever wanted our pretty boy? I'll take a man with muscles any time. It wouldn't be right for a man to have a wife who can beat him at anything, even if it's only lion taming."

Spear got a wide grin on his face. "Okay, Jill. But I'm warning you, I don't tame as easy as Jac, there. But if you want to know, I'd rather have my girl use her natural weapons without benefit of machine. Sort of gives a guy a fighting chance."

Jac Azad looked at them both, and flushed to the roots of his hair. But Kay Lin only laughed. She turned off the ray machine.

"Come here, soldier," she nearly whispered, in a cooing contralto.

"Do I look like a fool?" said Jac. And he came.

*　　*　　*

MEKKA was gone, but Jac and Kay Lin stood now on the hills of black lava that marked its ancient site, into the white dome over the many openings that marked the new Mekka being built deep under the surface.

"She will be more beautiful and greater than ever," said Jac.

"Yes my emperor," murmured Kay Lin, "and I am very glad that you are not made of metal."

Jac looked down at her. "So am I. For if I was, I would be afraid of melting!"

He took her in his arms, and for a long moment there was silence. Then she gasped and pulled away. "My," she cried. "The Vulcana must be erupting again!"

Jac grinned down at her. "That's one thing we need never worry about," he said. "That old cone is as dead as any volcano will ever be."

"And you know," she said, "I don't much care—as long as you are about."

THE END

If you've enjoyed this book, you will not want to miss these terrific titles…

ARMCHAIR SCI-FI & HORROR DOUBLE NOVELS, $12.95 each

D-1   **THE GALAXY RAIDERS** by William P. McGivern
SPACE STATION #1 by Frank Belknap Long

D-2   **THE PROGRAMMED PEOPLE** by Jack Sharkey
SLAVES OF THE CRYSTAL BRAIN by William Carter Sawtelle

D-3   **YOU'RE ALL ALONE** by Fritz Leiber
THE LIQUID MAN by Bernard C. Gilford

D-4   **CITADEL OF THE STAR LORDS** by Edmond Hamilton
VOYAGE TO ETERNITY by Milton Lesser

D-5   **IRON MEN OF VENUS** by Don Wilcox
THE MAN WITH ABSOLUTE MOTION by Noel Loomis

D-6   **WHO SOWS THE WIND…** by Rog Phillips
THE PUZZLE PLANET by Robert A. W. Lowndes

D-7   **PLANET OF DREAD** by Murray Leinster
TWICE UPON A TIME by Charles L. Fontenay

D-8   **THE TERROR OUT OF SPACE** by Dwight V. Swain
QUEST OF THE GOLDEN APE by Ivar Jorgensen and Adam Chase

D-9   **SECRET OF MARRACOTT DEEP** by Henry Slesar
PAWN OF THE BLACK FLEET by Mark Clifton.

D-10   **BEYOND THE RINGS OF SATURN** by Robert Moore Williams
A MAN OBSESSED by Alan E. Nourse

ARMCHAIR SCIENCE FICTION CLASSICS, $12.95 each

C-1   **THE GREEN MAN**
by Harold M. Sherman

C-2   **A TRACE OF MEMORY**
By Keith Laumer

C-3   **INTO PLUTONIAN DEPTHS**
by Stanton A. Coblentz

ARMCHAIR MASTERS OF SCIENCE FICTION SERIES, $16.95 each

M-1   **MASTERS OF SCIENCE FICTION, Vol. One**
Bryce Walton—"Dark of the Moon" and other tales

M-2   **MASTERS OF SCIENCE FICTION, Vol. Two**
Jerome Bixby—"One Way Street" and other tales

If you've enjoyed this book, you will not want to miss these terrific titles…

ARMCHAIR SCI-FI & HORROR DOUBLE NOVELS, $12.95 each

ARMCHAIR SCIENCE FICTION CLASSICS, $12.95 each

ARMCHAIR SCI-FI & HORROR GEMS SERIES, $12.95 each

If you've enjoyed this book, you will not want to miss these terrific titles…

ARMCHAIR SCI-FI & HORROR DOUBLE NOVELS, $12.95 each

D-161   **THE TIME-RAIDER** by Edmond Hamilton
WHISPER OF DEATH, THE by Harl Vincent

D-162   **SONS OF THE DELUGE** by Nelson S. Bond
THE COUNTRY BEYOND THE CURVE by Walt Sheldon

D-163   **HIS TOUCH TURNED STONE TO FLESH** by Milton Lesser
ULLR UPRISING by H. Beam Piper

D-164   **WOLFBANE** by C. M. Kornbluth & Frederick Pohl
THE LAST TWO ALIVE! by Alfred Coppel

D-165   **LET FREEDOM RING** by Fritz Leiber
THE MACHINE THAT FLOATS by Joe Gibson

D-166   **EXILES OF THE MOON** by Nat Schachner & Arthur Leo Zagut
DEATH PLAYS A GAME by David V. Reed

D-167   **DAWN OF THE DEMIGODS** by Raymond Z. Gallun
EMPIRE by Clifford D. Simak

D-168   **ARMAGEDDON** by Rog Phillips aka Craig Browning
THE LOVE MACHINE, THE by James Cooke Brown

D-169   **THREE AGAINST THE ROUM** by Robert Moore Williams
OUT OF TIME'S ABYSS by Edgar Rice Burroughs

D-170   **BEYOND THE GREEN PRISM** by A. Hyatt Verrill
ALCATRAZ OF THE STARWAYS by Henry Hasse & Albert dePina

ARMCHAIR SCIENCE FICTION CLASSICS, $12.95 each

C-67   **POWER METAL**
by S. J. Byrne

C-64   **THE PROFESSOR JAMESON SAGA, Book One**
by Neil R. Jones

C-64   **THE PROFESSOR JAMESON SAGA, Book Two**
by Neil R. Jones

ARMCHAIR SCI-FI & HORROR GEMS SERIES, $12.95 each

G-19   **SCIENCE FICTION GEMS, Vol. Ten**
Robert Sheckley and others

G-20   **HORROR GEMS, Vol. Ten**
Manly Wade Wellman and others

If you've enjoyed this book, you will not want to miss these terrific titles…

ARMCHAIR SCI-FI & HORROR DOUBLE NOVELS, $12.95 each

D-171 **REGAN'S PLANET** by Robert Silverberg
SOMEONE TO WATCH OVER ME by H. L. Gold and Floyd Gale

D-172 **PEOPLE MINUS X** by Raymond Z. Gallun
THE SAVAGE MACHINE by Randall Garrett

D-173 **THE FACE BEYOND THE VEIL** by Rog Phillips
REST IN AGONY by Paul W. Fairman

D-174 **VIRGIN OF VALKARION** by Poul Anderson
EARTH ALERT by Kris Neville

D-175 **WHEN THE ATOMS FAILED** by John W. Campbell, Jr.
DRAGONS OF SPACE by Aladra Septama

D-176 **THE TATTOOED MAN** by Edmond Hamilton
A RESCUE FROM JUPITER by Gawain Edwards

D-177 **THE FLYING THREAT** by David H. Keller, M. D.
THE FIFTH-DIMENSION TUBE by Murray Leinster

D-178 **LAST DAYS OF THRONAS** by S. J. Byrne
GODDESS OF WORLD 21 by Henry Slesar

D-179 **THE MOTHER WORLD** by B. Wallis & George C. Wallis
BEYOND THE VANISHING POINT by Ray Cummings

D-180 **DARK DESTINY** by Dwight V. Swain
SECRET OF PLANETOID 88 by Ed Earl Repp

ARMCHAIR SCIENCE FICTION CLASSICS, $12.95 each

C-69 **EXILES OF THE MOON**
by Nathan Schachner & Arthur Leo Zagut

C-70 **SKYLARK OF SPACE**
by E. E. "Doc' Smith

ARMCHAIR MYSTERY-CRIME DOUBLE NOVELS, $12.95 each

B-11 **THE BABY DOLL MURDERS** by James O. Causey
DEATH HITCHES A RIDE by Martin L. Weiss

B-12 **THE DOVE** by Milton Ozaki
THE GLASS LADDER by Paul W. Fairman

B-13 **THE NAKED STORM** by C. M. Kornbluth
THE MAN OUTSIDE by Alexander Blade

Printed in Great Britain
by Amazon

23421681R00142